THE MONITOR

THE MONITOR

A Randy Craig Mystery
by Janice MacDonald

Turnstone Press
607-100 Arthur Street
Artspace Building
Winnipeg, MB
R3B 1H3 Canada
www.TurnstonePress.com

Turnstone Press gratefully acknowledges the assistance of the Canada
Council for the Arts, the Manitoba Arts Council and the Government of
Canada through the Book Publishing Industry Development Program
and the Government of Manitoba through the Department of Culture,
Heritage and Tourism, Arts Branch for our publishing activities.

  Canada

The Canada Council | Le Conseil des Arts
for the Arts | du Canada

Cover design: Doowah Design
Interior design: Sharon Caseburg
Printed and bound in Canada by AGMV Marquis for Turnstone Press.

National Library of Canada Cataloguing in Publication Data

MacDonald, Janice E. (Janice Elva), 1959-

The monitor : a Randy Craig mystery / by Janice MacDonald.

ISBN 0-88801-284-5
I. Title.
PS8575.D63245M66 2003   C813'.54   C2003-905320-2

This is for Martina, Lasha and Cora

I cannot imagine better friends.

ACKNOWLEDGEMENTS

I would like to thank my family, without whom I would literally crack into a thousand brittle pieces. Randy, Madeleine and Jocelyn, you are the most special people in the world to me and I'm proud to be connected to you. Thank you for your patience with me, for not minding when I make odd references to blood and mayhem during otherwise sedate moments, and for reading drafts not fit for human consumption (and for eating some meals of the same calibre during the course of the writing). Thanks also to Dilly, who sat on my shoulder and kept me company for most of the writing of this.

I'd also like to thank the real Dr. Ray Lopez, who gave me some ideas on how to configure certain elements of the chat room; Ryan Sales, who told me about hunting bad guys; and Howard Rheingold, for creating Brainstorms, which is where you go when you grow out of the chats. Thanks also to all my "imaginary friends"—everyone who lent me your name or handle for characters and all the folks I've had pleasant chats with on various sites.

Babel contains elements of many chatsites I've visited over the years, and also has some bells and whistles I've often dreamed of having available. While I've had some wonderful advice and help in the creation of Babel, all the errors are mine and shouldn't be considered a commentary on any chat room in particular.

While most writers would agree that churning out the manuscript is arduous work, it's often what comes after that counts the most. I am very blessed when it comes to people who run this gauntlet with me.

I am so grateful that the folks at Turnstone believe in genre writing enough to have created the glorious Ravenstone line. Thanks to Todd, a publisher who believes in writers and treats us like an integral part of the chain; Sharon who keeps it all happening smoothly; and Kelly, a marketer who somehow makes shilling the product seem like great fun and easy, to boot.

Thanks to Jackie, Steve, Sharon, Laurie, Gail, Mary Jane, Linda, Henrietta, Gaylene and all other independent booksellers who hand-sell Canadian mysteries. Thanks to all the Canadian readers who support their local writers, and all the other readers who delve into Canadian books with such evident respect.

THE MONITOR

CHAPTER 1

Denise and I were sharing our monthly potluck supper of my Greek salad, her chicken enchiladas, and an inexpensive bottle of wine she'd pulled out of her shoulder bag. I'm not much of a drinker, but, since we both had things to celebrate, it seemed churlish not to indulge.

We were drinking to Denise's appointment to chair of a committee. It was at the department level, but it had larger implications. She was to be in charge of the writer-in-residence program, which was housed by the English department, but partially funded through alumni funds and some other administration purses. To me, it sounded like a headache and a half, but Denise was campaigning for tenure track, and from her tentative stance as a full-time sessional lecturer, this was the biggest opening she had been given. She was going to give it her all, I could tell, and Denise's all was no small thing. If anyone was going to get tenure in this climate, it would be her.

Being slightly older and armed with only an MA, I hadn't fared quite so well in terms of the University of Alberta. Cutbacks had been rampant, and I'd been lucky to land a couple of distance courses run through Grant MacEwan College. I was hoping that they might pave the way to more work, though it was impossible to predict what might happen in the educational scene in this province anymore.

However, I did have something to celebrate, too. In addition to my distance work, which barely paid the bills, I had just managed to land a job that was perfect for me, which paid very well and didn't even require a new wardrobe. While I had signed a confidentiality agreement, I didn't think it was going to be a big issue to tell Denise a bit of what I was going to be doing. After all, she did worry about me.

Her reaction wasn't quite what I had hoped for. "What the heck is a chat-room monitor? You mean on the Internet? Oh Randy, you mean you're going to spend your evenings peeping on cyber-wankers?"

"Not exactly, though the main reason for the monitoring is to crack down on kiddie porn for sure. In fact, I think that is part of the mandate that system operators have to agree to when getting that much bandwidth to operate." I took more wine than I had intended and coughed a bit as the power of it went up my nose. "Mostly, though, I am there to make sure that no one gets out of line and nothing illegal takes place. The other chatters won't even know I'm there."

"That's creepy."

"Well, sort of, but not really any creepier than having surveillance cameras in department stores. You know they're there for your general protection, because shoplifting makes everything pricier for everyone else, so you put up with the cameras and try not to take it personally."

"You know, I've never actually been in a chat room," Denise mused while pouring herself another glass of wine. I put my hand over the rim of my glass so she couldn't top up mine at the same time.

"Let me clean up this mess, and then I'll log us in and you can see what I'm talking about." We were seated at my small kitchen table, which is set along the wall of the eating area of my apartment. Since my desk—complete with computer and printer—is also in the room, as well as a rather large filing cabinet, movement can get problematic if everything isn't streamlined. I cleaned and washed off the table with a damp cloth, setting our dishes into a plastic dishpan in my old ceramic sink. I then lowered the hinged leaf on the table and brought one of the kitchen chairs over to the desk area. Denise, still holding onto her wineglass, settled in beside me as I booted up my computer.

"So this is a real-time sort of thing? The folks are all logged in to their various terminals at the same time as us?"

"Exactly. However, this isn't what you'd call Internet Relay Chat. That is a bit too fast, even for me, and I type pretty quickly. This is real-time chat through a web browser, what they call a cgi-bin program. There is a self-reloading component to the web site that activates every time someone posts something. It's as if you are hitting the reload button every so often and discovering that changes have been made to the site."

My desktop picture of the Edmonton river valley in full autumn color had by now appeared, and I clicked on my browser icon to hook onto the Internet. I had invested in a cable connection earlier in the fall and was gratified by Denise's admiration of how fast my connection time was. I hit the Bookmarks menu and pulled my cursor down to Babel, the name of the chat room I'd been hired to monitor.

I logged in as Denise, signing her in as a guest. I had

no problems telling her about the job, but I had signed a confidentiality agreement and I didn't want to appear in the room before my appointed time with my trainer. It wouldn't hurt, though, to just show her how chat worked.

There were several folks in the room who responded to the automatic posting: *Denise has entered the building*.

"You see, they're mostly friendly. I'll just post a quick comment for you, and you can see how the room works."

Denise: Hi folks. I'm a newbie. I'll just watch for a bit.

Maia: Jump on in, honey. We're pretty friendly around here, and newbies are always welcome. There's an FAQ up in the left corner there, if you want. *smile*

"What's an FAQ?" asked Denise, beside me.

"It stands for *frequently asked questions*, and covers basic netiquette for the room, directions on how to create a private message, or a private room, how to choose an icon, who to write to with complaints or problems, that sort of thing. Most people don't bother reading them when they come into a new community, but they should. It's very easy to step on toes in the cyber-world."

"What does that mean?" Denise pointed to the screen, which had refreshed a few times while we'd been talking. Several folks had posted, and, along with asterisked body language, they had added various acronyms to their posts.

"Well, that LOL means *laughing out loud* and ROT-FLMAO means *rolling on the floor laughing my ass off*. FWIW means *for what it's worth* and IMNSHO stands for *in my not so humble opinion*. There are others, like YMMV, which stands for *your mileage may vary*, and BEG, which means *big evil grin*. Chatters take pride in creating their own jargon, just like any other closed society. Besides, some of these are trying to get missing body language across to the room, while others are just compressing some really long phrases that tend to find their way over and over into general speech."

"Okay, so what's a private message?"

"Well, that is half of what goes on in any given chat room, though it had never occurred to me before I started monitoring. You wouldn't believe the amount of flirting and innuendo that is flying around in there right now, I'm betting. For instance, if you were to private-message Maia right now to thank her for her help, it might take a wee while for her to get back to you. I have a feeling she and Daniel in there are having a few private moments. Hang on."

I demonstrated by highlighting Maia's name in the chatter list to the right of the screen. Then I typed in the message box: "Thanks for steering me to the FAQ. I don't want to mess up."

As soon as I hit the Post button, it appeared on the screen above as:

PM from Denise to Maia: Thanks for steering me to the FAQ. I don't want to mess up.

A few more public postings came between, and then Denise gave a little whoop when she read:

Bonn: Have you ever noticed how pink cartoon pigs are? I mean, that's got to warp an urban kid's mind, right?

Gandalf: You don't think the fact that cartoon pigs tend to talk might be a giveaway that it's not quite National Geographic?

PM from Maia to Denise: Don't worry, hon. It's not like you're interrupting the brain trust here. *LOL*

"See, you and Maia are the only ones who can see that post. Of course, there are all sorts of things being posted that you likely can't see."

"But you can when you're logged in as a monitor?"

I shrugged. "Well, I think I can turn it off and on. I don't spend the whole evening reading other people's private conversations, but I can go in to make sure nothing ugly is brewing. Likewise with the private rooms; I can hover in the rafters and check on what's happening within. Usually it's private cyber-sex, and I don't spend much time lingering, if you know what I mean. We just have to be careful that nothing illegal is taking place."

With that, I hit the Leave button, and the chat screen was replaced with Babel's "See you next time" splash page, replete with banner ads and counter.

"Although you can't see it, *Denise has left the building* was posted after you logged out. Most folks announce that they'll be leaving, and then there are myriad goodbyes posted before they actually log out."

"So, in other words, you've made me look like a rude person," Denise offered a mock pout.

"Well, if you actually decided to chat, I'd suggest you register with a handle that offers you some disguise. Never forget, the chat population is constantly changing. There will be a core group of regulars, but anyone can walk in off the street, just like we did tonight. You have to keep some healthy paranoia about you."

"What is your chat handle?" Denise seemed interested, but I had a feeling I hadn't managed to sell her on the brave new world possibilities I was seeing in the Internet.

"Chimera," I admitted. "I know it sounds a bit melodramatic, but it felt right at the time, and now I'm stuck with it."

Denise laughed. "Not at all. I can't think of a better name. After all, truth in advertising, and all that."

It wasn't long before our conversation was back to

Denise's new position on the committee. We mulled over various of her fundraising ideas while drying the dishes, and I walked her to the front door of the apartment to watch her safely to her car.

Although Denise had seemed a bit contemptuous of my new job, I was glad I'd told her about it. I am not that good at keeping things secret from folks I care about. This is odd, in that I am very good at keeping other people's secrets. My own life, however, I prefer to live as an open book. Of course, it was probably a good thing I hadn't told her about the interview process to get the job. I'm not sure I'd have been able to put a spin on that whole thing that would sound anything but bizarre.

CHAPTER 2

I'd been surfing about the 'Net for a while, using it mainly to research my freelance work. It was cheaper than a membership to the university library, and far vaster. Then, to unwind after marking e-mailed essays or dealing with obtuse questions from students on the class conference board, I would pop into one of the myriad chat rooms set up on the 'Net, where there was always someone to talk to. It was like the coffee rooms in other workplaces, except that there you usually found yourself alone, drinking the swill from the drip coffee urn in the corner and reading the occupational safety posters out of boredom. Besides, with the irregular hours I was keeping, there was usually no one either unoccupied or sometimes even awake when I decided to take a break.

A notice one evening in Babel, my favorite chat site, had made me sit up and take notice. "Do you come here regularly? How would you like to chat productively? Get paid for your efforts? For more information, leave a private message for Chatgod."

Well, never let it be said that I was the nervous sort, but I thought about that notice for an entire evening before replying.

I figured no harm could come from a simple private

message, or, in chat parlance, PM, so I left my handle "Chimera" with a PM posting saying I was usually in Babel from 10:00 p.m. onward and that I could always use the job. It was the next day before I received a reply.

I'd seen Chatgod posting messages and announcements from time to time, but he'd never spoken to me before.

PM *from Chatgod to Chimera:* Be in Babel at 10:05 tomorrow evening.

I was intrigued. Nervous, but not a little bit flattered, too, that he should take my PM seriously. The next evening I showered and dressed nicely, even though I didn't have a Webcam and I couldn't afford the fancy bells and whistles that allowed chatters to see each other. I just needed to feel confident for the interview.

I went into the room at 9:45, and chatted a bit aimlessly with the few folks there. Some of the East Coasters were calling it a night, the Swedes had all gone to bed long before, and the Californians were just beginning to drift in. Evangeline was moaning about her exams, as usual, giving me the feeling that her parents had sent her to college for her MRS rather than for any intellectual training. Gopher was monkeying around, posting pictures of some nubile cartoon characters, and Kafir seemed to be marking time till his sweetie Kara arrived. I was just about to deselect images on my screen, to avoid yet another view of Sailor Mercury, when a small "ping" emanated from my computer.

While I've been computer-proficient since my thesis days, I am Luddite enough to worry about any new thing that happens, figuring I've finally broken the magic toy. I quickly pulled my hands from the keyboard and stared at the machine.

The screen shimmered for a moment, and then, where the usual advertising appeared at the top of the screen, there was suddenly a window with a man's face at the center, staring straight at me. I jumped.

The postings of the others disappeared and in their place came a message, without my even having to press the Post button. No handle appeared before his message, but it would have been redundant in any case. His message read, "Good evening, Chimera. I am Chatgod."

I was mesmerized by the face on my screen and felt as if he were looking right into me, although I knew he couldn't see me. I gulped, and posted into the message box: "Hello."

So this was Chatgod. He wasn't at all what I had expected. I guess I had imagined him to fit into the stereotype of cyber-tech geeks from university, bespectacled, pocket-protected, emaciated, and earnest. Instead, he was a startlingly handsome man in an ascetic, monk-like way. His graying hair was close-cropped to a perfectly sculpted head, and his high cheekbones and a thin aquiline nose gave him a look of ancient aristocracy. But it was his eyes that held me. They were blue, a piercing cold blue, as if they took their color from the depths of a glacier-fed lake. I shivered.

Chatgod: Chimera, your name has brought you to the top of my list of prospective employees. I sense that you are the one we seek.

Chimera: What exactly is the job?

Chatgod: Our world is a new one, and we feel our responsibility to our patrons keenly. We have decided that a monitor is required, someone to watch over the flock.

Chimera: The flock?

Chatgod: Many of the visitors to Babel are harmless;

most are quite amiable. Several are outstanding yet vulnerable people, about whom we worry. Into this mixture, from time to time, wander the chaotic, the anarchic, and those who are touched with a streak of evil. This worries us, in a world whose format restricts us from being able to lock ourselves away from the undesirable element before it has struck.

I cannot be everywhere, at all times. I require someone I can trust to keep an eye out for problems, to smooth waters, and to report to me. Your handle, the manner I've seen you use when posting, and the time zone factor all lead me to believe you would be ideal for this job. I am offering you $15 an hour, seven hours a day, six days a week. In return, I demand secrecy, total secrecy.

You are not to discuss your job with anyone, not your family, not your friends. No one in Babel must know your true role. If you must account to anyone for your employment, you may say that you have been employed by a 'Net server wishing to expand across the country, and that you do basic editorial work, some beta testing, some writing and content filler. Am I clear on this?

Chimera: Perfectly.

Chatgod: Good. This is a frontier, Chimera, a brave, new world. You are chosen to be a player in a game we are inventing rules to as we go along. Give me your time from 8:00 p.m. till 3:00 a.m. and I will give you a new land. The requirements are empathy, compassion, and occasionally ruthlessness. Like a gardener, you must control infestation to allow for growth. You will be a gardener, a shepherd, a watcher. Will you join us?

A little voice inside me was saying "run," but I wasn't listening, I was drowning in those icy eyes. "Yes," I posted.

This seemed to please Chatgod. For a moment, I thought he almost smiled.

Chatgod: Good. Tomorrow, my assistant, Alchemist, will contact you. He has been our sole monitor till now, and will continue while you are off-line. He will guide you in your role, and show you the various steps for watching without being seen. You report to him and he will report to me. Give him your name, address, and banking particulars, and your salary will be electronically placed in your account. Should you need to speak to me, I will always be a posting away. Courage, Monitor, and welcome.

The screen shimmered again, and once more I was looking at Babel as I had been used to seeing it. Although Carlin, one of my favorites, was cracking wise with some pretty funny material, I was too wound up to chat. I exited the room and went to bed, my head spinning.

CHAPTER 3

Because I had a night job now, I allowed myself to sleep in. It might have had something to do with last night's wine, as well. The morning sun had burned away my misgivings about Chatgod's messianic impulses, and what remained was the exhilarating thought that this job would suit me to a T. Not only could I indulge my preference to sleep in regularly, but I could also continue to teach the on-line distance courses in the afternoons, do chores and even catch an early movie, and be on-line again by 8:00 for my shift as paid Peeping Tom. Of course, this allowed no hope of a social life, but since I wasn't supposed to talk about my work, what sort of conversation cards could I bring to the table, anyhow?

I'd been finding the great smorgasbord of life pretty sparse these days. I'd broken off a serious long-term relationship at the end of the summer, and soon after that I'd got "sucked into the 'Net" (Denise's term for my new passion), and the mildly flirtatious, anonymous friendships I'd developed in the chat sites suited my needs for the moment. Chatgod had implied that I would still be able to chat while on the job, so things seemed pretty well perfect.

I was just hoping I would get along with this Alchemist, the guy Chatgod had said would be contacting me this

evening. From what I could gather, he was the only monitor at the moment and needed to take some time off. I was
wondering how grateful he would be that I'd been hired.
Folks tend to get a little turf-possessive at the best of times,
and cyber seemed to multiply this effect.

To celebrate my new job, I French-braided my hair,
pulled on my faded brown leather bomber jacket, and
headed out to stock up on some supplies.

I returned from my expedition with two pounds of
ground Kona coffee, the latest Rohinton Mistry novel,
some strawberry licorice, and a box of multicolored
recipe cards. It occurred to me I might want to start keeping track of some of the chatters. It was a technique I'd
devised during my grad student days, and it had stood
me in good stead through my freelance career. Mind you,
I had a large box under my bed full of little packets of cue
cards from old projects bound with elastic, the way some
women have stacks of love letters, but that's the price you
pay for not being around when they were passing out
eidetic memories.

After a hasty supper of pita stuffed with tomatoes and
lettuce, at 7:30 I booted up my computer and, after
checking my e-mail, clicked on my browser. I had seven
or eight chat sites bookmarked, but my mouse was
trained to aim for Babel, and pretty soon I was typing
Chimera into the handle box, and choosing an icon to
appear beside my name.

I'm not icon-loyal. While I think Kara and Lea probably would as soon leave the house without makeup as
enter the chat room without their pink paw prints, and
Virago was identified by his lightning stroke, I usually
just opted for a dot, and color-jumped, depending on my
mood. Tonight I picked red.

The East Coast crowd were out in full force, plus a couple of the Europeans I only had ever seen on weekend afternoons. Eros and Ghandhi posted some hellos to me, which was gratifying, and I blended myself into an ongoing conversation on whether garden gnomes were hideous kitsch or folk art. The topics that came up online never failed to amaze me.

I got caught up in things to the extent that the PM from Alchemist surprised me when it showed up at the top of my screen at 8:01. All it said was, "Come to Circle2." I had to pull down the Help menu to recall how to enter a semi-private room, but soon I was looking at another screen's wallpaper, this one a textured green. Alchemist was already there.

Chimera: Hi.

Alchemist: Hi there, Randy. I'm Tim. It's a pleasure to meet you. Chatgod is awfully impressed with you.

I began to wonder what use Chatgod had made of my user ID, the only information he'd required of me. I knew that some of my freelance work was floating about on the 'Net, but I also knew that high-tech searches could turn up a lot more than that. I had a feeling Chatgod probably knew by now what marks I'd got on old piano exams.

Chimera: Well, Tim, I'm pretty raw at all this, I hope I'm not too much bother to train. *smile*

Alchemist: *laugh* You should have seen me at the beginning. Don't worry, Chimera, you'll be fine.

Alchemist seemed very friendly and walked me through the various aspects of the monitoring job. With a Root command, I could link into anyone's PMs. I wasn't to let anyone in the chat room know I was a monitor. Chatters were told to address concerns to a mythical person named Alvin. I would receive all Alvin's messages, as did Alchemist and Chatgod, and in this way we could be contacted by the chatters. I learned how to determine a chatter's IP address, which stood for Internet Provider and was made up of a series of numbers that detailed where the connected terminal was anywhere in the world. I also learned how to do "screen captures" for evidence of bad behavior. This meant that I took a still photo of the active screen for future proof of what had transpired. While logs were kept of all sessions, they were difficult to access, and not all PMs were logged. Alchemist warned me that these took a lot of memory and to use them only when absolutely necessary.

He also gave me a list of chatters to keep a close eye on.

Alchemist: Some of them are troublemakers, some are really too young to handle things on their own, and there are a couple whom Chatgod just wants an eye kept on. I think I'll let you decide who's who, though, so as not to influence your opinion.

I jotted down the names, thinking they'd be the first I made cards for.

Alchemist: And that's all. If there's a problem you don't think you can handle, contact me, any time. It'll take me a while to change my sleep patterns, so I will probably be up.

So there I was, with a couple of handy-dandy commands, a list of people to watch, and a very nice guy as a co-worker. Could life get any better? Plus, I had strawberry licorice and the means to pay for it.

CHAPTER 4

The next evening, Alchemist and I PMed each other for about a half hour before he logged off for the evening. I was feeling pretty edgy about my maiden voyage.

PM *from Alchemist to Chimera:* Don't worry, Randy, you'll be fine. There's not too much going down today. Mind you, if Geoff L. doesn't stay on his meds, you'll have to toss him tonight! *grin* He was irritating some folks last night with the song lyrics he kept posting in blinking big font.

PM *from Chimera to Alchemist:* Thanks, I'll try to keep things under control.

PM *from Alchemist to Chimera:* Just have fun, that's the main thing. Ciao, Chimera.

I was on my own. I could post my own messages as Chimera, or I could post and receive messages from Alvin if I wished, although Alchemist had advised me to appear as Alvin only if there was trouble, since several women seemed to be enamored of the mythical Alvin and would clog my screen with PMs if I appeared unnecessarily. I could also read everyone's PMs, which in a way struck me as rather fun.

I have a voyeuristic tendency in me, I'm the first to admit. My favorite time of riding the bus is in the evening, when lights are coming on in houses but curtains aren't yet closed. I'll stare into those little lighted boxes and wonder about the people who inhabit them. If I worry about it at all, I put it down to having a healthy anthropological curiosity, rather than any form of prurience. I mean, I'd never even seen a pornographic film, nor did I want to.

Alchemist had advised me to spend some time right away trying out the various commands I needed for monitoring. "If something ugly starts to happen, it happens quickly. You have to be on top of things," he'd said. So, tonight I was obediently popping in to check on the various "Baby, I want you" messages that chatters were slipping into their conversations.

I'd participated in an interesting chat a couple of days earlier about the whole notion of cyber-relationships. Gandalf, someone I'd never chatted with before, was expounding on the tack that no one on the screen was real to him, that we were mere blips that he could obliterate with the flicking off of his computer. Fluff, one of the Babel regulars, a very intelligent and witty woman, was taking him to task for this attitude. Her reasoning was sound, for her. I really believed that she was, like she said, much the same in real life, or IRL, as she was on-line. To reduce her to a blip without feelings would be really reductive.

And yet, from the looks of things, no one seemed to take the risks of flirting too seriously. Innuendo bounced about like a squash ball in a very small court. Folks batted their eyelashes, bounced into people's laps with abandon, and administered huge, wet smooches, all couched in asterisks. And those were on the open screen. Behind the scenes, cyber-wolves prowled, looking for women who wanted to participate in cyber-sex, and some of the women were just as craven, offering some outrageous propositions to folks they'd not spent five minutes chatting to. It was an education.

It was about 10.00, and I was making a second pot of coffee when I noticed Venita appear. This was one of the names on the list Alchemist had given me. I was curious as to why he hadn't filled me in on the reasons for the names being on the list, but had to admit it was fascinating, the same way opening a new mystery novel can be compelling.

Venita was in a bubbly mood and didn't wait patiently to join a conversation. I wondered why I'd never spotted her in Babel before, but that soon became clear. "I'm usually on at noon" she posted in answer to someone's question if she was a newbie. "But I managed to wrassle a terminal this evening, and I am ready to meow."

A couple of the regular stud muffins stated some feelers her way, but Venita had disappeared as quickly as she'd appeared. That was odd. I flicked the Root command on her name and saw immediately where she'd gone. She was neck-deep in PM land with someone named Theseus, someone I'd never seen before.

PM from Theseus to Venita: How's my hot baby tonight? *evil grin*

PM from Venita to Theseus: Hi yourself, honey. I've been sitting here, all by myself, thinking about you . . . *looks deep in his eyes* getting hotter . . . and wetter . . .

PM from Theseus to Venita: Oh baby, touch me.

PM from Venita to Theseus: Baby, I love to touch you . . . to feel you getting bigger . . . and harder . . . *moan*

Sheesh. I was starting to wonder if this was some kind of joke Alchemist was pulling on me, to see if I could cut it as a monitor. I was feeling a bit unclean reading these PMs, but Venita was on the list and the list was my job. I cut and pasted a screen's worth of PMs and kept watching, pausing for a few minutes to check what was happening on the open screen.

ZZBottom, another of the names on the list, had appeared. I checked who he was talking with and popped in to see some PMs, but he seemed to be focused on the fate of Da Bulls for now, so I returned to Venita and Theseus.

PM *from Theseus to Venita:* *pulls her onto his lap, straddling him* Have you been a good girl today?

PM *from Venita to Theseus:* *wriggles in delight* Oh yes, Daddy, a very good girl . . . too good . . . wanna see how good?

PM *from Theseus to Venita:* *puts his hands under her skirt* You aren't wearing any panties . . . you *haven't* been good today . . . Daddy's gonna have to spank you.

Oh god. This was a bit too thick for me. I flicked back on to the open screen in time to see Geoff L's latest musical meanderings. This was something I could deal with. I counted the number of times four-letter Anglo-Saxon words were used as verbs in the lyrics and cleared the screen and locked him out. He'd be back with another handle, as soon as he fought his way out of Netscape limbo, but I could keep an eye out for him, and avoid having to think about kinky Venita and her mysterious satyr.

Oh well, it was a dirty job but, according to Chatgod, someone had to do it.

CHAPTER 5

My second solo night went a bit better. Alchemist stuck around for a while, and for some reason it was easier to read the more sappy PMs if there was someone else reading and joking in my ear about them. And he was funny and wittily caustic, without sounding mean. It was as if we were discussing the antics of tumbling, rowdy puppies, rather than oversexed lonely people with computers. For the first time, talking with Alchemist, I could understand the desire to meet up with cyber-friends IRL.

I'd read about taking cyber-relationships into real time but had never before felt the urge. To tell you the truth, half the time, I felt as if I was living in a Flann O'Brien novel, where the characters the writer was creating came to life as he slept and rewrote their stories. Until now, I had been content to chat with no push to imagine the people behind the words. I had jotted down Alchemist's (I couldn't think of him as Tim) phone number when he had given it to me my first night of monitoring. Maybe one of these days I'd get around to calling him.

ZZBottom came on again shortly after *Alchemist had left the building*, and I pulled a green card for him. Call it intuition, call it having once shared a house with a compulsive gambler, but there were some things he'd said about the basketball games the night before that made me suspicious.

Sure enough, I caught some PMs that made me realize he was running a loose sort of bookmaking arrangement through Babel. No wonder Chatgod wanted him watched. I jotted down a few of the names he was connecting with. It occurred to me it might be sort of fun to play with lag times, when on occasion the computer program just seemed to hang for hours without refreshing, if he got into horse racing any time soon. There's nothing like a player's inability to place a bet on time to make a bookie go out of business.

It was about 11:30, and I was thanking my lucky stars that Venita and Theseus hadn't surfaced on my shift, when someone named Sanders appeared in the room. Maia and Vixen had been chatting about sofa cushion binding, but perked up and welcomed him into the fold. He seemed nice, a little diffident, but polite. Since nothing else was happening, I pressed my own handle shift, and Chimera came out to play.

Sanders: Hello Chimera. Are you another regular denizen of these hallowed halls?

Chimera: *smile* Yes, I suppose so. Welcome Sanders. What brings you to our shores?

Sanders: I have heard from far and wide that the best chat to be had happens at Babel. Tonight I had some time to search, and I found my way here. Is it indeed all they speak of? *smile*

Chimera: All and more. Babel is what you make of it, Sanders. *grin*

We all chatted for a bit, and he revealed himself to be extremely well-read, something that always makes me partial. I checked the user lists a few times, but it seemed that only Sanders, Vixen, and I were about, Maia having left earlier because she was in a different time zone.

This was chat at its best. Sipping good coffee, feet tucked up underneath you, exchanging witticisms with an intelligent man. I know someone who once said that everyone on the 'Net is a thirteen-year-old boy until proven otherwise, but I doubted that Sanders had seen thirteen for a while. Few thirteen-year-olds I knew could make a joke about *Finnegan's Wake*, for example.

PM *from Sanders to Chimera:* Tell me something about yourself, to let me picture you accurately, unless that affronts your sensibilities. *smile*

PM *from Chimera to Sanders:* Dark eyes, dark hair, dark thoughts, long limbs, short attention span. *grin*

PM *from Sanders to Chimera:* Provocative picture *g* me—hair graying, middle thickening, heart young, mind wandering, eyes green . . .

PM *from Chimera to Sanders:* Nice picture, sir. *smile* You're right, of course, it does help to hang a picture on some particulars.

PM *from Sanders to Chimera:* I'm from Edmonton, in Canada. What about you?

I sat back so quickly, I might have bruised my vertebrae on the back of the chair. Ohmigod, it was one thing to chat with a fascinating, witty man over the 'Net. It was quite another to know he lived in the same small city. I stared at the screen, sweating slightly, as if he might suddenly appear at my main floor apartment window.

I couldn't help it. As much as I approved of basic honesty on the 'Net, I couldn't open myself up to this sort of thing, especially because it might jeopardize my job as monitor.

PM *from Chimera to Sanders:* I am from the ether. *smile* Everywhere and nowhere.

There was a long pause before I received a reply.

PM *from Sanders to Chimera:* Ah, a mystery woman. *smile* How fascinatingly enticing. Good night, my ether woman. *kiss*

It was a good thing Jackal came on about then, with some stupid fantasy pics he kept trying to post. Blocking the pornographic ones took my mind off the man who, somewhere in my city, was thinking about me, and probably wondering.

CHAPTER 6

I don't want anyone getting the idea that I'm some sort of cyber-junkie who spends her life in gray sweats in front of her computer, so I'd better explain something about myself. I'm thirty-something, in fact, more "something" than thirty, and after about ten years as a freelance writer, I had gone back to university to do an MA on an interesting Canadian author. After getting the degree here, I found myself settling in Edmonton, teaching freshman English as a sessional lecturer at the University of Alberta. I liked the hours and I had also more than liked the man in my life, one of Edmonton's Finest.

But both the job and the relationship had fizzled recently, the job because of university cutbacks, and the relationship likely because of my own insecurities. Steve had wanted something permanent, and I just wasn't ready for it. Frankly, I wasn't sure if I would ever be. There's an intensely selfish streak in me, and it makes me wonder if I'll ever be able to meld myself into half of a couple with any ease.

So, instead of working as a sessional at the U of A, I was now technically across the river at Grant MacEwan College. Except that I was really in the dining room of my apartment, since the only courses I'd managed to get for this winter term were distance ones. I had two sections of English 111, which was called Communications but really amounted to an essay-writing course. I wasn't knocking it, though. The whole world could use practice in formulating logical arguments, as far as I was concerned. Students worked from a packaged set of lessons and e-mailed me their queries, quizzes, and essays, and I responded in kind. The chair of the English department had halfway promised me some classroom work in the spring term, so I was biding my time, trying to make the salary from two classes stretch.

Thank goodness the rent on my apartment was cheap, and thank goodness I liked lentils. I'd dropped about fifteen pounds since the previous summer, but that was just fine, aside from having to shell out for a new pair of jeans. Life is just chock-full of silver linings. And, aside from Denise's admonitions, I was enjoying the monitor job. I decided I had time to head down to the Safeway for some salad greens before I needed to log in for the evening.

I was about halfway to the Safeway on Whyte Avenue when I happened to meet Dr. Flanders. He is a cute little button of a man, a retired professor of Canadian drama in the English department of the U of A. He has an uncanny ability to remember the name of every student he's ever met, I'm sure, and he greeted me like a long-lost friend.

"Randy! You look marvelous! How have you been keeping yourself? I saw your piece in *Alberta Views* last summer on the rise of bed and breakfasts in Alberta. Did you get to try any of them for the article?"

We went on to speak of the differences between English breakfasts, the horror of fried bread, and traveling in general, but after about ten minutes he seemed to collect himself.

"Well, it's been lovely to see you, but I must get these bananas home before they freeze! Take care, dear," and off he fussed down the street.

I found myself smiling the rest of the way. Dr. Flanders did that to me. I'm not sure why. Maybe it was the fact that I sensed he really liked me, the same way old boyfriends' mothers did. I am one of those incredibly unthreatening people, I guess. Old folks talk to me on buses, cashiers tell me their problems as they ring in my purchases, acquaintances at parties tell me their innermost secrets. I must have a trustworthy look about me, or maybe I just don't move quickly enough. Children don't seem to bother with me much, but it's a mutual thing. Although I've met a few I like, for the most part they seem to be just apprentice people. They can call me when they've got something interesting to say.

I was wandering the canned goods section, admiring the colors, when a man bumped into me backing away from the pear halves. We muttered our apologies and I continued down the aisle, but found myself glancing back at him. Might he be Sanders?

This was getting ridiculous, having my cyber-world infringing on my real life, and I cringed to find myself thinking *LOL*. I grabbed two packages of rice cakes and headed for the produce section. I picked up some bananas, apples, tomatoes, and lettuce and made my way to the fifteen-items-or-less cashier.

While it was interesting to muse about Sanders, the person who really had me daydreaming was Alchemist. His dry humor about the folks on Babel made me laugh, even when I was away from the terminal, but I never found it cutting or offensive. It was as if we were smiling at the antics of cute creatures a bit further down the food chain, like watching chimps in the zoo. I grinned to myself. I wasn't sure who would take umbrage with that statement more—the residents of Babel, or Jane Goodall.

It was five-ish before I got home again, and the waning sun was directly on a line with my kitchen window, making it enjoyable to unpack and shred lettuce. I tossed up a salad, sliced a hard-boiled egg from the fridge into the bowl, and put the rest of the salad-ready lettuce into a plastic bag for tomorrow.

I refuse to eat at the computer terminal. Somehow I feel that if I stay away from it during mealtime, I am not truly addicted. So, instead, I munched on my salad and read the latest Reginald Hill paperback at my kitchen table, approximately three and a half feet away from my computer.

Once dinner was out of the way, I tidied up the kitchen and took a general swipe around the living room. The downside of small quarters is that you need to keep things put away and clean in order to exist without madness encroaching. The upside, however, is you can practically stand in the middle of the room and reach anywhere to pick things up. I moved into the bedroom to pick up some clothes for the laundry, and then even swirled some toilet-bowl cleaner into the bowl for good measure before heading to my desk.

Quarter to seven. Well, I grinned, it was my first week on the job, it wouldn't hurt to look eager. I logged on, using the custom page Alchemist had designed for me the evening before. It was oddly gratifying to have "Welcome Chimera! It's so good to see you!" appear in bold white letters on the black screen. Several one-button choices appeared below that. I could log in immediately to any of the rooms, or lurk as Alvin. The Alvin choice could also be accessed later with a quick HTML code, so I went in as Chimera to see what was shaking.

There were several PMs listed for me, but I scrolled past them at first to get a sense of who was in the room, and what was happening currently. Not too much, it seemed. I counted Carlin, Kafir and Kara, and Maia, who was very likely waiting for Vixen.

Alchemist had pointed them out as probably the most stabilizing influences on Babel, and he was probably right.

Alchemist: It's the women who set the tone of the community, I think. We're just lucky we've got Vixen and Maia. They keep an eye out for newbies, and know exactly how far the general gaiety on the public screen should go. Others take their cue from them, at least on the public screen, and people are drawn to their good humor.

Chimera: What do you know about them?

Alchemist: One is from Arizona and the other from Halifax. They met here, and they're always saving money to get one of them enough plane fare to visit the other. They're good people.

I agreed with his thumbnail assessment. While the median age at Babel seemed to be about thirty, I sensed that both of these women were slightly older, perhaps in their early forties. They were both obviously well educated and witty. Maia, I had gathered, was divorced, and Vixen was a housewife with a computer jones. They shared a flock of male admirers and consistently made newcomers welcome. It amazed me that they were friends, since they could so easily have become rivals, but there was a bond between them that everyone could sense. They had each traveled to each other's homes, and were in the midst of planning a shared holiday to Mexico for the next winter.

These were the women who started up games of Truth or Dare, who teased other regulars, and who maintained the peace when the younger crowd began roughhousing with idiotic expletives. My job was bound to be easier when either one was in Babel, since everyone seemed to rise to their expectations. Tonight, I marked time with Maia, laughing at her descriptions of her day. She had a way of making everyday chores into adventures. Today her washing machine had packed it in, and she was busy describing the people she'd run across in the coin laundry she'd had to use.

Maia: There was one fellow there who kept his dryer going for three loads, just so he could watch my filmies whip round in the little round window. *grin* I wanted to ask him if he'd heard of cable, but thought better of it . . . *shudder*

Carlin asked Maia to describe her "filmies," and Maia responded by hitting him with the feather duster she and Vixen had invented to fend off the overly adventurous. Occasionally they would post it as a pictograph that looked something like ----------------------(((((((((((((((. Men panted to be thwacked with the duster, which only went to show.

Vixen bounced into the room, and I faded back while she and Maia caught up with each other's days. I didn't bother going into their PMs much. While they kept up a running flirtatious patter to the general room, to each other they mostly discussed Vixen's son's school triumphs and Maia's home-business ventures. Occasionally Vixen would give Maia a new recipe, or Maia would describe a hairdo she thought Vixen should try. It was like Mae West and Lauren Bacall with their hair in curlers talking over the backyard fence. I knew they received lots of PMs from the men in the room, but they were always kind and seldom sent anyone away miserable, although I doubted many got more than a batted eyelash for their troubles.

I read my PMs after posting my own *hugs* in return. Most were from Alchemist, who apparently had had to leave early this evening and so couldn't hand off, but would try to pop back later for a bit. I was surprised at my own disappointment not to find him there. It was as if I'd been cleaning the house for his visit on my screen, I realized. I was getting more and more confident on my own, but it certainly helped to have a mentor there beside me for the first week or so, anyhow.

There was also a PM from Sanders, posted some time in the middle of the night: "Couldn't sleep. I see you in the ether. Hope to connect soon."

I couldn't help myself. I was smiling. I shook myself and cleared my private messages to keep better track of the public screen. Although using the frames version of Babel slowed me down a bit, it helped me keep track of the current users as well as watch the board. Alchemist had promised me that a newer browser would speed things up a bit. I was hoping installation wouldn't be too onerous.

At about 9:00 p.m. my time, 11:00 Babel time, ZZBottom appeared. I had been making some notes and developing some ideas on how to chase him away from Babel without causing too much friction. That was essential, as Alchemist had advised. Although our business was to keep things smooth and legal, we had to be careful about angering potential hackers. A disgruntled hacker could wreak as much havoc as a disgruntled postal employee in a clock tower, even with all the safety measures that Chatgod implied were in place.

I gave him a few minutes to start contacting his gambling devotees, and then, just before he closed the bets, I pushed my magic button, which created a temporary freeze on refreshing in Babel and thus created the most dreaded of all chatting occurrences, lag. Although several innocent people would suffer "chattus interuptus," I had a feeling it was going to drive ZZBottom crazy. Crazy enough, I hoped, to take his bookmaking elsewhere.

Lag occurred for all sorts of natural reasons, of course. A hub on the Web could be down somewhere, causing the refresh rate to drop to negligible. Boze, a veteran chatter, had claimed he had managed to paint his entire house during lag times. I was hoping that some well-placed lags could keep enough regulars from placing bets on time with our resident bookie that he would decide to head for greener, faster pastures.

I watched the clock, reset Babel nine minutes later, and popped into ZZBottom's PMs to watch the results. I found myself giggling while watching his attempts to placate the angry bettors. I checked my watch against the racing form I'd bought earlier in the day. From my calculations, my next hit would be the 7:05 at Santa Anita. If I averaged two lags per night, I was betting ZZBottom might be taking his bookie joint elsewhere before the end of the week. That is, if I were the betting type.

CHAPTER 7

A couple of days later, Alchemist and I were crowing over ZZBottom's swift departure. I had a feeling, though, that my co-worker was ogling one of the newbies, a woman named Senta who had a slightly zaftig way about her. Although I had never seen him act more than mildly flirtatiously to anyone, he had seemed a trifle distracted ever since she'd logged on.

Regardless of Denise's opinions of chat rooms, and even barring my view of Venita and Theseus's liaison as warped, chat rooms held very little overt carnality. They reminded me of church potluck suppers at times, or half-forgotten parties my parents had either hosted or I'd melded with 1950s television, where faithful couples and bashful singles were somehow free to flirt and tease with no repercussions. The art of flirting had become a casualty of the 1990s, with all the fear of sexually transmitted diseases and political correctness.

With the anonymity of the Internet, chat rooms, at least the best of them, had managed to revive that art form. Of course, the better the chatter was verbally, the better the flow, and the more ardent the admirers. You could see that in Maia and Vixen. They understood the concept of flirtation and of the party atmosphere that Babel generated.

I was watching a couple I'd seen together on a more regular basis in the last few days. Relationships were so incendiary in cyber. Entire romances could play out in a matter of weeks. Thea, it seemed, had been introduced to Babel by another 'Net-girlfriend, Kara. She and Milan had connected very quickly, or else they'd already known each other from some other chat site. I wasn't sure. I wasn't too sure, either, about Thea's emotional stability; she had made a few comments about an unhappy marriage. They say nothing can break up a happy marriage, but the Internet was getting a very strong reputation for being an enemy of that sacred institution. If Thea was having trouble at home, a cyber-affair with Milan wasn't going to do anything to patch things up IRL. I pulled out one of my colored cue cards and made a note of their names. I had a feeling Chatgod wouldn't be too happy to have more gristle for the Ann Landers types to gnaw on.

I didn't know how I felt about the whole real-time versus cyber-time debate. There were people who could make a very good case for the concept that cyber-relationships could remain in the fantasy realm while real life continued, unscathed. However, the more of oneself one put onto the screen, the more intense the relationships one evolved. This was why I worried more about those with handles that were actual names than those who adopted personas like Vixen or Maia, or indeed Chimera.

The potency of words was what had attracted me to chat rooms in the first place, but they became a double-edged sword when coupled with the loneliness of those who were pulled toward computer screens. Lacking body language, folks invested more in terms of opening themselves up emotionally to others as they formulated relationships. Compared to real-time couplings, where the physical aspects often took over, leaving it longer to get to know the inner workings of your partner's mind, cyber-relationships plumbed the depths of emotions, dreams, and fantasies of people who had yet to lay eyes on each other.

Thea seemed to be lapping up Milan's attentions like she hadn't been noticed in years. If that didn't say something sad about the state of her marriage, I don't know what could. It may be that her marriage was on rocky ground, but she seemed to waffle when any of the more hard-headed women in Babel suggested she pack and walk. Milan struck me as a sensitive sort; he paid compliments to the shyer women and connected in a friendly way with various men. Moreover, he had a vocabulary that could melt ice in Inuvik, and that was the coin of the realm in Babel, for sure. Thea was blossoming like a time-lapse rose.

I made a note to keep an eye on them and clicked back onto the general screen. Almost automatically, I banned Geoff L, knowing he'd be back in another manifestation in a couple of minutes, foaming at the mouth. I wished his mother could keep him on his meds and gangsta rap out of his boom box. I was getting tired of him posting obscenities. I checked my watch. It would soon be time for the western shift to get on in full swing, and Geoff L lived somewhere on the eastern seaboard. He had about another half an hour before he petered out.

Alchemist popped back on my screen to say goodnight just as I returned to my desk with another cup of coffee: *grin* They're all yours, be gentle with the puppets, Chimera, see you tomorrow!

I posted back a quick goodnight *hug* and settled into my chair. One of the things I liked best about Alchemist was his ability to spell and type clean postings. Not that I

was immaculate. I had to watch my typing, I consistently seemed to get dyslexic with the word *just*. It usually
came out jsut. At least no one would think I couldn't
spell, though. Of course, they might think I was sloppy,
but heck, I could live with that.

Thea and Milan had created a private room by now. I
checked the listings and grinned. They'd titled it *motel*. I
wondered whose idea that had been. Geoff L had gone to
bed, Maia was gone, and Vixen was PMing with Teddy, her
current cyber-paramour. Lea, Kara, Carlin, and Twirp
were playing at having a hot-tub party, flicking each other
with cyber-towels and generally getting up to no harm.

My Notify list blinked as Sanders appeared. He must
have left the link open a long time, since his entrance
wasn't announced on the open screen. Although I was
visible to anyone searching lists of current users, I hadn't
posted anything recently, so it was a bit surprising to
receive a PM from Sanders almost immediately.

And how is the ether woman this fine evening?
Smile I've been thinking about you. . . .

I pondered a response. I had to admit the man
intrigued me, but I wasn't sure whether it was the hint of
danger I felt from his physical proximity, or his personality. From the general postings I'd read, he seemed nice,
but I had the feeling that, were he to realize where I lived,
he might request a coffee date or some such, and I wasn't
sure I wanted to go down that road.

Lots of Babellers had met up in real time, and most of
the time it seemed to enhance their friendships, but there
was still the thought in the back of my mind that any one
of these folks could be an ax-murderer. Just as I was
thinking up a suitably evasive reply to Sanders, my telephone rang.

It startled me. I picked up the receiver cautiously, my mind still half on the screen updating in front of me.

"Randy?" My heart still flipped a bit whenever I heard Steve's voice. It had been almost five months since we'd decided to cool it, and although I'd managed to persuade myself it had been all for the best, I still missed him desperately.

"Hi there, Officer. How's it going?"

"A lot better, hearing your voice." I could hear him smiling through his words. "I was wondering if you might like to catch a bite later. I miss you, you know."

"Tonight? I've already eaten, I think."

"You think?"

"Well, I'm not hungry, so I must have." This was likely not the right response, since Steve had always been on at me about my eating habits. "Actually, Steve, I'm busy tonight, but I'd love to get together. How about," my eye raked the calendar above my desk, "day after tomorrow?"

"Thursday? For dinner? Sure. How about I pick you up at, say, 7:00?" Steve sounded a bit deflated, but that could have been just my imagination.

"Sounds great, I'm looking forward to it."

"Me too, Randy. Me too. Well, I'd better get back to it. Crime doesn't sleep."

"Catch the bad guys, Officer. That's what I pay my taxes for. See you Thursday."

I hung up the phone, thinking I'd better notify Alchemist of my date on Thursday to see if he could cover for me. I'd offer to take one of his day shifts, I figured, although we hadn't yet decided what my day off would be, I realized. It would be good to see Steve again. I wasn't sure how much I would tell him about my new job, though. I had a feeling he wouldn't approve, although I wasn't sure what was giving me that idea.

I turned my attention back to Babel, where there was another PM from Sanders.

Still with us, lady of shadows?

PM from Chimera to Sanders: Nice to see you; merely contemplating life, the universe and the price of wheat in China.

PM from Sanders to Chimera: Overrated, too big to clean, and stick to rice.

I laughed. Sanders was funny, I had to give him that. To be on the safe side, I opened another window to watch the room in general as I chatted with him. I was certainly curious about him, but I couldn't very well ask any pointed questions without leaving myself open to having to answer in kind. I played along, hoping he would allow some personal tidbits to slip out. I had a wacky vision of him turning out to be my next-door neighbor, Mr. McGregor, tired of his Hammond organ and gone cyber, and almost spit coffee onto the monitor.

In a way, I had been lucky that Steve had called when he had, or I might have been tempted to tell Sanders a little more about myself. I had been feeling lonely. It was mostly my own fault, but it didn't help for Sanders to know that.

To be extra safe, I dialed up Denise's number and left a request for a coffee date on her answering machine. Sanders and I continued to quip as I kept an eye on the room at large. I checked in on Thea and Milan in their private room, motel, every so often, but they were getting rather embarrassingly explicit, and I felt uncomfortable. Sex has never been a spectator sport for me, even if only described in words. Alchemist might have the stomach for this sort of thing, but I didn't think I ever would.

Thea must have been a reader of bodice-ripper romance novels. Her postings had that faint edge of patchouli to them.

Thea: *breast heaving* The thought of your hands claiming territory, drawing me toward you, pulling me ever nearer . . . being impaled. . . . *moaning*

Milan: Darling, I cup one perfect breast in my hand and bring my mouth down on your warm nipple, my tongue licking it to attention, as I push deeper into your mysteries. . . .

I had to admit, Milan knew his audience.

Thea: *writhing* Oh . . . oh lord, I hear him coming down the hall. . . . *kiss* Bye.

Milan: Thea. . . .

I shook my head. I tried not to be judgmental, but this was ugly. I have never understood the penchant some folks have for starting things without finishing others. Thea might be unhappy in her marriage, but there was no excuse, in this day and age, not to simply walk away from that unhappiness before starting something new.

I'd always been puzzled as well by the acceptance of chivalric romance, the old Arthurian idea of pining for the unattainable. I had been too shy to ever question it in university English classes, and the professors, all male, come to think of it, had seemed to find nothing wrong in the concept of lusting after another man's wife. I wondered if Milan was truly in love with Thea as Thea, or if he was harboring some Lancelot complex.

It has been my opinion that Lancelot should have forgotten about Guinevere and checked out the poor old Lady of Shalott before she boarded the barge, but then where would Tennyson have been? Stuck with some bedraggled seabird for eternity. I grinned to myself.

Maybe it was a good thing I didn't have a classroom job this winter. With any luck, by May, when I was hoping for a literature course, I would be back on an even keel, maundering on about pastoral poetry and the need for informed readers to allow parody to exist, instead of sermonizing on the moral turpitude of the previous generations. There might be a paper in comparing chivalric romances to cyber-relationships, but I doubted I'd be the one to write it.

PM from Sanders to Chimera: Forgive my intrusion to your reverie. I must confess you have been the cause of mine.

I smiled, in spite of myself. Well, I wouldn't be teaching English literatrue for a living unless I could be swept up by words, now would I? I had to admit it; the man was getting to me.

PM from Chimera to Sanders: Perhaps if the shadows were highlighted a bit more, our reveries would take on a similar hue . . . tell me about yourself . . . I'm a very good listener.

I remembered an old roommate of mine, famous for having a date every weekend through undergrad days, even prior to exams, when most of us were busy trying to cram eight months' reading into forty-eight hours. Her advice, when pushed for her secrets to dating prowess, was relatively simple. She had admitted that she would look into her date's eyes and say, "Tell me about yourself," and spend the rest of the evening listening and nodding.

It wasn't that easy to just smile and nod in a chat room but it might work to get some more information without having to divulge.

PM from Sanders to Chimera: Certainly, but there is no

such thing as something for nothing in this world or any other. *smile*

Rats. Oh well, if I played my cards warily, things should be safe enough.

Lying in bed later that night, I was still mulling over some of the intriguing conversation I'd had with Sanders. It was so much more titillating, for me at any rate, to think that I'd been speaking to someone I might ostensibly one day meet, someone from my own milieu. And he was that, indeed.

While we had maintained a veneer of banter and metaphor, some salient facts had come through. I was hoping more had come to me than had gone out, but then one could never be sure just what anyone read between the lines.

He had said he was involved tangentially and occasionally with the arts, but not paid for those connections. I had divulged that I was between jobs at the moment. He was divorced. I was single. His reading tastes were refreshingly eclectic, spanning poetry, biography, and the Booker nominees. He frequented the Yardbird Suite for good jazz, he drank his lattes decaffeinated and his beers dark, he played backgammon for money and started each day with the *Globe and Mail* cryptic crossword. He knew his way around the south side and university area, from the sounds of things.

By the end of the evening I had almost blurted out a request to meet him for drinks. I chuckled. What would his reaction have been had I casually said, "Why don't we meet at The Second Cup in Old Strathcona for a latte tomorrow?"

This was something I hadn't prepared myself for—the thought of actually wanting to meet someone from the chats in real time. What if, after all the interesting banter, he turned out to be some acne-riddled nebbish with an overbite and body piercings? Or worse, short?

I eventually drifted off to sleep, and my dreams were crowded with visions of typing "Thursday" over and over onto a computer screen.

CHAPTER 8

Alchemist agreed to cover for me on Thursday night. I was nervous about seeing Steve for the first time in almost half a year. I warred against dressing up but didn't want to risk hurting his feelings by appearing too casual. As well, I needed a little help masking the vulnerability I still felt. I decided on black jeans, a black cropped sweater, and just a hint of eye makeup. I braided my hair and reached instinctively for my favorite silver earrings. My hand stopped midway to the earring wall, two panels of cork tile over my dresser on which my earrings hung from dressmaker's pins. Steve had given me those earrings. What would my wearing them say to him?

"Oh lord, Randy, you're going to analyze yourself into an early grave," I said out loud, and snatched the silver earrings off their pin.

I was ready well before 7:00. I wandered about the apartment, checking that all the dishes were washed, the towels hung up, the bed quilts pulled straight. I wasn't planning anything; at least, I didn't think I was.

I glanced over at my desk area in the tiny dining room. I had stowed all my cue cards in a yellow plastic recipe box, and, although there was a list of handles on the bulletin board to the left of the window above the computer,

I doubted that it divulged any secrets. Not that I was hiding anything in particular from Steve. I knew I would answer him honestly if he came right out and asked what I was doing with myself every evening from eight till three these days, but I wasn't sure I really wanted him to be too curious.

I was still trying to analyze whether I was ashamed of my involvement as a paid peeper in the chat room when there was a knock at my door. Seven o'clock; right on time. I felt my heart bounce upward as I moved to the door.

Steve looked just as gorgeous as he had the first time I'd seen him. His brown leather jacket emphasized his broad shoulders, and his shirt underneath was crisp and fresh. I wanted to run my hands through his hair, to pull him into me and drink in his scent, all warmth and clean shower soap, as I remembered so well. Instead, I smiled brightly and asked, "So? Ready to eat?"

We walked down the hall of my apartment building in silence. I found myself concentrating on the edge of the Persian carpet that ran down the middle of the floor. It was so strange to be awkward around Steve, who had shared my bed, my shower, my . . . well, it didn't bear thinking about. I darted a quick look at him as he opened the door for me and caught his eye. The same thoughts must have been coursing through his mind, because he cocked his head to one side and said, "Oh Randy," and all of a sudden we were locked in an embrace that would rival the hottest teenage couple in any bus shelter.

After a few minutes, we broke for air. We looked at each other and laughed. "Should we head back down the hall, do you think?"

I smirked. "No way, Browning. You promised me

dinner. First things first." I squeezed him once more, fiercely, before moving back a step. Who knows, it was very likely a mistake to go against all the well-thought-out reasons for not continuing the relationship, but I felt as if a part of me that had been missing had returned and brought me back to life. I felt like laughing, or singing and dancing.

Instead, I let Steve lead me to his car and drive me to Earl's Tin Palace, where the beautiful people that evening just had to take a back seat to us.

CHAPTER 9

We were back at my place, a bit disheveled and very mellow. Although I hadn't forgotten how easy I felt in Steve's presence, it was as if a fog had been lifted, having him back in my orbit.

Over dinner we had discussed Steve's work, his project for early intervention with troubled teens through the community precincts, and the paper he'd delivered at a conference he'd attended in August. He'd kept himself very busy since we'd been apart; I wasn't sure whether to be jealous or pleased.

Now it was my turn. Steve had ambled out to the kitchen to get us some water. I was drowsy and didn't notice how long he was taking. When he returned, he deliberately dribbled a bit of water into my belly button.

"You rat!"

"That's not what you were saying a couple of hours ago." I sniffed in mock hauteur and took the glass of water from him.

"I noticed a strange list of names over your desk there. You doing some research or something?"

"Yeah, something." A brief thought of Chatgod's strange, cold face flashed across my brain, and I remembered his admonition to tell no one about my job. But this was Steve, and in the afterglow of ultimate vulnerability, I had no desire to keep secrets from him.

I outlined my monitoring job for Steve. I found myself trying to make it seem as innocuous as possible and trying to gauge his reaction as I went on. He asked a few interested questions and seemed to agree that it wasn't bad work for the time being.

"How do you feel about spying on people, though? Don't you feel as if you're somehow infringing on their privacy?"

"Well, I guess I'm rationalizing, but I figure that everyone should be pretty aware that the 'Net isn't a secure place. I wouldn't ever write anything I'd be worried about being overheard in church. There are other sites that log everything that takes place on the screen and in private. I think, in a way, that is worse than a few watchers. At least we don't log private messages or do anything more than block people who are overstepping certain already posted rules against pornography and other nastiness. And they are never sure if they've been kicked out or if their link has just somehow gone down."

Steve shook his head. "This Chatgod guy seems a bit strange, though, if you ask me. What if you all end up eating poisoned pudding the next time a comet whips around?"

I laughed at the thought. "Oh yeah, he's a case, all right. And you aren't far off the mark. I think he does have some sort of messianic complex, but he pays my salary right on time and hasn't bothered me at all, so I can't complain."

"Well, I know there was a lot of talk about policing on the 'Net at the symposium I went to in August. I didn't give it too much thought, as I don't go on-line except at work, but I could get you the printout of the proceedings if you want. There might be something there useful to you, since you're setting yourself up as a private cyber-cop."

I'd not thought of myself as such, but the more Steve spoke, the more it rang true. Something told me that setting myself up as a private cyber-cop wasn't quite what Chatgod had in mind, but I pushed that thought aside.

"Some of the people are fascinating, Steve. As an old sociology major, you'd love it. It's as if folks are rediscovering the art of communication, or developing a new one."

Steve leaned forward and took the water glass away from me, setting it up on the dresser within easy reach.

"Speaking of alternate forms of communication, mind if I stay over?"

"You always said it was like 'sleeping at attention' in this small bed," I laughed.

"Who said anything about sleeping?"

What can I say? It never pays to argue with the law.

CHAPTER 10

It was even later than usual when I finally got in gear on Friday morning, but I didn't mind. Steve had gone home after having some toast and coffee, and I'd putzed about in my housecoat for a while longer, unwilling to break the spell. Finally, I roused myself and got dressed. Old Strathcona was calling, and I wanted to wander about.

I was halfway to Whyte Avenue, heading on a zigzag diagonal through the neighborhood of old homes and three-storey walk-up apartments, when I realized I hadn't thought about the 'Net once since Steve and I had talked about it the night before, nor had I missed being on-line. Maybe I wasn't quite the addict I feared I was becoming. I smiled, mentally envisioning an *LOL* sign. On the other hand, maybe I was a nymphomaniac. Well, all in all, neither addiction was going to kill anyone. There were worse vices.

I moseyed about in When Pigs Fly, an idiosyncratic little boutique. They always had something to look at. Some of their tee-shirts had very funny slogans on them. I found myself laughing out loud at one: "Inside this body is a thin woman screaming to get out; I ate her." It would make a great global for the chat room, those little bits of cyber-graffiti that appeared above the screen occasionally when you refreshed. I smirked inwardly. Maybe I was addicted to the chats after all.

After a latte and bagel at one of the myriad coffee shops within the three-block radius, I meandered over to HUB Cigar. It was an anachronism, even in this neighborhood of eccentric establishments: a news agency par excellence with the original old wooden floors, where business people, children, rubbies, and covert voyeurs mingled easily.

I love this store, where you have to keep an eye to which aisle you wander down to get to the literary periodicals. You mustn't catch anyone's eye, just in case they happen to be carrying several assorted issues of *Bouncy*, or indulging in a glut of X-MEN comics.

After picking up a couple of writing quarterlies and a *Quill & Quire,* I found myself in front of the wall of international newspapers. I'd never paid much attention to these before, in that I usually paid little attention to anything smacking of current events, but today they drew me. They were stacked in cubbyholes with the names of the paper crafted on crude cardboard signs beneath each opening. I stood and read the names of places that had never interested me before: Chicago, Atlanta, Singapore, Austin, San Diego. I spoke daily with people from these places now. On an impulse I grabbed three or four of the cheaper editions, although none of them was very inexpensive. It would be cheaper to log into most of these papers' on-line editions, but the local flavor wouldn't be there; the ads, the local interest feel-good stories, and the people-oriented articles seemed to get leeched out of what made it on-line.

It would be fun to sprinkle my conversation with some knowledge about what was happening elsewhere in the world. I smiled wryly, thinking that this would be a way to confuse the trail for Sanders as well. I kept worrying that I'd inadvertently say something too "Edmontonian" and give it all away. At least, if I dropped hints from various places, it might keep him guessing a while longer.

I paid for my papers and headed back out onto the bustling center of Edmonton's trendy area. I walked down a few doors and popped into one of the nicer coffee bars to reward myself with another latte.

Block 1912 was my latest favorite of all the coffee shops along Whyte. There was a postmodernist flair to it, but mostly I liked the fact that the chairs were padded. I dumped my coat and bag in a chair and went up to get a skim milk/decaf latte. Some wag of a waiter had once called my order a "why bother?" but I liked them.

Once I'd got my coffee, I scrunched down in my chair and hauled some of the newspapers I'd just bought out of the plastic bag. *The San Francisco Chronicle* was interesting, although I felt a bit pretentious reading it in public. For some reason, it just felt too foreign to be reading it in the middle of Edmonton.

I took out the *Austin American-Statesman*. It was a traditional folded newspaper, along the same lines as *The Edmonton Journal*. I cannot bear tabloid-styled papers—for some reason they make me feel tawdry—but I must admit that they are easier to handle in cafés. I peeled off the International section for later and began to read the city news.

One article caught my eye at once, which wasn't difficult, as the headline was huge: COMPUTER KILLS MAN.

I guess it is not that unusual to be electrocuted by a piece of electronic hardware. It gave me pause, though. I thought about all the times I'd worked straight through thunderstorms. It had never occurred to me to be cautious about using my computer. One more thing to get neurotic about. Maybe I should have a rubber mat under my desk.

It seemed that one Charles Banyon had been surfing the 'Net in the comforts of his own home when he had connected a circuit by touching the keyboard at the same time as he clicked his mouse. He was discovered by his wife, Theresa, when she returned from the hairdresser's. In her anguish, after cutting the power at the breakers, it seems she had bashed the computer tower to smithereens with a shovel.

The spokesman from the police was quoted as saying that there was as yet no explanation for the faulty electrics, but that they were investigating, and the possibility of foul play had not been eliminated. The article went on to list the number of deaths by accidental electrocution that happen yearly, although they neglected to point out how many of these might be from murderous computers.

I sat back. This was going to get blamed on Internet chatting somehow, I'd bet. How did they know he'd been on-line, anyhow? Maybe he was checking his accounts or writing a novel. But, no, they had to say he'd been surfing. It was no wonder folks like Denise were so wary of the on-line frontier. I was betting there would be folks talking about this in Babel pretty soon.

The café was beginning to fill up, making me feel guilty. I packed away my papers and bundled up. It always surprises me how many people seem to be at loose ends on a workday. For years, as a freelancer, I used to wander about in a wasteland of empty shops and cafés, seeing only the occasional "lunching ladies." Now, it was as if half the population of Edmonton was ambling through the workday world. Downsizing?

CHAPTER 11

It was about 10:00 when Sanders showed up that evening. Most of the folks were telling jokes on-line. My favorite was the knock-knock joke about the interrupting cow. "Interrupting cow wh—?" "MOOOOOO!" It made me laugh to see how much really could be transmitted by sheer verbiage, even without the handy asterisked moods, gestures, and smiley-faced "emoticons."

I'd been filling Alchemist in about the lag attempts with ZZBottom, and he was highly appreciative of my methods, even though he'd had to fend off about seventy-five messages to Alvin about the bad service. Neither of us had spotted ZZBottom around all week, and Alchemist passed on to me Chatgod's praises as well.

Alchemist: That's exactly the sort of thing Chatgod gets worried about. You done great, kid.

Chimera: Well, I've been watching Venita, but, beyond her being a borderline nymphomaniac, I'm not sure what might be amiss there. I have some spidey senses about Thea and Milan, though I'm not too sure yet. The rest of the list you gave me hasn't really made much of a showing.

Alchemist: No, well, people come and go; but they might be back. I'd say to always trust your spidey senses on this job. *grin* And well, about Venita . . . would it help you to know she is thirteen?

Chimera: 13????!???? That makes my skin crawl. I tell you, slutrock music has a lot to answer for.

Alchemist: Yeah. *shrug* Venita's not the one I really worry about, though. This isn't her first liaison. Keep an eye on her if she comes in at night. I usually ride herd on her while she's in computer lab at school. I think she only gets to the library to "study" at night once every couple of weeks at best.

Chimera: Okey-dokey. Well, I think I've kept you over-time. Thanks for covering for me last night. *hug*

Alchemist: Any time. *grin* Hot date?

Chimera: Well, hot-blooded at any rate, as opposed to silica chipped. *LOL*

Alchemist: *LOL* The best kind! Gotta dash. Have a good night! *hugs*

I was just belting my velour bathrobe and pouring another cup of decaf when I got a PM from Sanders.

Evening, Milady. *gallant bow and sweeping of plumed hat*

I chuckled as I scooted my chair into the desk and posted back to him.

PM from Chimera to Sanders: In a costume drama mood, are we, this evening?

PM from Sanders to Chimera: Indubitably. I am in the mood for wild, romantic, courtly gestures. The moors are beckoning, the winds are howling, and the dogs are bay-ing at the moon. How goest it with you? *grin*

Damn. There were times when I wished for nothing so much as a seventeen-inch monitor screen. Even with frames and two windows open, it was getting difficult to keep the banter running with Sanders and maintain an appropriate eye on what was happening in the general room. The jokes had petered off, and Milan was in talking with Vixen and Ghandhi. I was on the lookout for Thea to appear, but I hadn't seen her in a couple of days.

PM from Sanders to Chimera: Or it could simply be that I just finished seeing *The Man Who Would be King* for about the seventeenth time. *chuckle*

Rats. I hadn't even known it was on TV. Not that I watched much television any more, come to think of it, but I have to admit to having long adored Michael Caine. I stretched my hand out to the side table next to my desk, which held the remote. It still seemed vaguely ridiculous to have a remote control for a television that sat only seven feet away, but what the heck. I clicked onto CBC, which was starting into the news. Sometimes it helped to have a background drone of human voices in the place with me. I leaned back to read what had been happening in the open room. Sanders had surfaced there, to Vixen's delight, and perhaps to Ghandhi's relief. Vixen had a habit of teasing him unmercifully over his occasional malapropisms. English was his third or fourth language, and he was far clearer to understand than many of the people from the contiguous forty-eight, but that didn't stop Vixen.

Sanders: I hear that computers can be injurious to your health.

Vixen: Tell me about it. Mouse elbow! *LOL*

Milan: What do you mean, Sanders?

Sanders: I heard on the news this evening a fellow was electrocuted by his computer.

Vixen: WHAT???

Sanders: Well, that's what they're saying on the CBC.

I frowned. The news here in Edmonton had just

begun. I punched up the volume on the remote. They were still on the first story headline, something about a riot in Afghanistan. Maybe he had watched the 6:00 news or listened to *As It Happens* on the radio. I was impressed that the CBC had covered the story. It hadn't been in the local paper, just the Austin paper, which was four days old when I purchased it. Of course, maybe it had been in an earlier *Edmonton Journal*, if they'd taken it off the wire.

Chimera: Where did that happen, Sanders?

Sanders: Somewhere in Texas.

This was strange. The news on the tube had already moved from important international items to current Canadian content. They were interviewing a scientist in BC who had come one step closer to a vaccine against herpes. It would be the weather next, and no word yet of a computer death in Texas. Perhaps the earlier news had been more extensive. I'd always thought they ran the same clips for the 6:00 and 11:00 newscasts, but maybe something had been bumped for a newer story.

Milan: Did they say what had happened?

Sanders: *shrug* Just that a man had been electrocuted while on the Internet. That should give Luddites something to talk about. The police are investigating, though.

Vixen: Maybe Bill Gates is the culprit. Was he on a Mac? *chuckle*

Ghandhi: I always turn things off in a lightning storm.

Chimera: Vixen> *LOL*

Sanders: You might have something there, Vixen. *LOL*

Vixen: Oh, I never turn anything off. I likely should, but I like to live dangerously. *grin*

Milan: Well, I'll look out for that story. Wouldn't want to go out that way.

Sanders: Amen, Milan. No, I want to go soft and quiet into that good night . . . a long time from now. *chuckle*

The conversation started to segue into a comparison of deaths and funerals. I made my general goodbyes to the room and then went in quietly to check on any Alvin PMs that might have cropped up before the California crew got into high gear. I could see what Alchemist had meant; there were still some snarky anti-lag PMs from a couple of folks, seven from one fellow who ran a computer store in Ontario and knew more about computers in his little finger than Alvin could ever hope to know, blah, blah, blah. I cleared them and checked through the private rooms from earlier to clear them. Motel was still up, but from the looks of it, Thea hadn't been in to pick up any of Milan's rather urgent messages. I decided to leave it up for them. It didn't take all that much server space.

Sanders was still chatting in the open room. Quite a few folks had popped in, and it was beginning to get festive, in the way of all Friday nights. I doubted there would be much to worry about, given the mix of folks there. But, as I had been warned, when things happened, they happened quickly.

The phone rang, which, surprisingly, didn't startle me as much this time, with the television still murmuring in the living room. I clicked the remote off, wondering who would be calling this side of midnight. It was Denise, of course.

"I knew you wouldn't be in bed," she began.

I laughed. It wouldn't have mattered if I were, in her mind. "How are you doing? Do you have time for a get-together any time soon?" It would be great to spend some time with Denise, especially now that I could actually pay my own way.

"I would love it," said Denise, "and I have a suggestion. Let me buy you lunch after we do some shopping. I have to find a pair of shoes for a do next week."

"Sounds great. When? Tomorrow?"

"Yes, I'll pick you up. There is just one hitch. We have to go to the mall; I've tried everywhere else. But it will be painless, I promise you. And we'll eat at the Old Spaghetti Factory. Shall I get you about 9:45? Great. Can't wait. See you!"

She rang off quickly, probably afraid I would be forming a negative response. I sat with the phone still in my hand, envisioning myself at West Edmonton Mall on a Saturday morning in the company of a mad shoe shopper. I laughed and set the phone receiver back in its cradle. It could be worse. I could have been electrocuted by my computer.

CHAPTER 12

I don't want to be cast out as some pariah from the human race, but I have to admit that I don't count clothes shopping among my favorite pastimes. However, in the company of a good friend, it can be a diversion. In the company of a good friend on a mission, it can be a blast. I was leaning against a table of shoes that looked as if they had been made by disconsolate Russian workers, listening to Denise explain her predicament to the third manager along Phase One of the mega-mall.

"I have a ridiculous dress to wear next Thursday, and it requires ridiculous shoes to go with it. Shoes that are delicate, frothy, impractical, beautiful. Do you have anything like that?"

The last shop manager had just laughed. This one seemed to commiserate. "We have nothing like that this year. Look what they send us! These big, clunky heels. They don't even have the redeeming quality of being practical, look at the last on this one. You would break down your arch in ten minutes! And for what? So your calf can look like it's soldered to a block of cement? Where is the elegance in that? Pah!"

Although I doubted this was the way to sell shoes, I enjoyed seeing someone who seemed to take his business seriously. He leaned in and whispered something to Denise. She smiled and shook his hand, then slipped back into her loafers.

"C'mon, Randy. I've been given a lead," she whispered in high-drama, spy-movie mode, as she grabbed my arm and spun me out of the shop.

I was having a great time. Part of it was being with Denise, whose conversation was always witty and intelligent. Besides, she was so damned gorgeous that the crowds seemed to part and melt to let her through. She just shook her head, allowing her smooth, thick blond hair to fall into place, and, despite her strong feminist convictions, took it as her due. I tucked an escaping tendril from my braid behind my ear and followed along, graced by association.

I was intrigued with her quest. I couldn't wait to have her rationalize both her search for what our mothers would have dubbed "hooker shoes" and her costume for the event with her own rigid ethical code. I figured I would get it all from her over lunch. Right now, she was hot on the trail.

We passed two more stores filled with Russian Realist footwear, then she pulled me into a small store near the ice rink.

"This is where André told me to try."

"André?"

"The man at the last shoe store," she grinned. "He said if anyone had Cinderella shoes, it would be this place."

André was probably right. There was a crystal chandelier hanging in the center of the small shop, lighting glass and marble shelves on either side. Two round banquettes for sitting were placed down the center of the store. A young woman in black tights, a black jumper, and dead-black hair appeared from the back of the store. She wasn't really as anachronistic as she might have been; in this milieu she seemed more like a milliner's apprentice than a goth.

"May I help you?"

Denise launched into her spiel. I sat on one of the banquettes and counted the number of opera bags on the wall behind the back counter. The girl seemed to be nodding, and she disappeared.

Denise giggled. "I think we may have found the mother lode."

The girl reappeared with several boxes. Denise positively gurgled with delight as she opened the first one and pulled out a black sandal with tiny spaghetti straps, perched on a clear Lucite heel. A three-inch heel. My feet cramped as I looked at it. Denise was kicking off her loafers and rolling up her wide-legged wool trousers. She eased the straps over her toes and wound the ankle strap twice around before belting it, then she stood up and made her way to the mirror.

"Perfect," she announced.

"We have them in gold as well," offered the clerk.

"I think that just might be gilding it," Denise said seriously.

I made strange, strangled noises into the shoulder of my jacket.

Trust Denise's luck. It turned out that the wonder shoes were also on sale and the only ones left in black just happened to be her size. Life just works out that way for her. True to her word, we were on our way to the Old Spaghetti Factory as soon as her treasure was bagged.

I love this restaurant. It is one of the great redeeming features for me when I go to visit the mall, beyond the

$1.50 second-run cinemas and the funny fountain in the entrance to Galaxyland, which is no longer as charming because of all the pastel statuary built up around it. The original Old Spaghetti Factory in the Boardwalk downtown has all sorts of great antiques, like the one in Vancouver's Gastown, but all of them have that amazing Mizithra cheese, which supposedly is what Homer ate while composing *The Illiad.* I tend to expect epics to burst out of my forehead, fully bound, after a meal there.

I was digging into the hot sourdough bread as Denise tried to defend her position on stiletto heels.

"It's all about costume, I think. There is a time and a place for this dress-up gear. And if I can't wear sequins and three-inch heels to a gala, then when will I ever get the chance? Besides, I factor in the concept that it's for a good cause. The only way to get money for the writer-in-residency program is to make it appear glamorous to hordes of rich alumni. So, glamorous we go. I don't think anyone ever said that feminism meant not being allowed to feel beautiful. I think the idea is to really examine our concepts of beauty, and live by our decisions. And, having examined them up the yin yang, I am getting dolled up on Thursday."

I grinned. I had nothing against the concept of looking like the belle of the ball, either, although Denise had a far better shot at pulling that sort of thing off than I ever would. Besides, she was going to be emceeing the gala. As Emma Goldman had once said, "If I can't dance, I don't want to be part of your revolution." Not that anyone could dance long in those shoes.

We were halfway through our meals when Denise got around to asking me about Steve. I told her we had seen each other recently, which seemed to make her happy. She then asked about my job.

"So, how's your cyber-peeping job going?" Maybe it was the glow of having found her dream shoes, or the mellowing effect of the food, but she seemed less condemnatory than before. I decided to risk it and gave her a more detailed rundown than I had planned.

"So the concept is to be just a sort of guardian angel for the tribe, is that it?" She rolled a long noodle around her fork with the concentration of a Buddha.

"Pretty much," I allowed.

"Well, if you like the people and the atmosphere, and you don't have to dress up and go out in the cold to get to work, it sort of sounds like money for jam to me." She shrugged. "You don't even have to create a lesson plan or mark anything, and you still get paid. That makes me suspicious. But that's just me."

Trust Denise to hit on the raw nerve every time.

"Believe me, I think that as well. And I think my guard is always up. I talked to my bank manager, though, and there is nothing they can do with my account number except deposit money into it, which they are doing with efficient regularity, so honestly I can't see where the snare might be. I really quite like the fellow I work with. Oh, did I tell you, there is a fellow from Edmonton in the room these days? I haven't told him where I'm from, might be too, too awkward, you know."

"Ewwww, no kidding. I still cannot honestly see what the attraction is, Randy. Granted there is the language aspect of things, I can understand that part; but it doesn't strike me that there are a whole lot of rocket scientists out there in chat rooms of an evening."

I laughed. "Actually, there are likely more rocket scientists than people interested in discussing the works of Trollope."

"No, I would figure the trollops on the 'Net were spelled slightly differently," Denise intoned, batting her eyelashes and laughing.

"Well, that's true enough, but at least they can all afford computers and are somewhat literate."

"There is that. And speaking of literate, how is your Grant MacEwan distance teaching going?"

We ended up over lattes, gossiping about the tenure-track folks at U of A, as per usual. Denise managed to guilt me into buying a ticket to the gala, which was to be held the next Thursday night. I was praying that Alchemist wouldn't mind covering for me, although I was half-inclined just to write it off as a charitable deduction. Denise was urging me to be seen, however, just in case some more courses at the university turned up at the last minute.

"It helps to be in their faces," she said, "unless you want to marry one of them, that is, in which case you can be a sessional for life. Besides, there are a couple of nice new grad students whom you haven't met. Women and men. You need to get out, after all. Oh, and Steve can get a ticket at the door, if he can come. Just a thought." She smiled, catlike.

Scratch a feminist, find a yenta.

Chapter 13

There were two phone messages from Steve blinking for me when I got back from our girls' day out, and several e-mails. I adore getting e-mail, and now there was one from Steve. Double happiness, as my friend Andrea Chong used to say. I chuckled, thinking that he was finally getting around his block of the new-fangled technology enough to send e-mail. It was a start. I opened the e-mail from Alchemist first, though; he'd never before sent me a high-priority note.

```
TO: rcraig@uofalberta.ca
FROM: alchemist@babel.com

Hey Chimera,

Have you seen Thea in the room recently? I have
been getting several distraught sounding PMs
from Milan, asking if I've seen her. Looks to me
like he's canvasing everyone. Just thought I'd
check. Hope your day is good. See you later.
*hugs*

Al
```

It sounded like Milan was getting frantic. I knew he'd been asking after her, and I hadn't seen Thea in almost a week, but that sort of thing had not really troubled me. If anything, I guess I had just thought they'd had a tiff. People operate in divergent rhythms in any given chat site. Some folks stay loyal to one place and frequent it daily for a time, then move on. Others hit various places and only stay to chat if the spirit moves them. And there were always the "tourists," who happened in and left, never to be seen again.

I made a quick note on some scratch paper to keep an eye out for Thea, thinking I should transfer it to her cue card later, when I was on duty. That was one thing I had taken to heart from an article I'd read on telecommuting to the office place. The boss tends to consider you accessible and "on" at any time, given that he can e-mail you with requests and orders. You have to remain firm to your hourly workload to avoid being overloaded with duties during your downtime.

I busied myself with clearing out the papers and bottles for the recycle pickup. I had more than usual this week, given my splurge at Hub Cigar earlier in the week. I'd read through the various papers I'd bought, and, besides coveting the production of *Carmen* at the San Francisco Opera, which sounded magnificent in the review, there was not much there that interested me. News was news everywhere. Or maybe it was just that it all seemed so pasteurized, given the few truly independent papers these days. I piled up the papers for the collection box in the laundry room and bagged the rest for the back curb. One of the neighbors saved newspapers for a local church fundraiser, and most of us added to his stock.

When I came back in from taking the papers to the laundry room and the blue bag to the back alley curb where we all put our recyclables, I stood for a minute in my postage-stamp kitchen, trying to decide if I was hungry or not. I'd eaten with Denise, but that had been a good four hours before. I decided to forego an evening meal and just snack on a bagel during my shift if the need arose. That was another good thing about Internet work, you could get a lot done during lag time. I very rarely announced to a chat room that I'd BRB, or *be right back.* Most folks thought the acronym stood for *bathroom break,* and I didn't think the world needed to know my every little biological rhythm. Besides, I had rarely ever been caught out with an "Are you still there?" query. Either my plumbing was very efficient, or their modems were slower than mine.

I called Steve back on his pager, and he rang a few minutes later. His reason for calling was to invite me to a matinee movie on Sunday, which sounded fine to me. I flew the idea of Denise's gala past him and, to my surprise, he sounded interested. It occurred to me that he might actually have liked and be missing some of the friends he had met through me. He promised to check his week's assignments and get back to me. I made another note to ask Alchemist to cover for me on Thursday. I guess Cinderella was going to go to the ball, after all.

CHAPTER 14

I logged into Babel about an hour early, partially to let Alchemist off early, thus softening him up for the Thursday appeal, and partially to find out what the skinny was on the search for Thea. Sure enough, there were a couple of PMs from Milan addressed to Chimera as well, asking if I'd seen his lady. If he was asking me, he was likely swamping everyone.

The place was hopping, which is sort of unusual for a weekend. A lot of people seemed to have only weekday access, or make other plans for weekends, but tonight there were names I hadn't seen in a long time dotting the screen. I hauled out the list of To Watch For names as a precaution, though I was pretty sure I had them memorized.

Alchemist seemed pretty jolly. He was in the open chat bantering with Lea, Carlin, and Jackal. Vixen was in fine form, hitting folks with the duster as the need arose. Maia came sauntering in, and Vixen gave her massive hugs. I gathered from a quick look at their PMs that Maia had been on a blind date and Vixen wanted all the details. The lull in Vixen's duster attacks was all that Carlin seemed to have been waiting for. He began waltzing Lea around the room, and then began some sort of tango.

Jackal was laughing it up with Teena and Ophelia. The atmosphere seemed pretty highly charged, sexually. The innuendo was flying, and it was just 7:00 p.m. by my watch.

Alchemist agreed to cover for me again the next Thursday as long as I took his Monday afternoon shift, since he said he wanted to get out to a lecture. He left me to the rabble with a laugh and the offer of some virtual saltpeter.

PM from Alchemist to Chimera: I think you're going to need to hose this lot down a couple of times tonight. *grin*

PM from Chimera to Alchemist: Sure looks that way. I'll make the coffee extra strong. *LOL*

PM from Alchemist to Chimera: You can do it. *poof*

Oh boy. Vixen had started a game of Truth or Dare. Maia had demanded that Carlin detail the strangest place he'd ever made love. After relating a tale of an elevator stopped between floors, he then dared Vixen to print the last PM she'd received. Laughingly, she posted a rather innocuous flirtation, without the sender's name attached.

I found myself wondering who was cozying up to Vixen these days. With sheer idle curiosity, I flicked into her PMs, and discovered that the PM she had just posted to the room had come from Sanders. I was a little shocked, not at the posting, but at my reaction to the discovery. Could I be jealous of attentions in a cyber-chat room? It seemed preposterous. I rubbed the skin between my eyebrows to erase the furrow. Good thing I was a monitor and above all this, I told myself firmly. Yeah, right.

I found myself hovering in the background instead of joining in. I told myself I was just being prudent, since, with the atmosphere the way it was tonight, anything could happen. Every now and then, I can almost fool myself. I shrugged mentally. It wasn't as if I'd given Sanders any reason to hope for anything from me, anyhow. And it certainly wasn't that I was jealous or interested in him myself. I think I was just annoyed with myself for assuming he was being exclusive in his charms when he was talking with me.

Alchemist had been right. I was glad I'd put on regular coffee. About midnight, after Vixen and Carlin had both disappeared and Sanders hadn't been in sight for a while, I noticed that Jackal and Gopher had gone into a private room. The thing that intrigued me about this was that they were both purported males.

While private rooms can often be used for business meetings and areas to discuss computer games and play with HTML, usually folks tended to take those into other open areas of the chat. The truth was, private rooms were mostly used for sexual liaisons, no matter how people tried to whitewash the vision of the Internet. I didn't necessarily agree with those who believed that the Internet was destroying families and ruining marriages and was inherently evil; however, I wasn't so naïve as to believe that everyone was there just to visit and play word games.

When folks went private, I usually respected their wishes, especially as cyber-sex wasn't something I cared to read. However, when two men went private, in a room that was tolerant but not openly welcoming of homosexuality, I was curious. Who has a business meeting at midnight, after all? I checked the private list and found one that was just numerals: 482840. I decided to have a peek.

I am so relieved I never had an urge to become a gynecologist. There is, to me, nothing really attractive about the urethra or vulva, not even their names. Gopher seemed to have a different esthetic sensibility, though. He was salivating over all the pictures Jackal was posting, especially the ones involving more than one woman.

That is something else I have never understood about heterosexual men. So many of them have this absolute antipathy toward gay men, and yet the pornography they subscribe to often depicts two or more women wandering over each other's bodies. Of course, when it comes right down to it, I've never understood the lure of pornography at all. One thing was certain. There were strict rules against porn in Babel, and it was part of my job to enforce them. I logged in as Alvin, cleared the room completely, and sent both Gopher and Jackal their warning. Folks get one warning, then they are blocked completely. Alchemist told me he sometimes didn't bother with the warning, since he judged some people to be more difficult to deal with once they'd been caught out, and more likely to cause bigger trouble.

This was my first situation, however, so I decided to run it by the books. I made a note of each of their IP addresses on cue cards, just in case they decided to pull the same stunt under a different handle. I also made a note that it wasn't kiddie porn. We had a number to contact if any of that showed up. INTERPOL had a 'Net watch on those creeps and would trace an IP address to the perpetrators.

Gopher ran. Jackal made a half-hearted attempt at an apologetic, man-to-man justification to Alvin, who merely posted back: "Read the rules. Get with the program and be welcome, or get out."

I sent a PM to Alchemist to let him know about the two names to watch, and what I had done. Tracy from

Singapore had just logged in on the open screen, as had Ivories, a blues musician from LA. Since I liked them both, I decided it was time Chimera made another appearance. We chatted about Korean food and dim sum for a pleasant while, making me ravenously hungry. I grabbed a handful of graham wafers with my next cup of coffee, which this time I made decaf. It was almost quitting time, and I wanted to be able to get to sleep. I was going to the movies tomorrow.

CHAPTER 15

I have to admit there is nothing quite like a Jackie Chan movie. He has got to be the most charming man on celluloid since Cary Grant. This one involved some missing jewels, a beautiful woman who was deadly with her hands and feet, the ruination of a major restaurant, and plenty of great gags, too. Steve and I laughed our way through a large bag of popcorn and were still laughing as we wandered out to the car.

"I'm the good guy, I should get the girl!"

"Hard to see that happening in movies any more, isn't it? It always seems as if the hero is incredibly flawed these days, or he's seventeen. Maybe that's why I like Jackie Chan movies; he still believes in the fairy-tale way of making movies."

"Isn't it true, though, that women go after bad boys?" asked Steve. "I mean, look at all the women who correspond with murderers in prison. What about that writer who married the convict?"

"Well, not everyone likes a bad boy. After all, look at us. You're as good as they get."

"Well, you, my dear, have exquisite taste. There is no denying."

By this time we were back at my apartment, and Steve

followed me in and hung his jacket up on my brass coat tree next to the door. I headed to the kitchen to put the kettle on the stove. When I came out of the kitchen with cups and the milk pitcher, I found Steve standing in front of my desk, surveying the set-up.

"It looks like Command Central here," he remarked. "Is all this for the monitoring job?"

"Well, this stuff over here is my distance course. I have twenty-five students who are working relatively at their own speed through English 111, which is basically an essay-writing course. While I was bummed out by not getting courses at the university this year, I have to admit that doing this work for Grant MacEwan is very satisfying. I've been to two staff meetings so far, and I really like the atmosphere of the department. And teaching in your sweats is a bonus," I grinned. "Actually, the chair has said I might get some real-time classes next term, which would be great."

Steve smiled at me. "I'm glad to hear it. I think you need to be in front of a class, Randy. I sure think the class benefits, at any rate."

I curtsied with mock flourish to make the moment pass, but I was touched by Steve's endorsement of my teaching skills. He had seen me in action once or twice, so I knew it wasn't mere sideline cheering. Truth was, I did miss standing up in front of the class, as much as I was enjoying e-mails with my distance students, especially Annette Standing Bull from up near Redearth, who wrote the most gloriously descriptive essays of her early life on the traplines with her father.

Steve was now pointing to the other side of the desk, where I'd put up a new set of cork tiles along the window's side for a bulletin board.

"What about this stuff? Is this your Internet job?"

I followed his glance. There were two or three lists of names. One was the To Watch For list Alchemist had given me. Another was the list of regulars on my shift, folks who were likely to be there five nights out of six; and the third was my list of folks I had to watch out for since I'd bumped or banned them.

As well, I had Alchemist's phone number on a pink card tacked to the corner, a couple of HTML lines of code to remember (I always forgot which way the numbers went to increase font size), and a funny cartoon of a woman in sweats at a computer ordering in pizza and coffee.

"Yep, pretty much. It's funny. This Internet job, which was intended just to augment the college stuff, is actually paying much more than the distance ed classes. It does mean I have to punch a clock more regularly, but I can't really complain about that. Lots of people in the world have worse schedules. I can see matinée movies, keep my days free, and still get the occasional night off. Oh," I broke off, "that reminds me. Did you really want to come to this writer-in-residence benefit that Denise has roped me into? I've got the night off, and she says there are bound to be tickets at the door. I want to go mainly to see her glitter, but it's a good cause, and a night out.…"

Steve smiled, pulling me close to him. "I would love to come and see you shine. When is it?"

"Thursday, at the Timms Centre. We could walk from here, since I don't intend to wear anything nearly as silly as Denise's new shoes."

I ended up telling Steve about the wild shoe-shopping trip we'd had, and we laughed some more. It was so good to have him back in my life, so real and solid. That was one thing about dealing in the printed computer-message world. It lacked the solidity of real people.

I hugged him tighter than usual as he left for his own evening shift. He laughed and again promised to give me a call when he found out if he could free up Thursday evening.

"I gather you'll be home tonight?"

"Oh, you bet. Just me and my imaginary friends."

CHAPTER 16

When I logged on that evening, after treating myself to a pita stuffed with tuna and chopped celery, I was juiced. It was probably from being with Steve, I admitted to myself; there is just nothing like the obvious admiration of a gorgeous guy to make you feel like you can conquer the world. After chatting a bit with Alchemist, who was sounding pretty flirtatious himself that evening, I waved him out the virtual door and scanned the notes he'd left about the folks in Babel that day.

Milan had posted several PMs to Alvin, all having something to do with finding Thea. Apparently she still wasn't answering his e-mails, and he was sounding more and more frantic as the messages progressed. I tried to think of the last time I had seen Thea in Babel; it must have been nearly a week. It was hard to sort out time frames on-line. There is a saying that a week in cyber is like three months in real time, so no wonder Milan was so edgy. They had been thick as thieves for several weeks before, and now nothing. Seemingly, according to Milan, she had vanished without any reason; they hadn't fought or broken up; she wasn't planning a vacation.

I was trying to think up how to reply when I noticed with relief that Alchemist had posted back something soothing to Milan under the guise of Alvin, so I went on my rounds.

There were a couple of private rooms open. Vixen was showing Maia pictures of her new car in one of them, and two middle-aged lovebirds, one in Nebraska and the other in Melbourne, were cozying up. All in all, it looked like it was going to be a quiet night.

I popped into the general room as Chimera after pouring myself a cup of coffee. Grace was organizing a word game whereby you could only speak in haiku for the next half hour. Carlin and Maia were up for it, Vixen was playing along, though I could sense she found word games tiresome, and Theseus popped up with a great one:

Theseus: **Nothing on TV**
Cursor invites connection
So here I am, folks!

I *LOL*-ed in response but then tracked back to see when he had slipped in without my seeing him. I hated to get caught like that. I found him, logged in from the early morning, way up on Alchemist's shift. He must have left his connection open all day long and just wandered back in. I couldn't imagine anyone lurking in Babel all day. Anyone who wasn't getting paid, that is, I grinned to myself ruefully.

I figured he must have had a cable connection. No one would leave his phone line tied up that long. I decided to check through and see if anyone else was lurking in the background, and I thought I should make a note to Chatgod to see about a program that tracked that sort of activity. As it was, we only had log-on times, log-off times, and posts to go by. If I wanted to make sure of someone, I had miles of transcript to scroll through.

The haikus were flying fast and furious, and of course

getting a bit bawdier each time. Oh well, it was past 9:00 in the evening in most parts of the western hemisphere; and most of the occupants of Babel were over the age of majority. That thought brought me back to Venita, and what Alchemist had said about her. I hadn't seen her in a while, and I wasn't at all sorry. She made my skin crawl, I had to admit. Of course, with all the schoolgirl-uniform poses of the pop stars, and barely there clothing pumped at the teen set, what could one expect in behavior from the very young? Patterning has to come from somewhere, after all.

Sanders logged on, and tonight I was up for him. While I was still very circumspect about where I lived in the real world, I managed to banter without feeling too awkward. Again, the residue of a day with Steve made me feel invincible. As that thought came into my mind, it occurred to me how close that word was to another: invisible. There was a lot to be said for anonymity and invisibility, I had to admit.

PM from Sanders to Chimera: Good evening, lovely lady!

PM from Chimera to Sanders: Hail, sir! And how has been your day?

PM from Sanders to Chimera: All the better now that I am here with you.

PM from Chimera to Sanders: *smile* I am sure you say that to all the truly lovely women you chat with.

Sanders: Ah, you have caught me out. It's true, I only flirt with the very best. I am an elitist. Shoot me now. But let me die in your arms.

Damn, he wasn't bad. When you considered that he was simultaneously posting this to Vixen:

PM from Sanders to Vixen: Hey, darlin'!

PM from Vixen to Sanders: Hey yourself, hotstuff! How are you doing, sweetie?

PM from Sanders to Vixen: Fantastic as always, angel. So what are you doing this evening? Is your dance card full?

PM from Vixen to Sanders: Not since you walked in, sugar. Why don't I just sit here real close beside you and we'll see what pops up? *wink*

I'll admit I was a little miffed, but not overly surprised. Moreover, I was honestly impressed. His manner and style were almost completely different with each person he was talking to. Meanwhile he was also participating in the haiku extravaganza and keeping up with a discussion of various laptop advantages that Ivories and Gandalf were pursuing around and through the zaniness of Grace's game. He tailored himself to fit the conversation, and I had to admire it. He was truly the ideal writer for each script, throwing his own persona into a back cupboard for the sake of his diverse audiences. I wondered what that real persona was like and whether I would like it half so much as the world-weary roué he seemed to have chosen as the mask he showed me.

I had popped into the kitchen to pour myself another cup of coffee and make a note to pick up more milk the next day when I saw a pulsing on the Alvin window at the top right of my screen.

Someone new had signed on. This wasn't in itself unusual, since many of the folks in Babel lured real-time friends into the fold, and strays surfing through chatroom listings happened upon us from time to time. Chatgod had created the pulse program just to let monitors know that someone was new. Occasionally, Alvin would pop in with a PM to the newbie, welcoming him or her and pointing out the general rules of conduct. It was up to us to decide whether the new person required a full-fledged Alvin welcome or just a general group howdy. Since Lea and Kara were in the room, I was loath to bring Alvin into things. Both of them had a thing for authority figures, and they would spend the rest of the evening trying to coax a flirtation out of Alvin. If I could avoid that, I would.

I checked the board. Tremor had arrived. Vixen had already said hello, and Sanders was asking him if he'd been to Babel before. Maybe Alvin didn't have to appear at all. Virtual community is such a cool thing. It has to evolve naturally, and the folks in the virtual community have to take pride in their place on-line, but if that all happened, then monitoring became simply a matter of cleaning up the odd teenaged expletive off the screen; the community took care of the rest. Babel was almost at that stage, I sensed. However, as Chatgod and Alchemist had pointed out, it didn't take much for an unscrupulous person to bring it all down if we weren't vigilant on the sidelines.

Tremor seemed to be an old hand at chat rooms and knew enough netiquette to hang back a bit, typing when typed to. He introduced himself as an acquaintance of Milan's, and asked if we'd seen him this evening. No one had, and I chimed in with a thought that he had been in earlier (his posts to Alvin had been time-stamped, the last one at 5:00 p.m.), but that I hadn't seen him since then. I figured no one there would pay much attention to the fact that Chimera hadn't been in the room until 7:00. For all they knew, I flitted in there a dozen times a day, just barely missing them by moments. After all, unlike me, they didn't have access to the time logs.

Tremor seemed slightly distracted by this, but it didn't stop him from sticking around. Vixen was trying to pry some information from him, which was her general way.

She liked to pigeonhole people a bit, but she had a point. If you know someone is an engineer, there is really no point arguing Camus with them. Tremor was vague, saying he did some contract work on-line. Sanders laughingly called him a hit man, and Tremor *grinned* back at him. Vixen was charmed. She was taking some computer courses herself and was always ready to talk shop.

Tremor began to PM with her, mainly getting the general idiosyncracies of the room down. She was telling him how to create a private room, how to leave a message for someone not currently logged in, and how to choose an avatar or icon for his own use. I had to admit, she had it covered. I knew why she was telling him; she was always on the prowl for a new conquest. Vixen liked to think all the men in the room were pining for her, and she was a nice enough woman that everyone played along, even those who probably had no real interest in her, or women of any kind. I wasn't too sure why Tremor figured he needed to know all this immediately, though, and made a small note to keep an eye on him. I decided to leave a small note for Milan to the effect that his friend had dropped by and was looking for him. As I posted it, I saw that there was another note for Milan waiting, from Tremor himself.

PM *from Tremor to Milan:* Remember, a deal's a deal.

I wondered what Milan had got himself into, on top of losing his girlfriend. Oh well, it wasn't my business. As long as folks were conducting themselves properly in Babel, that was all that counted. I tuned back into the conversation on the general board, parried a few more flirting darts with Sanders and signed off at 3:30 a.m. For notes to Alchemist, who would be logging in at 10:00 a.m., I listed Tremor's arrival, and the haiku games, and listed the evening as uneventful. No fights, no problems. I shut down my portal to the global village, which was very rarely frequented by anyone from the Far East through their evening hours, and padded off to bed.

CHAPTER 17

Monday morning brought two essays in the mail and one tortured e-mail from a student pleading for an extension of a week. I granted it, with stern warnings not to get too far out of sync, and marked the two papers. I made copious notes on both their papers and on bright pink bond paper, thinking that the verbiage would substitute for the lack of a physical presence and the pink would make up for the jokes and smiles there would have been in a real-time class. I decided to walk the mail up to Whyte Avenue and catch a bus from there. I was heading off to get something to wear to the writer-in-residence gala. There was no way I would match Denise's splendor, but as her friend I couldn't arrive wearing overly drab clothing; it would mock her decision to go glamorous.

Besides, it was turning out to be quite a production. Not only was the present writer-in-residence going to be reading, but they had also invited back all the past writers-in-residence, who were a stellar crew, and many of them had written to say they'd be there. I doubted they would lure Margaret Atwood back, but there were some pretty fancy names responding, according to Denise.

She, of course, was thrilled that Steve was coming with me. She was absolutely sold on Steve. I was just relieved that Denise and Steve never had been attracted to each other, unlike any other man who came near Denise. She had that effect on men. She had been dating a reporter for a while, but that had fallen through about three months ago, and she was starting to look a bit "lean and hungry," if you asked me. I figured anyone caught in the path of that sequined dress on Thursday would be fair game.

I had nothing that would be up to a sequined dress and no budget that could remedy that obvious oversight in my wardrobe. However, I did have an ace in the hole, and its name was the Value Village. I caught the bus across from the TD Canada Trust corner and headed down Whyte Avenue to bargain heaven.

It wasn't too busy today in the Whyte Avenue store. I wandered down the jeans aisle by habit, just checking. Nothing today. That was the thing about shopping thrift shops, though. You had to be open to whatever was there, not dependant on discovering exactly what you were looking for. I had once come in hoping for a red sweater and left with three bathing suits. Fatalists tend to do very well in thrift shops.

I strolled through the skirts and blouses but couldn't see anything that sent me reeling. This wasn't going to be a picnic, after all. I wandered into the dresses aisle, hoping something would hop out. I ran my hand along the fabrics when I got to my general size, letting a tactile impression in as well as the obvious visuals. Sometimes the feel of a fabric would lead me to a great find. Inside the size category, things were organized by color, with patterns grouped at the end. If you squinted down the aisles, it was like looking at rippling rainbows. I looked through the blues carefully, and then checked out the reds, even though I couldn't see myself blazing in scarlet. I'm just not quite that showy. Cream would mean careful undergarments, so I didn't spend much time on that section.

Finally, I headed to the fitting rooms with four choices: a moss green dress that looked almost floor length, a black dress with an interesting twist of straps at the back, a gray wool sheath with a long slit up the side of the left leg, and a gold, shiny, sleeveless dress with a draping cowl neckline.

The gold one felt itchy going on, so I didn't even bother doing it up. Besides, it had that game-show pointer-model look. The black one was the most promising, I figured, so I slid my way up through the maze of straps and slid my own bra straps down into the sides of the dress to see what the final effect would be. I'd just try to overlook the enormous gray work socks on the ends of my legs.

I backed out of the changing room, holding my hair up on top of my head with one hand. It wasn't bad, but it wasn't anything outstanding, either, as most little black dresses aren't. They're safe and standard. Oh well, there were two more to try.

The gray was nice and warm. Somehow, though, it looked more like something you would wear to the symphony than something you would wear to a gala. I grinned at my own pronouncement; like I went to the symphony and galas every other weekend. I checked the ticket stapled to the sleeve. The gray was $7. With high black boots and a clutch purse, it would look fine.

One more dress left. It was a simple cut, of light velour in a moss green. I dropped it over my head and it fell in waves. It had a scoop neck and long sleeves, and it wasn't full length but hung to lower mid-calf, hitting my leg nicely above the turn of the ankle. I looked at myself in the mirror and liked what I saw. The color of the dress picked up on the green of my eyes, making them larger and more vivid. I stepped out of the dressing room to turn fully around. As I did so, an old woman sitting on a chair set at the end of the aisle said, "Yes! That's the one!" I looked at her, startled. She smiled at me, saying, "You'll be the belle of the ball, honey." I grinned back at her. I'd found my dress.

I picked up the gray dress, too, on the grounds that Steve might like the odd symphony this winter, and headed for home.

CHAPTER 18

It was a nice evening for chatting. There was no great horror in the news to discuss, the weather was okay wherever anyone was, and everyone seemed in a pretty happy mood. Alchemist told me he was heading out to a movie, and wished me well. I hung about in the background, watching, and at the same time reading the Stephen King memoir on writing I'd been given for my birthday last year. There is a luxurious feeling that comes over one when the apartment is clean, student papers are marked and graded, and the computer is humming along with the coffee maker. It was cold outside and cozy within. I had a new dress and a man to take me partying. Could life get any better?

Apparently it could. None of the potential troublemakers had logged in this evening, and the folks in the room were inclined to be mellow. Tracy and Dion were having a sweet time trying to pretend they weren't hooked on each other, discussing their favorite board games and why they liked them. Tracy liked Monopoly, a game I had always nicknamed "Monotonous." Dion was describing the game Sorry to her, which apparently either had never made it to Singapore or had just never made it onto her radar. Some of the other folks were chiming in with their ideas of great games. Bean liked pinochle, Maia enjoyed Scrabble, Kara was into bridge in a big way, but we all knew that. She was forever heading off to tournaments, or inviting folks into Babel from her on-line games. They never seemed to stay; I guess we weren't the bridge sort of crowd, and Kara was just an anomaly.

I was wondering what sort of board games I could even remember, let alone consider my favorite, when Sanders popped in and added cribbage to the list of games.

Chimera: Cribbage! Yes, I remember playing that with my grandma's Golden Age group when I was little. I have no idea how to play it any more. All I can recall is saying "fifteen two, fifteen four, and a pair is six."

Sanders: That's the gist of it, all right.

Chimera: Do you still play it?

Sanders: All the time.

Bean: Can you play it on-line? Or solitaire versions?

Suzy: Oh now, solitaire! I can play that for hours! I just get caught in it!

Maia: And mahjong! Before I found y'all on-line, I used to play mahjong for at least an hour a night.

Vixen: Half an hour of heaven and eight great hours of sleep! That's my kind of game, folks.

Trust Vixen to bring things back to suggestible topics. It was annoying at times; I liked the atmosphere in there so much better when everyone was at ease, rather than trying to outdo each other in sexual innuendo. Take it into whisper mode, was my idea.

Not that they didn't. I think that the ratio of private messaging went up threefold whenever the open discussion got suggestive. No wonder advertising worked so well on people; at times we really are sheep.

PM from Sanders to Chimera: So tell me about your grandmother. She sounds like someone I would have admired.

PM from Chimera to Sanders: I thought she was wonderful. I used to stay with her on summer holidays, to give my parents a chance for some grown-up time.

PM from Sanders to Chimera: I used to long for that sort of summer holiday. My parents demanded we all go on a long road trip every summer. My sister, my brother, and I were all close to murdering each other, and my parents were keen to leave us at a service station. However, we managed to drive each other crazy past the Grand Canyon, across Canada all the way to Prince Edward Island, up the Alaska Highway and, of course, always through to the Okanagan, the tropical jewel of Canada.

PM from Chimera to Sanders: Oh, I have always wanted to do that Alaska Highway trip!

PM from Sanders to Chimera: Well, let me know if you head through Edmonton on your trip. I would be honored to show you around.

PM from Chimera to Sanders: Why, thank you. So Edmonton is on the route, then?

PM from Sanders to Chimera: Pretty much, unless you're joining it from northern BC. Would that be better for you?

I decided I had better back out of this conversation pretty quickly, or he was going to get into where I was from again, and, while I didn't want to let him know I was likely just down the street, I had an aversion to lying to him. Even if he was flirting in PMs with Vixen, he was one of the most literate and certainly one of the kindest of the whole Babel crowd.

I had been toying with the idea of telling him where I was from until I'd seen him playing with Vixen.

Somehow it had jolted me that he was no better than the others, which was odd since I accepted it from most of them as a natural form of communication.

I just didn't want any cyber-man of mine behaving that way. Not that I was even looking for a cyber-man, of course, I reminded myself silently. I had a terrific man and a relationship worth working at. I didn't need to flirt on-line. In fact, given my job, it was far better that I remain aloof.

I had to admit, though, the power of words was so deliriously enticing that I would veer close to the edge every now and then with someone who could wield phrases the way a matador whipped his cape about. Sanders was like that, in my mind. He was so above the rest of the crowd in his literacy, and so clever in his ability to discuss without ever resorting to argument, that I was naturally drawn to him.

Maybe there was a high-schoolish thing to it as well. It seemed as if folks in Babel paired off, and we were all playing the beautiful people in high school, leaning against the lockers with our arms slung over our girl-friend's shoulders, or our thumbs hooked into a back belt loop of our boyfriend's jeans. Not that many of us were those characters in high school really, I was betting the farm. To be interested in computers bespoke a level of nerdishness that didn't equate with the in-crowd of any high school.

There was a pecking order in cyber, though, much like in high school, or, I suppose, any congregation of people. Vixen and Maia were definitely on top, with Carlin and Ivories and Tracy right there as the most solid of the evening regulars. A lot of it had to do with regularity, and some of it with plain old popularity. After all, Kafir and

Kara were in there almost as much as Vixen, but they talked to almost no one, and very few folks bothered them in cyber.

I wondered how popular Chimera was. It seemed as if I was welcomed happily whenever I appeared, and no one minded me joining in any conversation. I felt like an accepted regular, but I realized it was Sanders alone who made me feel special. Well, Alchemist, too, of course, but Alchemist was a work buddy.

I did wonder just as much about Alchemist as I did about Sanders, come to think of it. He wouldn't show a picture and was very self-deprecating any time I had asked him to describe himself. I was glad I was working there, though, because he was certainly a friend worth having. I thought of him as personable and easygoing, and I always pictured him with a smile on his face as he typed.

They were talking about shopping now, and I figured it had a lot to do with the fact that both Sanders and Dion had left. Tracy was going to some function at the hospital where she worked in Singapore and was describing the traditional costume, which was a long tunic over a matching, wrapped, long skirt. The way she was describing the wrapping of the skirt reminded me of a cross between a sari and a kilt, and I said so.

Tracy: That is a great description, Chimera. It has the pleating at the front, though, and not the back. I like to wear them, because in them all women look graceful.

Chimera: They sound lovely. Do most women there still wear traditional clothing?

Tracy: Many do. Some uniforms, as for air stewards and such, are based on the traditional style. Many older women wear them every day, and most of the rest of us wear them when we dress up. :)

Maia: Are you going to send us pictures, Tracy? Get someone to take a shot before you head out!

Chimera: What day is the reception?

Tracy: Oh Maia, I can't promise you, but I will try! :) I won't be in on Thursday, because that is the reception, but I shall try to get someone to take my picture and I will post it on Friday!

Chimera: I'm going out on Thursday, too.

Maia: Pictures, pictures! We want pictures.

Chimera: No luck, I'm afraid. I don't have a digital camera, and even my old camera is shot.

Maia: *pouts* That just isn't fair. It sounds like just no one will be in on Thursday and now there will be nothing to show for it, either. That is, unless Tracy can get someone. Vixen won't be in, you two won't be here, Ivories has a gig, and Sanders is heading out somewhere, too. I think Babel is gonna just dry up and blow away.

Chimera: I predict you'll start some word game and have 75 folks dancing attendance, Maia. I am not going to be worried about you!

Maia: You're always going out these days, Chimera. Tell us, have you got a fella?

Chimera: :) Well, I don't know what would give you that idea. Besides, I am hardly ever anywhere but here!

Maia: I wish I could go out sometime, but there is just no way I can support an on-line habit AND a babysitter!

Tracy: ~laughing~ Like you would trust anyone with Jacob.

Maia: This is true. *grin* Okay, so you ladies can go to the ball, and poor Cindermaia will stay home and pick lentils out of her hair, or the fireplace, or wherever.

Chimera: You do that, kiddo.

Maia: However, I expect full reports when you return! In fact, that might be how Friday works. Instead of how you spent your summer vacation, I'm going to ask y'all how you spent your Thursday!

Maia had a weekly question that folks were invited to respond to in a bulletin-board room she set up for that purpose. Usually it was a silly question, much like the old journal topics I used to assign my students at the beginning of each class. She would leave it up for the weekend, and people could check in on what everyone had posted. It was fun, and the result was much like those wild boards on the old TV show *Laugh In*. Some folks tried to answer seriously, while others just riffed on what the previous person had posted. All in all, it was another interesting experiment in communication.

Maybe that was why chat fascinated me so much. I felt as if we were in on the vanguard of some new form of rhetoric, the future as Marshall McLuhan had predicted. For once, I was in on the happening scene. I may have been too young to appreciate the 1960s, but here I was right smack dab in the middle of the Silicon Age. And making the most of it.

CHAPTER 19

Wednesday was nothing much. I spent most of the day cleaning the apartment and marking the one essay that arrived in the mail. Chat that evening wasn't all that stimulating, either.

Geoff L was back and posting the offensive lyrics to an insipid, if angry, song by yet another band I'd never heard of. Your cross-section of music is a bit more limited when all you listen to is the CBC. As Alvin, I gave him two warnings, and he finally calmed down just before leaving for the night. Alchemist had warned me that Venita might be in that evening. He had been monitoring her that afternoon, doing her Lolita number from her school's computer lab. The guy she had been with wasn't Theseus, either, and if he got wind of that there would be hell to pay in big, sweeping, Greek drama motions. I didn't consider myself a prude, but the whole concept of teenaged girls as sexual predators just made me want to shower. Venita should have been sitting in a school gym, preying on a basketball player, not getting old men all hot and bothered.

So I was pretty alert when, as Dr. Evil said, "things got weird."

First off, Sanders seemed distracted. I couldn't put my finger on it, but he was not quite as fluid in his conversation as usual. Then Milan showed up, again wanting to know if anyone had seen Thea. I checked my logs and notes. Thea hadn't been around in over three weeks now. I sent him an Alvin PM to that effect. Milan was all over that, asking Alvin what he should do, if Alvin could contact her, and whether Alvin thought he should call the police. "What police?" Alvin responded. Did Milan even know where she lived? I tried to imply, as gently as possible, that Thea might have simply got tired of chat or Milan, or both.

Milan wasn't having any of it. Apparently he knew for a fact that Thea was not only in love with him but she was also willing to leave her marriage for him. They had been in the middle of discussing the ways and means of her escape when Milan lost contact.

PM from Alvin to Milan: I'm afraid I cannot divulge her address to you.

PM from Milan to Alvin: I don't need it; I tell you, we had a serious thing happening. I just can't get hold of her right now, and it's worrying me.

PM from Alvin to Milan: Did you have a falling out? Do you know any of her real-time friends? Maybe she's ill. Or, I hate to bring it up, maybe she has taken the coward's way out of the relationship and is avoiding you.

PM from Milan to Alvin: She wouldn't do that, Alvin. You don't know her like I do. We've been completely open with each other. I mean, completely.

That could mean anything from long telephone conversations to passing risqué shots of themselves back and forth. I wondered how long Thea had been chatting, and how long with Milan in particular. It took a bit for women to expose themselves, I thought. Milan answered that for me without being asked.

PM from Milan to Alvin: We've been chatting for

almost a year now. I met her in Yahoo Chat and we eventually drifted over here. I am sure I am the first man she met here. This is a serious relationship, Alvin. I am so worried.

I tried to comfort him as best I could. I left notes for both Chatgod and Alchemist about the situation and watched him flit out of the room. Poor guy, he was transmitting his worry to me. I wasn't sure Thea hadn't blown him off, but, still, he seemed so sure something must have happened to her.

There was the real problem with cyber-relationships of any kind. You could chat with folks day in and day out, establishing strong friendships and a real sense of community, yet, if any one of them were hit by a bus, how long would it take for their cyber-community to learn of it? Possibly, if their families knew of their on-line friends, word would get to you. However, if they were loners, they could just disappear off the screen, and that would be that. You would never really know why.

Shortly after he left, Tremor logged in, again looking for Milan. Out of curiosity, I shot him a private message:
PM from Chimera to Tremor: Milan was in here a little while ago. He's really worried about Thea, because he hasn't seen her around lately.

PM from Tremor to Chimera: What is he worried about?

PM from Chimera to Tremor: He hasn't been able to contact her in two or three weeks. I guess she isn't on-line, but he says they haven't fought or anything.

PM from Tremor to Chimera: She'll be back. Maybe her 'puter died on her or something.

PM from Chimera to Tremor: Well, I hope she gets back soon, because it's driving him crazy.

PM from Tremor to Chimera: I should e-mail him and

talk some sense into him. Do you have his e-mail address, by any chance?

It wasn't regular, but Milan was in such a stew that I decided to bend regulations slightly. Besides, I'm sure Tremor could have found the information elsewhere if he really wanted to dig.

Tremor thanked me, and I clicked on the member list and scrolled down as quickly as I could. The darn thing refreshed every ninety seconds, but I managed to get to the Ms and copy Milan's e-mail before the screen went momentarily blank. In a minute I was back in the main room and sent it in a PM to Tremor.

PM from Chimera to Tremor: Tell him what you told me, that she's bound to be okay. He is so bent out of shape about this. I think he really loves her.

PM from Tremor to Chimera: Don't worry, I'll reach him. Thanks.

Computer trouble could account for Thea's being incommunicado, I reasoned. However, I knew of folks who raced off to Internet cafés and moved heaven and earth if their connection went down for one evening. How on earth could a dedicated chatter like Thea manage to stay off-line for three weeks?

CHAPTER 20

Thursday was a study in fairy tales. I went from little match girl to ugly duckling, trying to wend my way toward Cinderella. First off, my hair wouldn't do what I wanted it to do, but that wasn't an unusual occurrence. I washed it a second time and tried to be patient while it air-dried. If I messed with it before it was dry, all the body it was capable of fell out and it began its imitation of brunette spaghetti. While I was waiting, I decided to do something to my nails and began soaking the cuticles in softening gunk to find room on the nail to paint.

My mother used to swear that eating Jell-O was her secret to great nails, but I have a feeling she just inherited great hands from her mother while I got my dad's hands. For one thing, I cannot recall ever seeing her voluntarily eating Jell-O. My nails, no matter how much Jell-O I had room for, never seemed to do much more than crack or peel. Whenever I had the time to hit a beauty college for a manicure, they would comment pityingly on the state of my nails. Regular manicures were something I intended to fit into my regime if I ever made steady money. After all, with all the on-line chatting and distance marking I was doing, I had to look at my hands in front of me more often than ever. A little voice in my head told me that if I were a better typist, I wouldn't have to look at my hands at all, but I dismissed that noise immediately. Manicures were way more fun than typing lessons.

Dial M for Murder was the afternoon TV movie, which I had on for company as I primped. If getting dolled up meant I could look like Grace Kelly, I would be all over this girlie stuff. As it was, makeup had never been a big thing with me. I had been blessed with clear skin and nice straight eyebrows, so there had never been much reason to fixate on the mirror as a teen. I think that's what kept me from using makeup as an adult. My makeup routine consisted of washing my face when I shampooed my hair in the morning and adding mascara on days when I had to do any lecturing in big classrooms.

On a big night like tonight, though, I would break out the eyeshadow and the lipstick as well. Denise had said it was a gala, and I couldn't remember the last time Steve had seen me dressed up. Since I did it so seldom, it held a sort of Hallowe'en quality for me. I was becoming something I was not. I wondered if anyone would recognize me, or, better yet, give me candy.

I slipped the dress on about 5:30, and a sense of delight at being in the right clothes for the right occasion made the rest of the preparations easy. My hair was full and wavy, and I braided one thin section from above my left ear and drew it over the top of my head in place of a tiara, nailing it behind my right ear with a bobby pin. Now my loose hair wouldn't be falling forward into my face.

I laced up my little black witch boots, minding my shiny nails. I was as ready as it was possible to be, and it was still half an hour before Steve was due to pick me up. Out of habit, or perhaps addiction, I logged into Babel.

Carlin was cheering the grades Evangeline had received on her mid-terms, and Eros and Ghandhi were still awake, which was unusual for them. Maybe there was some sort of European holiday on and they didn't have to work the next day. Most of the Europeans were well in bed by the time I logged on in western Canada.

Alchemist sent me a quick PM, wondering if my plans had changed. I told him, a bit abashed, that I was still intending to go out but that I couldn't seem to keep away from the place.

As Chimera I made my hellos and replied to Maia's cheery greeting of "what's up?" with the information that I was all dressed up to go out tonight.

Chimera: I don't normally dress up, so this is feeling a bit weird, but nice weird.

Maia: What are you wearing? Inquiring minds want to know! *giggle*

Chimera: Well, it's not the fanciest dress in the world, but it's pretty fancy for me.

Sanders: I'm all dressed up, too! Maybe this is an international evening out! Maia, are you going out, too? I am off to a gala for the university.

Oh my lord. I was so relieved I hadn't mentioned the color of my dress. Sanders was going to be at the gala. My mouth went dry.

Maia: So, are you wearing a tux, Sanders? I am going nowhere, I'm afraid. Just me and my keyboard, strolling down the avenue. . . .

Sanders: Nope, just a navy suit. My budget doesn't run to tuxedos, I'm afraid. Anyhow, this will likely be an eclectic bunch, not your average formals, I'm guessing. It's for the Writer in Residence program. They bring in a writer each year to sit in an office and write, when not being interrupted by students and the public to read their manuscripts and give them advice.

Maia: You mean anyone can go see them?

Sanders: Sure. That is part of the purpose of the programs. Check the libraries and the universities near you . . . whereabouts are you?

Maia: Near Halifax.

Sanders: Right. Well, I'm betting there will be two or three folks around there to take your work to. Try the Dalhousie English Department.

Maia: Oh, I don't have anything worth looking at. Just some old poems from college days.

Sanders: Don't sell yourself short! You have a real sense of rhythm here.

Chimera: He's right, Maia. You should think about writing. Not that there is that much money in it. Unless you're Stephen King, that is.

Sanders: What about you, Chimera?

Chimera: Me, write? A little bit, but not enough to pay bills with.

Sanders: I interrupted you before. You never told us about your dress for your evening out.

Chimera: Well, it's red.

I said the first thing I could think of that wasn't what I was wearing. I stared down at the moss green velour, and plucked at it a bit nervously.

Chimera: And short.

Maia: That should get the heads turning, girlfriend! So where are you going?

Chimera: A party, an anniversary party for my uncle and aunt.

I didn't know I could lie with such facility. This was mainly because I never lied, knowing full well that my face would give me away. Steve had once told me never to take up poker. My typed font didn't blush, though. Who knows? I could get used to this.

Whatever I did, I couldn't let Sanders know I was going to be in the same room as him tonight. It was going to be bad enough wondering which guy in a navy suit he was, and worrying that my heretofore unknown telepathic powers would have him zoning in on me before the opening speeches were over.

Chimera: And I think I hear my ride now. Gotta run!

I logged out, not bothering to wait for the inevitable goodbyes. I was breathing hard, as if I had navigated a dangerous passage on a fallen log across a gorge.

I still wasn't sure why I didn't want Sanders knowing I was in his town. Cerebrally, I knew that the chances of his being an ax-murderer were pretty remote, but I would have felt a whole lot easier if he were pretty remote, too. Or, if I was being completely truthful, maybe I was scared of introducing another man into my real life and messing up the good thing I already had. Whatever. I wasn't going to get all analytical about it; it was important to me at a gut level, and I had learned to trust my instincts as I aged. Just as I was about to head to the washroom to recheck my makeup, Steve knocked on the door, saving me from being a complete liar on-line. He looked fabulous, as tall men always do when dressed up, in a navy double-breasted suit. I twirled around and felt delighted with the look of approval in my Prince Charming's eyes. Yes, my ride was here, and Cinderella was going to the ball. Now if only she knew what Rumplestiltskin looked like.

CHAPTER 21

Denise looked fabulous, like a fairy in a children's book. (Bruno Bettelheim would have been proud of me: I couldn't seem to get fairy tales off my mind.) Her dress picked up the light and reflected it off every little sequined surface, and the transparent heels of her shoes made it appear as if her feet seemed to float, rather than walk. She greeted Steve and me as we wandered into the Timms foyer.

"You are so lucky you could walk here! The parking is horrendous, which means that we either sold more tickets since I checked at noon or everyone came in separate cars. Grab a drink."

She handed us a couple of drink tickets.

"I am too keyed up to use these. You can buy more over there, but since it's a benefit, the prices are jacked up on everything. Check out the silent auction stuff upstairs, too. Oh, I hope this goes well."

We assured her that it would go marvelously and thanked her for the tickets. She said she'd try to find us later, and we split up. Steve decided he'd have a beer, and I ordered a spritzer. We angled our way to the windows, where there were some low, upholstered benches. Someone was playing the grand piano that sat under the staircase. It was classical and familiar, but not immediately so. The gala was to be confined to the upper and lower foyers of the Timms Centre, not spilling into the theater itself. We didn't need the theater; there was enough drama walking around the lobby.

Steve looked so great dressed up that I would have to watch out for predatory single women. I looked at him and a wave of lust came over me. It was so strong that I blushed, thinking it must have been physically obvious. Maybe not, because Steve just smiled at me and squeezed my hand.

"So, do you know all these people?"

Not all, I assured him, and decided not to tell him about the one I might know better than I realized. I am not sure why I didn't confide in Steve right then. I suppose it had something to do with our just getting back together, and something to do with the presuppositions folks had about chat rooms. I wasn't sure he'd understand about Sanders. To be totally truthful, I wasn't too sure I understood, myself.

It wasn't as if I was interested in Sanders in a relationship-forming way; at least, I didn't think so. The whole concept of flirting on-line, though, seemed so refreshing. It occurred to me that my parents' generation had had an easier time of things. They had been repressed about a lot of things, but innocent flirting had been mowed under along with larger issues of harassment and free love. We got more honest with each other but the cost was that we lost some of the fun qualities of social interaction.

I was musing about this and at the same time counting eight or nine men in blue suits while Steve went off to get us another drink. Two was my limit, even of spritzers, so this one would have to last longer than the first one had. I had gulped it nervously. I was going to have to settle down a bit.

It wasn't as if Sanders was going to find me, after all. I had the entire advantage. I knew what he would be wearing, and he thought I was in another color, at another party, in another town. So why was I so jumpy?

I wanted to know who he was. It was that simple. The part that wasn't at all simple was why I wanted to know. I knew that part of it had to do with safety, a sort of belling of the cat. If I knew what he looked like, he wouldn't be able to sneak up on me unawares in any other situation. The other reasons were darker. There was a real fascination involved in putting a face to an on-line persona. One thing I was sure of, no one looked the way I imagined them looking. Any time anyone posted a picture of themself, I was usually shocked by how different they were from my image of them. He or she would be larger, or balder, or younger, or dressed in clothing I'd never have imagined them wearing. The slogan-spouting activist who stood waving, wearing a tee-shirt with the notorious swoosh on it, was a case in point.

I thought of Sanders as a raffish-looking intellectual; the sort of fellow who wore a Harris tweed jacket that likely had belonged to his uncle (or bought at the Goodwill) with a school tie or an old woolen scarf that had a darned hole in one corner. A turtleneck, corduroy trousers, low, shapeless, leather shoes, and a bookbag slung over one shoulder completed the look. I was pretty sure he was a shadowy stand-in for Leonard Cohen or another, lesser-known, Beat poet, but I didn't care. This was my imaginary friend, after all. He could look however I wanted him to.

There was no one here that looked too raffish, though.

Or maybe what I meant was that even the raffish-looking ones were clean and tidy. After all, some of the professors and hordes of the writerly set in this town could be considered seedy-looking in a good light. Tonight, though, the lights were dim enough for any Blanche DuBois, and everyone looked marvelous.

I could name many of the people here. Some of them I had worked with before moving over to do distance courses at the college. Some of them had been my professors; many of them had been fellow students. Some of them were writers whose readings I'd attended and books I'd bought. Of course, some of them were complete strangers, too: the stratum of society who supported the arts in principle without hands-on involvement. These were the modern equivalents of the Renaissance patrons, and there were far too few of them, in my opinion, for us to ever have an autonomous arts scene in this country. Blessings on the ones who did exist.

Greg Hollingshead was wearing a blue suit. So was Timothy Anderson. I couldn't imagine either of them as Sanders. For that matter, so was Steve, I realized, as he reappeared, proffering me another white-wine spritzer. Blue must be this year's lime green in men's fashion.

"You are so lucky," I said to Steve, as he perched beside me.

"Because I'm out on the town with a beautiful woman? I know," he said.

"That's not quite what I meant. I was just thinking about fashions. Look at all the women here; if two of them showed up in the same dress, there would be a wave of whispers so strong it could budge the piano. Meanwhile, look how many of you show up in blue suits, and no one blinks an eye."

"Ah, that's what you think. You just don't know how to read the signs. See that fellow over there?" He pointed toward Timothy Anderson, a poet and opera singer I knew slightly. "That longer jacket is very stylish, sort of a Will Smith, Samuel Jackson look. He can pull it off because he's so tall. Meanwhile, over there, that fellow with the three-inch lapels is probably wearing the same suit he bought for his sister's wedding fifteen years ago. And see the fellow with the Nehru collar?" I nodded. "Retro. Very big in Toronto at the moment, I hear." Steve looked around the room and gave a low whistle. "And see that fellow by the window? Look how that jacket swings from the shoulders. That has to be Armani."

"So you're saying that there are levels of fashion even in men's suits. Touché. I guess I was just looking at the general concept. I didn't realize it was quite so intricate. I knew about tie widths but not much about style or cut. What about your suit? Is it au courant?"

Steve shrugged modestly. "It's about two years old, and cut classically enough that I can get away with it for another couple of years, or until Letterman goes off the air." He grinned. "The trouble with suits is that they are expensive and made to last. You can't justify buying too many, and you can't afford it, either. Unless you're working right in the city five days a week, you won't be buying a new suit for every occasion. So you have to choose on the conservative side if you want staying power."

"I think that double-breasted style looks great on you. Very wide-shouldered Johnny Weismuller-ish."

"And I'll bet you're imagining what I'd look like in a Speedo," grinned Steve. His grin turned into outright laughter as I blushed bright red.

"You are so transparent, Randy. It's almost too much fun to tease you."

"You'd be surprised. I am getting pretty good at being coy and opaque on-line, for your information," I said, rather archly, because I knew he was right. I couldn't lie to someone's face to save my life.

"How's that going?" Steve asked casually. He seemed almost too casual about it, seeing as he hadn't been very approving of the whole idea. I looked at him but couldn't read anything more than general interest in his face. Now, Steve, he could win any poker bluff.

I shrugged. "Not bad, I guess. It's a lot like being cruise director on a ship, I think. We have to make sure that folks are playing nicely, that no one is feeling too left out, and that they're not throwing things overboard or peeing in the lifeboats." I stretched my legs out a bit, with my little witch boot toes straight up. Steve smiled and then pointed to my left. There was a fellow balancing a drink in one hand and a plate of nibblies in the other, trying to get past my outstretched legs. I apologized and pulled my feet back in under the tent of my dress. As he passed by, I noticed that he had a slight pinstripe in his, of course, blue suit. I'd have to ask Steve whether that was a fashion faux pas.

But not at that moment. Steve stood and reached out a hand to me, saying we should try to see the silent auction stuff before too many more people crowded us out. We walked up the stairs, seeing our reflections in the darkened windows to our right. It felt so grown up, being out late in fancy clothes. Actually, what it felt like was my idea, when I was a child, of what being grown up must feel like. Really being grown up had a lot more to do with paying taxes and minding budgets and checking the triglycerides on the label, I knew that. Those weren't what I'd rushed through childhood to get to, though. Walking through a glittering party with a handsome man who thought me charming, along with making an entire dinner out of ice cream or talking back to a rude sales clerk—those were the things I'd had in mind.

Denise must have depleted several lifetimes' worth of charm to coax the donations she had. The silent auction was amazing. There were weekends at the Jasper Park Lodge, and weekends in tipis; tickets to the symphony, the opera, the Citadel Theatre, and the Canadian Finals Rodeo. Folks had already filled a page and a half for a busily peopled painting by Toti of Whyte Avenue, and there was a lot of interest in some hammered silver napkin rings.

I found the most wonderful prize: a library containing a signed volume from every writer-in-residence who had ever spent time at the University of Alberta. Since some of those writers had already passed away, this was indeed a special collection. I jotted my bidding number and a bid of $50 onto the sheet accompanying the books. Steve, whose tastes were amazingly eclectic, bid on a Ted Harrison print. I then bid on a handwoven shawl, a gold U of A watch, and tickets to next year's opera production of *I Pagliacci*. If no one else bid, I would be in trouble.

The thing was, people were bound to keep bidding at a silent auction, and eventually you got what you wanted, either at an exorbitant price, or through dogged diligence, or both. I usually got too tired to keep checking on the tables I was interested in, and lost things by five dollars or so. I decided I would keep an eye on the library until it hit $100 and monitor the opera tickets up to $75. That was about my limit for philanthropy.

"I think there is food around here somewhere," I said to Steve, who was eyeing a Golden Bears melton and leather jacket a little too keenly. "C'mon, you would never wear that. You know it."

"I can dream, can't I?" He was willing to be led away, though, and it occurred to me that I knew very little about Steve's U of A career.

"Were you ever on a team when you were at university?" I asked as we headed back downstairs toward the food table.

"Who, me? Nah, I didn't have the talent or the discipline. Besides, I was trying for prime minister, not premier." I laughed. Several Alberta mayors and provincial officials were former football players.

"I wasn't really athletic at university, either. I sometimes went for a swim, but mostly I spent my time in three places: classes, library, and student pub."

"Indeed. Of course, when we were of university age, there were rules where the college pubs weren't allowed to start serving beer until after three o'clock."

"Isn't that the same now?"

Steve shook his head. "Sadly, no. They can open at eleven, just like any bar in the province, and they can sell any hard liquor they wish, not just beer and wine. I have a feeling this leads to much less productivity in afternoon classes."

"That is one of the great pleasures of distance education; you don't have to see whether they are drunk or not." Steve laughed, but I wasn't completely joking. "Truth is, I have no great desire to see them at all. I have no curiosity about what those distance students look like. To me, they are words on a screen, or mailed to the college. Some of my colleagues make a point of being at the department office on the days their students book to write their final, but I am perfectly willing to have the secretary hand them the exam envelope and pop it in my mailbox when they've done."

"Is that the same with your on-line chat-room people, too, or just your students?"

"Well, sort of, although I do admit I have a bit more curiosity about the folks in the chat room. I tend to wonder where someone has disappeared to if I haven't seen the name pop up on the screen for a few days. Some folks are as regular as every day. Others are less frequent, but they don't seem to be what you'd call haphazard. They seem to have rhythms to their on-line use, and if you're a regular, you begin to sense those rhythms. So, when someone disappears, I get to wondering what's keeping her. Do you see what I mean?"

Steve nodded. "Do people disappear and return?"

"Well, from the time I've been monitoring, a couple of folks have taken some time off for holidays, or to move house, but only one person has really vanished, and I don't know if I'd have noticed that if it weren't for her boyfriend continuously looking for her."

"Her cyber-boyfriend?"

I grimaced. "Yes. That sounds sort of grotty, doesn't it? Believe me, it doesn't seem that way on-line. It really does feel like a community."

By this time we had managed to make our way through the cocktail-sausage-and-raw-veggies-with-dip line and were sitting on the floor-level radiators that lined the windows, with styrofoam plates perched on our knees.

"What makes it a community? Isn't one of the first determinants of a community a shared background and space?"

I'd forgotten that Steve's background was in sociology with a minor in anthropology. This argument was right up his alley.

"That might end up having to be redefined, Steve. From what I've seen, this really is a community. Folks care about other people. They come to the site to share their gossip, their stories, their triumphs, their grief. They remember each other's birthdays and sit vigil with the mourning. There are in-jokes and running gags and cliques and even scapegoats. It's got all the markings of community."

"Except that you all hide behind masks and nicknames." Steve shook his head and stole one of the mushrooms left on my plate to swipe up the rest of his ranch dressing dip.

"Well, there is that, I'll grant you. However, look around you here. How many people do you see showing you their unvarnished faces in this room? Do you think Denise teetering about in her glass slippers is the real Denise?"

"Well, there's you."

"Right. I am always made up to the nines in low-cut velour. Steve, you only see me that way because you know me. For all we know, the fellow over there leaning on the piano thinks I'm a kindergarten teacher and the woman by the bar sees me as a underworld spy."

"No, I see you because you are absolutely open in your outlook and attitude. Whatever you are involved in, you throw yourself into entirely. You lean into people you care to talk to, and slant back from those you instinctively don't trust. You smile with your whole body and, when you laugh, the whole room feels like it missed out on a really great dirty joke. That's Randy Craig. That's who I see."

The entire room, aside from the center of my vision where Steve's face smiled at me, went fuzzy, as if Frank Capra had jumped into my head to start directing. I halfway expected little bells to start ringing in the corners of the screens.

"You think you can win your point by utterly disarming your opponent, I see."

"I only tell it like I see it," he whispered, leaning in to kiss my forehead.

It was getting difficult to recall whatever it was I had been about to say to Steve, because my mind was definitely moving out of the concept of general community and into the more rarified world of nuclear unit. There had been something, though, and danged if I could remember what it was. Something Steve had said that triggered a thought.

Oh well, he'd triggered a whole bunch of nerve endings, too, and these were far more interesting. Denise chose that moment to bustle up.

"So, tell me, is it the most magnificent event you've ever attended? The best time you've had since the pigs ate your sister? Better than a monster truck rally or a poetry slam?" She collapsed gracefully onto the square stool in front of us. "If I take one more trip up those stairs, I swear I'll collapse. I've been wandering around, trying to add up bids in my head and calculating how far that would take us into the year for the program."

"Does the department put any money at all toward the writer-in-residence program? Or the province?" I asked.

Denise grimaced. "Well, there are a few bequests that have gone into the pot designated for the residency, and the province usually coughs up a partial grant through the Arts Foundation, but we really have to beat the bushes to keep it going. At least we can fund it the entire year. Grant MacEwan College can only support a writer-in-residence for three months of the year, and usually at a time when most of the students are up to their ears in assignments and exams or have disappeared."

I had a feeling I'd tapped in to one of Denise's high-powered "campaigning for donations" set pieces. She hardly needed to take a breath as she continued. "One of the best things about our program is that the writer is here throughout the school term, and can be a resource for instructors as well as one-on-one sessions. Sometimes, if they have the qualifications, one of them can teach a class, too, which helps defray the costs of the program." She looked around the room, which was successfully crowded with beautiful people, or reasonable facsimiles thereof. I figured she had to be pleased with herself. I looked where her eyes traveled and realized there were whole segments of Edmonton society that I would never lay eyes on in the course of an average day. Where did these folks come from? How did they know to turn up, all gleaming and gorgeous? Maybe there was some special signal, too high a pitch for the average ear.

"How widely did you advertise this, Denise?" There was likely a more reasonable explanation than the one I'd come up with.

She wrinkled her forehead. "We put out an ad on CKUA and a notice on CBC radio. Then we had some coverage on the books page of the paper, and some leaflets on bulletin boards, and at bookstores. I took posters to Roberston-Wesley United and St. Joseph's Basilica, too, thinking to locate money as well as bibliophiles. The thing is, while the silent auction is just good fun, there is a tax receipt for all straight donations to the fund, so it's got its appeal."

I wondered just how Sanders had heard about it. Maybe if I knew that, I'd know a bit more about him. Three more fellows in blue suits walked past me. What was it with blue suits?

Steve stood up, and Denise and I did, too. Someone was approaching.

"Steve Browning?" A man in, what else, a navy suit was smiling with a touch of incredulity. "Of all the folks I thought I might run into, I never suspected you. How are you?"

"Chick! Man oh man! Randy, Denise, I'd like you to meet Chick Anderson. We were in residence together. Chick, this is Denise Wolff, who is in charge of this whole evening, and my friend, Randy Craig, who is bidding on the library, so be warned."

Denise gave Chick one of her most dazzling smiles, so I figured he must be one of the people she'd been targeting with her sponsorship campaign.

"I've heard of you, of course. It's so nice to actually meet you. So, you know our Steve, do you? We'd love to hear stories of his wicked youth." No man is immune to Denise at any time, but now she was turning on the high beams, and Chick was a goner. He moved toward her the way sunflowers follow the sun, and I caught the amused look in Steve's face.

"Don't you dare, Chick. Actually, I wasn't joking about the library bidding. Would you mind if Randy and I dashed up to check the bidding sheet and left you here to keep Denise company?"

Chick nodded vigorously, and I laughed lightly as we climbed the stairs to the silent auction level. As if Denise would ever lack for company.

"So who exactly is Chick Anderson?"

"Have you ever heard of Anderson Fryers?" Steve answered.

"You mean the poultry barns on the way to Morinville?"

Steve nodded. "Yep, and more by Red Deer, and I think some in Saskatchewan somewhere. Well, that's Chick's family. Hence the nickname. His real name is, uh, David, I think."

"No wonder Denise is cultivating him. That's got to be some sponsor, if she can land him."

"No doubt. I can't figure out what he's doing here, unless he's just a representative for the family at all these shindigs. Chick avoided books throughout university, as I recall. He mainly went to football games and house parties. Of course, that was several, ahem, years ago. People change, I suppose. Chick may have discovered the joys of Robertson Davies since I last knew him."

I looked over the balcony to see Chick still gravitating toward Denise's aura. "I have a feeling he's being converted to literature as we speak." Steve laughed, too.

We got to the library table, and, sure enough, there had been a few more bids, but only upping the ante by five dollars at a time. I scribbled down a bid of $70, and we pushed along toward the opera tickets. Alex Danvers and Valerie Bock were standing nearby, and it was my turn to introduce Steve. Valerie worked full-time at Grant MacEwan College, and Alex was a part-timer doing distance courses and one evening session of English 101. I'd met them at the start of the term department meeting and we'd clicked. I'd known Valerie vaguely when I was working on my thesis, and I'd heard of Alex, but we'd never had any classes together. I wasn't surprised they were here, though. Both of them seemed dedicated to their field, and funding contemporary writers seemed to feed right into that concern.

Besides, they really were beautiful people in their own right. Valerie's auburn curls were dusted with sparkles that twinkled in the lights. There was a shimmery thread in her wine-colored dress, too. Alex was wearing the requisite blue suit, with a Bugs Bunny tie. I supposed it was his mark of rebellion against authority.

"How did you get roped into this bunfight, Randy?" Alex asked. I pointed Denise-ward and mentioned our connection. He nodded and admitted that Valerie was on the Grant MacEwan College writer-in-residence committee. I had thought there might be something romantic between them, but it's hard to gauge these things in general department meetings. Here, it was obvious, as Valerie tugged on his suit sleeve and asked if he'd get them more drinks.

"I've heard the U's getting Yann Martel next year," she said wistfully. Apparently, when you can only offer three-month stints, you can't attract the high flyers. I shrugged, admitting I knew nothing more than that funding was in place for at least one more year, and perhaps more if the take from this evening's fundraiser was high.

"Would you like to meet Denise?" I asked. Valerie nodded, making her sparkly hair shoot lights all over. Steve and I threaded our way back through the auction tables with her in tow. Denise and Chick were still close to the bottom of the staircase, and Denise seemed genuinely happy to meet Valerie. I left Steve with them and went over to the bar area, where Alex was getting more drinks. I intercepted him just as he was headed for the back stairs. We were stopped, just looking for the path of least resistance back to our people, when a voice at my side spoke to Alex.

"Professor Danvers?" Alex turned, and so did I. The fellow speaking looked slightly older than Alex, which I figured made him at least ten years older than I. His hair was a little bit longer than fashionable, but stylish in a classic way. I was no longer surprised that he, too, was wearing a blue suit. It seemed that only the bartenders and Rudy Wiebe were wearing black at this do. Alex smiled at him and introduced me by gesturing toward me with the hand carrying the Manhattan rather than the one carrying the beer.

"Winston! Nice to see you. Winston Graham, I'd like you to meet Randy Craig." To me, gesturing toward Winston with the bottle hand, he continued. "Winston was in my very first class of English 101, years ago. He's one of the true remaining Renaissance men or polymaths, as far as I can tell. Learns for the sake of learning. Are you still taking courses, Win?"

Winston bowed his head to me, acknowledging the introduction and the reputation. "For my pains, yes. I've moved toward the sciences in the last few years, although I am still dabbling in comparative religion, and, for fun, I'm taking an art history class this year."

"I don't know how you do it, but I envy you the ability to do it," said Alex.

"You just have to decide on your priorities, Professor Danvers."

"Call me Alex, please."

"Alex. I decided a long time ago that achieving success according to the societal norm wasn't something I cared very much about. Once that came clear, things got much simpler. Now, all I have to deal with is subsistence and tuition."

"It sounds ideal," I admitted.

He smiled at me. "I grant that it's not the route for everyone, but I find it very fulfilling. Well, it's been delightful to run into you, Alex, and to meet you, Ms Craig." He tilted his head in that mini-bow again, bringing to mind some Prussian officer in a Shaw play, and turned back into the crowd of blue-suited beautiful people.

Alex and I got back to Steve, Valerie, Denise, and Chick just as the band was starting into "Love Letters in the Sand."

"They've played 'Who Wrote the Book of Love' and Three Dog Night's 'Black and White' already," Steve laughed. "What do you bet they'll play 'I Write the Songs' and 'Paperback Writer' before the night is through?"

"Maybe they'll get around to that Moxy Fruvous song, 'My Baby Likes a Bunch of Authors'," I added.

Alex was telling Valerie that we'd run into Winston the Perpetual Student.

"Isn't he odd?" she responded. "I mean, I realize none of us has technically left academe, either, but just to hang about taking course after course seems a bit warped to me."

"Not all of us are still in academe, either," I reminded her, gesturing to Steve and Chick.

"Well, you know what I mean. We all went to university for a purpose, right?"

"I don't know," said Denise. "If we keep advocating a liberal arts education as the way to go, rather than a technical market-driven training ground, surely we have to support this fellow's life work."

She turned to Alex. "When did you have him in your class?"

"It was my first class—I was TAing while writing up

my MA thesis. That must have been what, sixteen, seventeen years ago? Yikes." Alex shook his head, obviously startled. Valerie patted his shoulder comfortingly.

"And this fellow, Winston, has been steadily taking courses since then? I assume he couldn't have started earlier, or he'd be beyond freshman English, right?"

"Well, maybe he'd been at things a year or two before getting around to English. He was a mature student then, as I recall."

"How does he avoid graduating, I wonder," I added.

"I suppose that's not impossible, if there is no real advisor assigned to the student within a program. The part I can't figure out is how he keeps afloat. After all, tuition has doubled and tripled since he started, and rents have increased. Unless he inherited a house and annual income, I can't figure out how he keeps going."

Chick looked a bit bemused at this, but I expect that chicken heirs never have to think about where their next drumsticks are coming from. Denise smiled brightly and excused herself from our circle. It was time to shut down the first half of the silent auction, and she had to make her way to a microphone to let folks know. I watched Chick's face grow even more distant. It looked as if Denise had made another conquest. I wonder if she cared.

Alex and Valerie were talking to Steve about a great Vietnamese restaurant and Steve claimed to be always in the mood for noodles. I excused myself to run up and check one more time on the library and opera bid sheets. The opera sheet was closed, and I was the last bid at $60. It was a darned good thing I'd bought the gray dress, too. I decided to let the bids on the library go and settle for just this prize. I popped back downstairs to let Steve know I was going to stand in the line to pay for my tickets. He was still talking to Alex and Valerie and Chick. Winston, the odd student, was being introduced to them by Alex, and two other fellows, both in blue suits, had also joined the group. It turned out they were members of Chick's golf club, and Steve, too, knew them slightly from his youth, as well.

I mentioned the opera tickets, kissed Steve lightly on the cheek, and went off to the cash table near the coat check to redeem my prize. After what seemed like an hour, I paid my dues, received the envelope containing my tickets, and turned to find Steve again. There he was, three feet away from me, coats in hand. The band was still playing, but things were beginning to wind down. Steve had to work the next morning, and I had essays to mark and e-mail back to a couple of students.

We waved to Denise and made our way out into the chill evening. Even though it was cold, there was no wind, and it was a pleasant walk home. The walk, coming on the heels of all the reminiscing during the evening, gave me a sense of déjà vu, shifting me back to my first days on a university campus, walking home across the quad with a handsome boy. No, wait, that was Barbra Streisand in *The Way We Were*. Easy mistake to make.

CHAPTER 22

Steve hadn't been able to spend the night because he had to be up early for the morning watch, so I was all alone, still buzzing away, sitting in my bathrobe with eye make-up remover stinging my eyes. There was no way I was going to get any sleep in the near future, despite the two drinks I'd had at the gala. The crisp night air on the walk home had cleared my head and invigorated me. I was ready to settle in for a good gossip about everything folks had been wearing and what had been said, but I was all on my lonesome. Denise would still be at the Timms Centre clearing up, and, if she wasn't there, she'd be flitting off somewhere with her committee to celebrate, I was sure.

I leaned over to the desk and pushed the mouse with my fingertips, setting the screen of my monitor alight. Three clicks and a password would get me to a whole slew of folks. I pulled out my desk chair. No wonder there was such a boom of involvement in the Internet. I couldn't be the only person out there with no one to talk to late on a Thursday night.

It was technically my night off, since I'd traded with Alchemist, so I logged in and showed up on-screen as Chimera, without checking the room or any notes for my next shift. Things were hopping, from what I could see. A round of hellos came my way from some of the regulars, and Button, a university student in Melbourne, bounced up to tell me about her trip to the Great Barrier Reef.

Button: Oh, it was absolutely brilliant. I was snorkeling at one point and a tiger shark came right up to my mask. Not a very big one. Maybe two metres long.

Chimera: Yikes. I'm about two metres long. I don't think I'd want a shark that big anywhere near me.

Button: Well, they're not very bright.

Chimera: They don't have to be bright when they've got teeth like that.

Button: Doh.

Dion: You know, that reminds me of something I read by Desmond Morris about human babies. He said that human babies have to smile early and be adorable and charming and coo because their mothers don't have furry bodies.

Tracy: Say what?

Gandalf: What do you mean? Like they used to have fur?

Dion: No. Monkey babies grab their mothers and don't let go, so they aren't left behind. Human babies can't do that, so they compensate by being charming and therefore tricking their mothers into picking them up and carrying them along.

Chimera: That makes a certain odd sense.

Sanders: Of course, it would be handier if they could put them in a convenient pocket.

Hmmm, Sanders obviously couldn't just crawl into bed after getting home, either. I didn't feel so flighty, after all.

Maia: Sanders! How was your gala affair?

Gandalf: Sanders is having an affair? :)

Maia: He was at a fundraiser tonight.

Sanders: Well, in the words of Noel Coward, "I have been to a mah-vellous party!"

Maia: Spill all the details. The most excitement I've had tonight was trying to get the kitchen window opened to clear the fumes from the spray-on oven cleaner. I need to live vicariously.

Dion: Maia. *LOL*

Sanders: Well, let's see, what can I say? It was a fascinating evening, and the conversations weren't too bad. I've been spoiled from on-line interaction, though; I tend to judge group dynamics and conversations a lot more rigorously than before.

Chimera: I know exactly what you mean.

Sanders: There was a nice selection of nibblies, and a pretty good band, although, this being Alberta, they had to throw the Chicken Dance in there somewhere.

I couldn't recall them playing it, although it wouldn't have surprised me. It had been an enormous hit for The Emeralds, the premier dance band from Edmonton for the last forty-odd years. Maybe the combo had covered it after Steve and I had left.

Maia: So, were there speeches? Or dancing?

Sanders: Blessedly few speeches, and unfortunately no dancing. There was a silent auction, though. That was the high point of most folks' evening—checking on their bids.

Chimera: Did you bid on anything?

Sanders: No, I didn't, but one of the women I met managed to snaffle some pretty decent opera tickets.

Gandalf: Y'all got opera up there in the frozen north?

Sanders: My friend, you would be surprised what we have up here. This place is the greatest little secret in North America, I tell you.

Maia: Sure it is, except for that bit about forty-below six-month-long winters.

Sanders: *chuckle* Well, there is that, I'll grant you.

I'm not quite sure how long I sat there, staring at the screen, but it refreshed itself automatically two or three times, pushing that amazing sentence to the top of my screen before I could think to type anything. Sanders had been part of the group I'd been talking to. But who had he been?

I couldn't trust myself to chat any longer, so I made my farewells and logged out. I rinsed out my cup, and set it in the sink. My computer whired itself into shutdown as I walked back through the office-slash-dining-area toward my bedroom. Who on earth was Sanders?

CHAPTER 23

The greatest thing about telecommuting is the ability to appreciate the morning light in one's own apartment. I did half an hour of crunches and stretches on my yoga mat while the coffee was brewing, and then sat in my sweats and work socks while sipping Colombian Supremo and watched the lines of light and shadow created by the venetian blinds on the hardwood floor. I loved the old, fat venetians that had come with the apartment. They might be a bugger to clean once or twice a year, but they felt so much more sincere than their skinny, plastic, modern children. My apartment had an eastern exposure, but, what with working for a living and all, it had been three years before I got to experience this light and shadow interplay on a regular basis.

It had been way more than three years since I'd been this adrift in terms of scheduling. Although the year off I'd taken to get my MA had been far from nine to five, more like seven to eleven, I'd been working about fifteen years or more before that, and this loosey-goosey way of logging in my teaching time had taken some getting used to. In a way, having to punch a clock at Babel had been a blessing in disguise. Now, at least, I had some sort of structure to answer to.

Still, on a lazy Friday morning like this, having had a lovely mid-week evening out the night before, with no place to go and no clock to punch until eight this evening, it felt as if I was getting away with something. In fact, I knew I was getting away with something. There were plenty of people putting in longer hours to make what I was earning. I was lucky that I didn't need too much overhead to keep myself afloat, but, on the other hand, I took some pride in staying simple in my needs. While I enjoyed eating out more than I likely should, I did economize in other ways. My home-cooked meals were simple and very often meatless, which brought down my grocery bills considerably. I shopped for clothing at thrift shops, all except for underwear and shoes, and I tried to wait for the second-run cinema offerings, if I couldn't wait for the video rental.

Books were another matter. I had to admit, I can't recall ever looking at the price on a book, except to see how much to pull out of my wallet. I can spend more than twenty minutes pondering the differences in the price of chicken pieces or cheese blocks and occasionally go away empty-handed. I don't think I've ever left a bookstore without something.

I guess, all in all, it was a good thing I economized in some measure, or I'd have gone broke years ago. Of course, with all the books I owned, I didn't ever have to worry much about heating bills. Any place I lived would have to be rated R40 on bookcase insulation alone.

So here I was, wiggling my toes in the sunny dust motes and wondering what the poor folks were doing. Truth was, I was trying not to think about Sanders, but it wasn't really working. All I had to do was look up at the corkboard beside my study window and see the opera tickets I'd pinned there the night before, and it set me back to wondering which one of the men in a blue suit he'd been.

The Man in the Blue Suit. It sounded as if it should be the title of an Alec Guinness movie, not a conundrum to ruin a winter morning. Oh well, I sighed, and hauled myself off the yoga mat. When all else fails, make a list. Or two.

I rolled up my mat and tucked it behind the non-functioning gas fire that sat where it had probably sat for the previous sixty years or more. My knee was acting up on me. I wasn't sure whether it was due to the witch boots I'd been wearing the night before or if it was acting as a harbinger of the weather changing. Such fun to have your own built-in barometer, but, as you aged, and assorted aches and pains added themselves to the mix, the old faithful quirks stopped being quite so useful. I could no longer state with certainty that we'd be getting snow tomorrow; it could be me just wearing out.

I went over to the desk, which was also bathed in stripey sunny splendor. It was a good thing I didn't have any marking to do; I was obviously having too much of a Wordsworthian moment to be entirely useful. I grabbed a pad of lined paper, a few colored cue cards, and a pen, and pushed the book and magazine on the table closer to the condiment basket.

If Sanders knew that I had successfully bid on the opera tickets, then he had been one of the men I was talking to at the end of the evening. Surely I could determine who Steve and I had been talking to and extrapolate his identity from what I knew of both Sanders and the folks I'd met at the gala.

It would be like one of those logic puzzles I used to do

on long, boring car trips. Woody, John, Curtis, and Clem live on this street. Their wives are Leslie, Susan, Kristie, and June. With the following bits of information, determine who lives in what colored house with which wife. Simple. Easy-peasy.

Okay. I had spoken with Denise and Chick Anderson. I then talked with Valerie and Alex Danvers and met that fellow Winston the Perpetual Student. We had seen Timothy Anderson and Greg Hollingshead, but they hadn't been around after I'd paid for the tickets. Maybe Sanders had been near when they'd closed the table of silent-auction items and had just seen my name on the bidding sheet? No, that couldn't be. He had mentioned that it had been someone he'd been talking with. Besides, whoever would recognize my name on a bidding sheet would have to be someone I knew well enough to talk with at the gala. That brought it back down to the people I'd already listed on my pad of paper:

Chick Anderson

Alex Danvers

Winston Graham

I couldn't conceive of Sanders being a woman, although I had read plenty of scary stories about how people on the Internet disguised their gender and ages and marital status to dupe the people they professed to love and respect. The thing was, I knew it couldn't be Denise and I just couldn't imagine it being Valerie, even with her background in creative writing. There were just far more interesting things for her to be doing with her creative energies, and I am sure that with her full-time teaching schedule and her publishing credits, she was definitely using her time more wisely than by cross-gender chatting.

There was one other person I hadn't put on the list, of course, and although I really couldn't see it, I wrote his name down just for the sake of absolute precision. I looked at the list and stood up to get some distance and perspective on it. Also, to get another cup of coffee. The list was still there when I got back to the table:

Chick Anderson

Alex Danvers

Winston Graham

Steve Browning

Now, I needed to list everything I knew about each man, beyond his sartorial taste in colors. I laid out the cue cards like a tarot reading, after labeling each one with a different name. There wasn't all that much I knew about most of them, but Chick Anderson's was the least. I could, I suppose, get some more information from Steve, but he would want to know why, and, besides, it didn't seem fair to use him if I was also going to list him as a suspect.

All I knew about Chick Anderson fit easily on four lines of the cue card. He was relatively the same age as Steve, he came from a wealthy family that had been situated in the Edmonton area for at least sixty years, he wasn't, as far as I could see, an intellectual, but he did profess to admire the arts. Being the western Canadian chicken heir apparent meant that he certainly would have enough money to indulge in computers, and not having to punch a time clock would allow plenty of time for chatting. I wasn't too sure how much computer knowledge he would necessarily have. I knew that Steve had bitched a bit last spring when the police department had brought in a new networking system, which meant he would have to relearn things. If Chick was anything like his old residence mate, he wouldn't be racing out for the latest megachip. I couldn't be sure of that, though. Maybe he was a diehard ham-radio operator who had made the jump to bulletin boards and chat rooms early on. Maybe he was a complete Luddite who still wrote with a quill pen. Maybe he'd just been "here for the beer" in his university days and was now living on the family reputation and trust fund.

Alex Danvers had an MA in English literature, with a focus in modern British novels. He was in a committed relationship with Valerie, had a part-time job at Grant MacEwan College, had his degrees from the U of A, and had taught there for a few years during and after his MA. With marking and prep time for courses, his chatting time would be negligible. Of course, given the strange timetables for Grant MacEwan English courses, his ability to come into Babel at odd hours might be understandable, plus two of his courses this term were distance ones. He was awfully proud of his credentials, though. I wasn't sure he would subsume all that into the persona I knew from the chat room.

Winston Graham was a perpetual student and seemed in many ways the most likely to be connected to an on-line chat community. I figured that he would have the time and inclination. As well, there was a greater chance he had slid into computer courses over the previous twenty years and might be more fluent on-line than Alex and Steve. Enigmatic, I'd written on his card, mainly just to fill up another line. Damn him for even being in the circle near the coat check last night. I knew nothing about him, and had no real line on checking him out.

I flicked the Steve card in irritation. Here was the one blue-suited man I could write reams about, and I still couldn't be sure of anything. He had a BA from the U of A, knew his way around the arts, was quick with general repartee, and able to hold his own with anyone. He professed to be non-conversant with the chat-room end of the Internet, but I had learned in the past that Steve kept his job and private life very much apart. Maybe he was part of the INTERPOL task force organized to sweep the Internet for child pornography. If he was, I would never learn it from him.

I shuffled the cue cards. This wasn't going too well. Now I would have to create a card for Sanders and see what I could possibly glean that would attach itself to the suspects.

I knew from his level of discourse in Babel that he was educated. He was literate without being showy, although I seemed to remember that he could quote some lines of modern poetry when the need arose. The sheer fact that he thought there was, on occasion, a need for poetry lifted him well above the norm in my books. He worked odd hours, if indeed he did work. He was very coy about his profession, much more likely to speak about current events and cultural concepts than work issues.

I knew that he was flirtatious, that he seemed to be single, and that he lived in Edmonton. If I could believe him, he had been wearing a blue suit last night at the writer-in-residence gala. (I was hoping this logic puzzle stuck to the men on the street with their wives and variously colored houses and didn't turn into the one about the blue-eyed island elves who lied or told the truth.) He had been near enough to me to know I'd snagged the opera tickets. And his name was Sanders.

I pulled the other four cards back toward the edge of the table. Handles in chat rooms were strange things.

Some folks used nicknames very close to their own names. Some people tried on personae that seemed to match their mindsets at their time of entry into the community, and then were stuck with that moniker for better or for worse. No one, to my knowledge, had ever gone into a chat room disguised as a Bertha or Eustace. The names were sexy or cute or meaningful to the bearer in some iconic way. Maybe if I could come at it backwards, figuring out why Sanders called himself Sanders, I'd have a better idea of who I was dealing with.

Well, Sanders could be another diminutive for Alexander, which I was assuming was Alex's full given name. I wasn't sure why he would have pluralized it, but I pulled the blue cue card toward me and jotted "Alexander - Sander" across the bottom.

I stared at the name I'd written across the top of the pink cue card. What did Sanders mean to me? Had I never paused to wonder at all what the label implied?

Well, it could be a surname. It might be a carpenter's nickname—someone who used a sander a lot. It reminded me of a gypsy or circus name, but I think that would have had to be Sandor, instead of Sanders. Sanders sounded more like the name of a man in a Tom Stoppard play, a small, insignificant man who trudged instead of ambled. Maybe it was the name of a theatrical character. I would have to check that.

I glanced at Chick's yellow cue card. His last name was Anderson. I wondered if his given name began with an S. I couldn't remember if I'd been told his real name. Then he might be offering a handle of S Anders, the way some e-mail programs cut your name off after eight places. That was a distinct possibility, except that *Sanders* was only seven letters long. I'd have to ask Steve. Heck, I could probably ask Denise. By now, she probably knew his shoe size.

I took a glance at the green card on which I'd written the pitiful little I knew about Winston Graham. I couldn't imagine how on earth he could possibly make a leap to being called Sanders in an Internet chat room. Maybe he worked in a fast-food place to pay for his university jones, and the nickname his friends gave him for making sandwiches all night was Sanders. Okay, that was stretching it. Especially the part about him having a set of nicknaming friends while holding down a full-time service industry job and attending university courses. He did seem the most Sanders-like of all my possibilities. There was just no real connection I could make. If only the man I knew from Babel was calling himself Churchill or Cracker.

I glanced at the cards I'd made for Steve and Valerie. They were too ridiculous to contemplate, and I pushed myself away from the table. Here it was, almost three in the afternoon, and I was still in my sweats. What was more, I hadn't even made the bed. I could see the chaos of duvet, sheets, and blankets through the doorway. That was the trouble with a small apartment. If you didn't keep things incredibly tidy, it could drive you insane.

I went in to the bedroom and pulled my bedding into order. I plumped the reading pillows and set them over my space-aged polymer sleeping pillow. My Pooh Bear nightshirt was lying on the floor at the end of my bed. I shook it out before hanging it on one of the hooks on the bathroom door.

I was halfway out of my sweatshirt on my way to the shower when it hit me. Pooh Bear. Winston equals Winnie equals Sanders. Of course!

CHAPTER 24

I allowed myself a fully adequate shower, but I have to admit, I skipped the conditioner. I was eager to get out and test my memory of my favorite children's story. I toweled and scrunched my hair, and I tried not to wrinkle my face while applying moisturizer with sunscreen, my one concession to daily face care. Sliding into my jeans and a denim shirt so faded that Mary-Chapin Carpenter would be envious of it, I dumped the sweats into my laundry bin and hung the towel over the shower curtain rail to dry out.

My *World of Pooh* was hardcover with a rather fuzz-edged dust jacket, all cream and brown with the Shepard drawings wrapping entirely around. I kept it beside my complete Shakespeare, my *Oxford Student's Bible,* Janzen's *History of Art,* and my hardcover Bartlett's. Most every quote worth finding could be found in one of those books, I figured. As long as I could keep "The Love Song of J. Alfred Prufrock" set in my memory, I would be fine.

I slid it off the shelf, smiling because you just can't help but smile at the chubbiness and good-natured bemusement that shines out of those original drawings of Winnie the Pooh.

I flipped the book open and there it was, on page 8,

right where I remembered it being. The narrator tells Christopher Robin that his bear, Winnie-the-Pooh, lived in the forest, "under the same of Sanders." The illustration showed a sign with "Sanders" written on it tacked over the doorway to a small tree house. I had always been charmed by the matter-of-fact way in which A.A. Milne had played with the various idiosyncracies of the English language. Today, though, all I could think about was Winnie-the-Pooh and his assumed name.

Winnie-the-Pooh was named, I knew, as did all good Canadians, for a small black bear in the London Zoo sent from Canada in the early twentieth century, whose name was a shortened form of "Winnipeg." Most folks tended to confuse it, though, and assumed the bear of little brain had been named to honor the prime minister of the time, Winston Churchill. Here was a case of life imitating an approximation of art.

Winston lived under the name of Sanders.

CHAPTER 25

Damn. Now I had three men, all in blue suits, all with a more than tenuous connection to the handle Sanders. An Alexander could easily be Sanders; Chick Anderson might be nicknamed Colonel Sanders, and Winston might "live under the name of Sanders" with literary aplomb. This wasn't getting me any closer to a decision on who Sanders was.

I decided I would just have to initiate some sort of discussion about nicknames and handles at Babel one evening and see if Sanders volunteered any information. The trouble was, if I did that, I would set myself up for some revelations, too. I had been very careful up until now about veering away from any sort of discussion that got too personal or focused too much on background information. If I were to start one, it would look odd if I didn't join in.

Of course, none of this was really all that problematic. It was no skin off my nose if I never discovered who Sanders was. If I could just keep aware enough of Sanders not to blow my cover of anonymity, I could make things tick along just fine. After all, aside from the occasional gambler and Venita the teenaged harlot, there wasn't all that much to worry about there.

I logged into Babel at 6:00, so that I could chat a bit with Alchemist about the night before. He wanted to know how my big date had gone, and I told him a little bit of it.

He let me know that Tremor had been in, looking for Milan again early in the evening, and that Milan had been in shortly after but didn't seem to be all that concerned with Tremor. He had PMed everyone about Thea, though, including several to Alvin. Alchemist was wondering whether this obsession was healthy. Maybe they'd had a fight and he was cyber-stalking Thea, or planning to. Alchemist had tracked back through the logs. She hadn't been in for almost a month.

I wasn't all that worried about Milan or Thea. I had been watching relationships begin, rev up, and disintegrate on-line at the speed of light. As Alchemist had once said, a week in cyber-time was like half a year in real time. It made me feel vaguely like someone was designing some cosmic Alpo commercial around me, and the old joke of "in dog years, I'd be dead" echoed in the back of my mind, but I could sort of understand what he meant. Folks without the opportunity to hold hands or neck passionately, or even just wander through IKEA on a Saturday afternoon, tended to get a lot more into personal and emotional background quicker. I would bet I knew more about the inner workings of several people I would never meet in my lifetime than I did about most of the folks I went to grad school with. There was just something about the cyber-medium that pulled old dreams, neuroses, and memories onto the screen.

So Milan couldn't find his lady fair. Maybe real life had interfered with her on-line time. Life had a habit of doing that. I was betting we'd find out she'd had a rush order at work, or maybe she'd had to single-handedly manage the flea market at her church and just hadn't had time to check her e-mail for the last few weeks.

Hah, who was I kidding? I checked my e-mail every five minutes, to the chagrin of my service provider, who kept sending me little messages about setting my auto-check to half-hour intervals at the most frequent. So, if I —who wasn't intimately involved with someone on-line—was that connected, how could I imagine Thea wasn't?

Because Thea did not want to be heard from. Simple as that. There were all sorts of reasons a woman might want to keep away from a man. I decided to keep a closer eye on Milan than I'd at first planned.

Alchemist was going grocery shopping at an all-night grocery store. He was sure that this was the way to meet a dream date. I told him to hover in the organic vegetables where the more sincere people would be. He LOLed and signed off, leaving me in charge of Babel for my shift.

CHAPTER 26

Kafir and Ghandhi were teasing Lea and Maia about the fact that they knew nothing about golf, from what I could gather on first entering the main chat area. Milan had left several more PMs for Alvin, asking about Thea, and Vixen had also left Alvin a note, telling him about Milan. Vixen saw herself as a friend of Alvin's and would often imply that there was a closer relationship than she was willing to talk about when she discussed him on the open screen. I wasn't sure what Alchemist or possibly Chatgod had ever fed her under the Alvin guise, but I was always very businesslike when replying as Alvin. Still, if she wanted to pretend she had a relationship with Alvin, it only helped our mythification. I would PM her back later in my shift. I didn't want to have to parry a PM conversation with Vixen at the same time as having to watch over everything else. There was something happening in the room, I could feel a tension, but I couldn't pinpoint it. I decided to make a tour of private rooms, to see if there was something murky making my spidey senses tingle, or if it was just a general edge to the tone folks were taking with each other. That could happen. It was as if every once in a while everyone woke up on the wrong side of the bed and decided that, rather than punch a pillow or bite something, they would log in and spread the joy. If it was going to be that sort of an evening, I might as well pull out the ibuprofen now.

There were only three private rooms going. Vixen was in one of them with Bean, a relatively new fellow who liked to post lines of self-indulgent poetry. I had been watching him for a few days, not sure if he was being deliberately obscure to hide a rather libidinous nature, or if he really was as obtuse and dreamy as he seemed at first glance. It looked like Vixen was wondering the same thing. She was dangling a very flirtatious line, as she often did, hoping to add him to her harem, I supposed. As far as cyber-sex went, this was nothing more than petting, so I left them to it and clicked onto another virtual room where I could be a virtual fly on a virtual wall.

Jackal and Virago and Eros were telling some off-color jokes. I popped in as Alvin, thanking them for taking the vulgarity out of the main room without having to be asked. Mainly, I just wanted them to know I was around and watching. I didn't trust Jackal, but we could only toss him after he had posted porn. If he knew I was hovering, maybe he would behave himself while on my shift. I moved on before I had to read the punchline of what gynecologists drank at weddings.

Tremor and Milan were in the third room. This was where the tension was coming from. I could feel it the minute I clicked into the room.

Milan: Have you heard from Thea? I haven't heard a word from her. Even without a computer at home, I should have heard from her.

Tremor: Well, I wouldn't call her if I were you. Now is the time to be careful.

Milan: There are libraries, though. Cyber-cafés. If she wanted to, she could get hold of me.

Tremor: Then think about it. Maybe she doesn't want to get hold of you. That doesn't matter. What matters is the check, and it's time to settle up.

Milan: But until I hear from Thea, how can I be sure?

Tremor: Read the paper. Check your facts. And then remember your side of the contract.

Milan: But.

Tremor: No buts. I know where you live. I obviously know where she lives. That's all you need to think about.

Tremor left the building, and I quickly made a screen capture of the room before Milan could pop an erase on it. Even erased, it would be stored somewhere in Chatgod's backlogs, but I thought this might warrant a dated screen capture just in case.

What the heck were they on about? What had Milan and Thea hired Tremor to do? What was he asking to be paid for? Why indeed wasn't Thea on-line? Milan seemed to be implying that one of their computers wasn't functioning, and surely he meant hers, since he'd been on-line every day, but with the level of on-line canoodling they'd been up to, I would have thought they'd have exchanged phone numbers by now. Perhaps not, though. If Thea's husband had a call-monitoring device on the phone line, they'd be crazy to let him see a large number of calls coming from the same number.

Thea's husband. Now, there was a wild card in the hand. Something gnawed at me when I tried to put the thoughts of Thea's disappearance, Thea's lousy marriage, and the Thea-and-Milan cyber-romance together with the conversation I'd just read between Milan and Tremor. Where was Thea, anyway?

I moved back through the main room where Gerri and Carlin were riffing on book and movie titles to maintain a conversation. It looked like Sanders, who had just strolled in, was getting involved, too. Maia was always ready for a word game, and was bouncing about, laughing and thwacking folks. There was no tension here.

I went back through the private rooms. Interestingly, Sanders was in there before me, and they were no longer telling racy jokes. I couldn't catch the gist of all of it, but I didn't like what I did see. This was the night for screen captures, I guess. I would send a copy to Alchemist and see what he made of this:

Virago: I dunno, man, what if you got caught?

Eros: Then you're dead, man. Simple.

Sanders: The trick is to not get caught. But you have to realize there is always someone after you, even when you are getting a bead on your target, you are in someone else's sights.

Virago: Is this sort of thing allowed?

Sanders: Are you kidding? It's an assassination.

Eros: I wouldn't think so, man. That's why you have to find out where people live, instead of doing it out in the open. But you'd have to have a witness, right?

Sanders: Indubitably. Without it, how would you get credited with the kill?

They could have been talking about video games, but I was spooked enough to attribute all sorts of other meanings to that conversation. I was still focused on finding out what had happened to Thea. I would start by finding out where she lived.

I pulled down the menu list and clicked on to member details. While nothing more than a handle appeared in the chat room itself, all users had to register initially, giving their names and e-mail address. Captured at that time was the IP address they were logging in from. Sometimes that address shifted, and whenever a person logged in, the IP address showed in a box Alchemist and I had lit in the upper right corner of our monitor screens. Chatgod tried, in his opening salvo, to impress on people the need for disclosure in registration. The more information folks were willing to release, the feeling went, the likelier they were to behave themselves on-line. The registration form asked for real name, e-mail address, age, telephone number for emergency contact, and there was an optional area for snail mail addresses, since at one point I think Chatgod had been thinking of creating a magazine subscription list.

Thea's registration had her listed as Thea Banyon, with a phone number area code of 512. She hadn't filled in the snail mail address, but her e-mail address was thea@houyhnhnm.com. Trouble was, anyone could get a Houyhnhnm address. I would have to dig a bit deeper to find out where she was from. She didn't have a web site connected to her registration, either.

On a whim, I popped Milan's name into the search box. He was listed as david@cheesehead.com. I was assuming that this placed him in Wisconsin, as I couldn't imagine someone from anywhere else being proud to be a cheesehead. He did have a web site, and I clicked it to open in another browser window. I was hoping it wasn't too graphic-happy. With all of Babel open in front of me, it wouldn't take too much to crash me, and then we had to fill out reports detailing the amount of time Babel had remained unmonitored until we were up and running again.

I breathed easier as Milan's page opened. I couldn't be

too sure about it, but I was betting that this site was up completely for the benefit of Thea. There was a poem to Thea, a picture of Thea, a picture of Thea and him, a description of his love for her, and a couple of links to sites they liked. I noted with proprietory pride that Babel was the top of the list of links.

So, if the pictures were anything to go by, Thea and Milan had met IRL. I wondered if they had mentioned it on Babel, or if it was a deep, dark secret. I would have to nose about a bit. Surely someone would recall their arrival, or perhaps what the movie writers would call their "meet cute." I clicked my way back into the Babel-protected files to see who some of the oldest netizens were. My money was on Vixen and Leah, and I was half right. Vixen was the woman to engage in gossip for sure. If she had hung Bean out to dry by now, maybe we could dish a little dirt and I could find out the answers to a few burning questions.

It occurred to me that I was going to have to get a bit more easy with my own privacy if I was to receive any of the confidences I might need. So be it. As long as Sanders was an okay fellow, I guess it wouldn't matter too much that he eventually discovered that we shared a city. On the other hand, with all that talk of assassinations, I still wasn't sure how close I wanted to get to Sanders.

CHAPTER 27

There was something gnawing at me, something unpleasant, but I couldn't quite make it come into focus. I thought that, if I could find out where Thea lived, the picture would somehow be more clear. Lucky for me, Tremor had left and Milan was nowhere to be found. The boisterous boys were back out of the private room and joining in the main room fun and games. Several folks were playing a modified version of hangman, and I caught Vixen in a slow moment.

She was an interesting character and I couldn't quite get a handle on her. I knew she was married and that she flirted quite heavily on-line, but I didn't sense any marital woes in her background. Maybe the Internet would be to the bored housewives of today what Valium had been for the women of the 1960s. Much of Vixen's daily joy came from minding everyone's business in Babel. I was hoping she had been watching the romance of Thea and Milan with interest.

PM from Chimera to Vixen: Hi there! Have you been getting loads of PMs from Milan lately?

PM from Vixen to Chimera: Hi doll. *LOL* Have I ever. And I thought our dog looked bereft when we left him in the kennel last summer vacation!

PM from Chimera to Vixen: So you think Thea is just on a vacation? Or has she dumped Milan?

PM from Vixen to Chimera: Well, I saw her in here just before she left. She PMed me and told me she might be gone for a little while. I just thought she and hubby were going off on a cruise or something.

PM from Chimera to Vixen: Is that what she told you? I've never been on a cruise.

PM from Vixen to Chimera: Me either. *sigh* I wish old FD would get his act in gear and take a hint.

It took me a minute to recall that FoxyDog was how Vixen referred to her husband, a fellow who never appeared on-line, although Vixen was a little worried sometimes that he might sneak on in disguise to spy on her. Alchemist had promised to keep an eye on IP addresses for her, and, unless hubby was logging in from work and routing it through Patagonia, he had never done so.

PM from Chimera to Vixen: But Thea's on a cruise? Have you told Milan that?

PM from Vixen to Chimera: Well, I'm not sure she is. I just figured, given the time of year, you know. And I think her husband is older. *shrug*

PM from Chimera to Vixen: Did she meet Milan here? Or did they come here together?

PM from Vixen to Chimera: I think they must have met somewhere else, y'know. But they pretended to meet here. Thea arrived shortly after school started last fall. I remember because my kid's teacher's name is Thea, and I thought it might be her at first. That would have been one for the books, doncha know? *grin* All I know is that Thea was looking for something she wasn't getting at home, and Milan had been divorced, what, maybe two months? It was bound to happen. At first I thought she was desperate, then I figured they knew each other because she pretty well pounced on him the moment he walked through the virtual door. *LOL*

I figure that Vixen might have tried the same move herself, but that was being catty. With some folks, flirting was as natural and as necessary as breathing, and Vixen was one of those people.

I wondered if Thea's husband had ever seen Milan's web site. If he had put his wife's name into a search engine, mightn't it have taken him right to her picture and the shrine Milan had created?

Unless Thea wasn't actually her name, of course. Holy epiphany, Batman.

PM from Vixen to Chimera: You still there?

PM from Chimera to Vixen: Sorry, a bit of lag on this end. So, where is Thea from, anyhow? Are she and Milan in the same town?

PM from Vixen to Chimera: No, he's racking up the frequent flyer points, from what I hear. I think he's in Milwaukee or somewhere near the Great Lakes, and Thea's from somewhere in Texas. Haven't you ever heard her go on about it? What the heck is it about Texans, anyhow? Did you ever hear the joke about the cowboy funeral? The minister asks the congregation to stand and offer their memories of the dead man. No one moves a muscle. Finally, from out of the back, a long lanky drink of water stands up and hitches his thumbs in his belt loops and drawls, "Well, if there ain't no one who has anything to say about the dearly departed, would y'all mind if I said a few words about Texas?" *ROFLMAO*

PM from Chimera to Vixen: *ROTFL*

Texas. Thea was from Texas. I continued to kibbitz

with Vixen about various couples who had met and left each other in Babel, and I came to see that she really did envision the place as her own virtual soap opera. Well, I guess we all create what we need. For me it was a lunch-room filled with interesting people and occasionally a lively cocktail party. The banter and discussions were what drew me. For Vixen, who loved the intrigue and the flirting, it was *The Days of our General Restless Children,* a living, breathing soap opera. I wished her a good evening and took my public leave of the room, switching back into complete monitor mode. The gnawing feeling grew stronger.

On impulse, I slipped into my clogs and crossed the hall to the laundry room. I had brought my newspapers for recycling just yesterday and I knew there wouldn't be a collection for at least three or four days. Yes. There were my papers. I walked back across the hall, bringing them back into the apartment. As soon as I had the door shut, I dumped them on the coffee table and sat on the edge of the sofa, pawing through the pile. Finally I found what I was looking for: the *Austin American-Statesman.* I flipped through until I found what I recalled reading before.

Theresa Banyon was the name of the woman in Austin whose husband had been electrocuted by his computer. Thea was a perfectly common and acceptable nickname for Theresa. Chatgod was not going to like this at all.

CHAPTER 28

I flicked on the computer on the way to the kitchen the following morning, my usual routine. After filling the kettle and grabbing my vitamins, I was on my way back to the bathroom for a shower when I noticed the e-mail notice blinking in the corner of my screen. I clicked on the shortcut to Eudora, and waited for the mail to load into my Inbox. There were the requisite number of spam offers to enlarge my package and a couple of newsletters from academic and writing organizations with listservs to which I subscribed. What caught my eye was the urgently flagged message from Chatgod. I had sent him a message the night before, detailing what I'd discovered about Thea. I had transcribed most of the newspaper article, attached the screen capture of Milan and Tremor, and offered some sketchy comments about the perceived relationship between Thea and Milan, both my observations and those I'd culled from Vixen.

I had thought he might get back to me at Babel, leaving me a message, but it seemed like he was going to take it a bit more seriously. The e-mail gonged when I opened it, a notification that he had tagged it so that he would be notified when I had received and read the message. I just hate that toggle. It means I have to act on what I've read immediately or risk the wrath and ire of whoever sent me the message.

The e-mail read:

```
To: rcraig@uofalberta.com
From: chatgod@babel.com
Subject: YOUR REPORT

Randy,

I read your report with alarm. If what you sug-
gest is true, then we might have a hired killer
working from the aegis of Babel. That cannot be
allowed. I would like to speak with you. Please
click on <this link> as soon as you are able to
talk.

Chatgod
```

Well, confident now that he wasn't going to bounce onto my screen without warning, I left the e-mail open and went off to have a much shorter shower than I'd been planning. To be on the safe side, I closed and locked the bathroom door.

A few minutes later I was dressed, but my hair was still wet. I clicked on the e-mail link Chatgod had given.

Just because I'd seen it happen before didn't make it any easier to take. The entire screen shimmered and melted away, to be replaced with a view of Chatgod's ascetic visage. He looked up and straight at me. I knew that he couldn't really see me, since I didn't have compatible hardware in my monitor to capture visuals, but his manner of looking straight into his Web camera gave me the eerie impression that he would notice if I even twitched.

He pointed to my keyboard, toward the sound

buttons. I quickly hit the non-mute button, and I could hear his voice. I felt like Nipper, the RCA mascot dog.

"Randy, thank you for responding so quickly. I appreciate your report from last night. It seems I was correct in my assessment that you were indeed the person for the job. However, this situation cannot be allowed to continue."

I typed into the white box at the bottom of my screen: "Are you going to contact the police? Which police? Austin?"

His gaze flicked downward just a hair when I hit enter. Maybe my type wasn't quite at my eye level on his screen, but so close that I had to believe that he'd engineered it to give that eye-to-eye sensation in the first place.

"I would rather not bring the police into it as yet. Perhaps we can arrange something along the same lines for this Tremor as you dealt out to the bookie."

Chimera: I'm not sure that's such a good idea. For one thing, if this Tremor is what you think he is, then it seems like he's pretty good at what he does. I'm not sure I want to tick off a guy who seems to be pretty successful at killing people.

"I am not suggesting that you become a vigilante, Randy. I am just thinking that while it is not up to us to stop him, it's not healthy to anyone to condone this tacitly or implicitly in Babel. If he is using our community in which to conduct his illicit business, then it should stop. We need to make Babel a much less likely place to do business."

Chimera: How?

"For now, I think I will leave that to you and Alchemist to discuss. Let me know what plans you two come up with and I will exercise a power of veto. All in all, though, I would prefer to let you begin with an open mind. Many problems can be solved much more easily before a yardstick of behavior is laid down."

Fine for him to say. I grimaced, thinking of the horrors of monitoring every PM and every private room in Babel, night after night. Of course, that technically was what I was paid to do, but still it seemed highly invasive.

It was as if he could read my mind and see my facial expressions.

"Yes, it does seem like an invasion of privacy, doesn't it? However, you have to remember that this is a new frontier for so many of these people. They are behaving as if the old rules apply, those rules that tell them to trust people as soon as those people know a certain number of things about them and have achieved a certain level of intimacy. When the timing for that intimacy is foreshortened, all the old rules go out the window. And after all," he echoed my thoughts, "it is what you are being paid, as a monitor, to do."

I shrugged. Yes, it was, however 1984ish it might feel.

Chimera: I see what you mean.

Chatgod nodded, a short decisive movement that was almost a forward movement of his erect head, rather than a bob.

"I'm glad we can agree on this. I am counting on you, Randy. Between the two of you, you and Alchemist should be able to contain this cancer. Meanwhile, I am going to cull the logs for all transmissions by Tremor and see if I can isolate a constant IP address for him. Or her."

Chatgod nodded once more, and the screen shimmered again, leaving me staring at an e-mail offer for receiving my doctorate of divinity through the mail.

For a few minutes, to take my mind off the whole mess at Babel, I contemplated The Church of Randy. For one thing, there'd be a whole lot of singing and just the one rule: Be good to each other. I recalled a joke wherein God told this to Moses, who replied, "Listen Lord, I know these folks; you're going to have to be more specific."

I was afraid to think how many of Moses's specifics had been broken recently in Babel. Even the biggie—thou shalt not murder.

CHAPTER 29

I went into Babel about an hour before my shift began. Alchemist was hovering about in the background. He appreciated my coming in during his shift, and I knew that if our brainstorming went on into my shift, he wouldn't complain about having to stay on. He was amazingly loyal to Babel.

Chatgod had sent him a copy of my report. He opened a secure private room for us to talk in while we both kept an eye on the general room.

Chimera: I was going to talk to you about it tonight, but the pieces didn't fall together till quite late last night.

Alchemist: No hassle. You did exactly the right thing, Randy. Chatgod would have been livid if we'd waited before taking something like this to him.

Chimera: So what are we supposed to do? I am not even sure what Chatgod really wants us to do. Are we supposed to catch this killer? Or just chase him away from our playground?

Alchemist: This is like those ethical dilemmas in social studies class. Who do we throw out of the lifeboat? Who do we eat?

Chimera: *laugh* Yeah, a little bit more serious when

it comes out of the hypothetical, though, don't you think?

Alchemist: I think we're almost better off trying to keep it as much in the hypothetical as we can. After all, we aren't sure of any of this, right? We know that Thea's name is Theresa Banyon and that someone by that name in Austin, Texas, is the widow of a man electrocuted by his computer. The whole business of Tremor demanding money from Milan for services rendered could be for anything. He might be a sexual surrogate, for cripes' sake.

Chimera: A what??!!?

Alchemist: Well, we leap to the conclusion that he is a hired killer, but really, check your screen capture. Does it say anywhere that he is asking to be paid for killing Thea's husband?

Chimera: Well, would you expect a hired killer to be broadcasting that on-line where anyone can take a screen capture? He would have to be aware that chat room conversations are invariably logged, right?

Alchemist: You're granting him a lot of brains. I'm not so sure he can be Alpha *and* Omega. There aren't as many Hannibal Lecters out there as fiction would have you believe. Those who by nature are destroyers can't also be creative thinkers.

Chimera: I'm not so sure about that. I've met one pretty clever killer in my lifetime.

Alchemist: Randy! There are hidden depths to you, girl-friend! One of these days, you're going to have to tell me all about your personal relationships with killers! But right now, we have to rid ourselves of a pest.

Chimera: How he can appear without logging in like everyone else? I've been meaning to ask you.

Alchemist: Well, he could be on cable and just

constantly logged in to Babel. Or, if he's a hacker, he could have created himself a back-door program where he can maintain a constant open access to Babel even when he turns off his browser. On the other hand . . .

Chimera: Yes?

Alchemist: Maybe he is transmitting from his own server, which he would have to keep on at all times himself. If that's the case, it should be pretty easy to locate and fix his IP address. Thing is, I think we're going to have to operate on the assumption that he is either a really, really clever hacker type, in which case, I am betting he's not an actual murderer, or he is a killer who has a certain amount of savvy around machines like ours.

Chimera: That's two different trails entirely.

Alchemist: Yep. Of course, there are two of us.

Chimera: Why do I get the feeling I'm not going to be tracking the clever non-murdering type?

Alchemist: Do you think you have what it takes to track a hacker?

Chimera: Well, when you put it that way . . .

Alchemist: Kiddo, before we do anything that might bring you to his attention, we are going to do a little hacking of our own and get you routed through some circuitous patterns to Babel so that he can't easily ping backward and find where you are. It wouldn't fool a really good hacker, but if it's someone using us to wreak havoc of his own, it should do the trick.

Chimera: What if he is both hacker and murderer, though?

Alchemist: *shaking head* I guarantee it. That doesn't profile at all.

Chimera: Well, I just hope you're right. Otherwise, he's going to be on top of one or both of us.

Alchemist: Randy, you can contact me any time. I will be at home for the next three weeks almost exclusively, and I'm not planning on being far from my computer. I've got a program I want to test for bugs before I submit it to my bosses. So, day or night, I am yours.

Chimera: Speaking of, it's past your sign-off, hon. Thanks for sticking around. I'll talk to you some more tomorrow about it.

Alchemist: Yep. In the meantime, I should have a program set up by tomorrow that will list all private rooms as soon as they become active. That should help our monitoring considerably. You can just leave it up in a corner of your screen at all times.

Chimera: That would be great. 'Night.

Alchemist: 'Night, Randy. Take care.

He logged out, leaving me to wander through the place, checking corners for murderous intentions. Even before the limerick contest started up, I felt pretty silly about the whole thing. Still, it was my job and whatever I'd suspected earlier was obviously enough to get Chatgod nervous, if you could detect nervousness in that glacier-like demeanor.

I just hoped Alchemist's instincts for what hackers were made of was accurate. We hadn't discussed the whole Sanders conversation about assassinating folks, either. Babel was turning into a rather bloodthirsty place altogether.

At the end of my shift I wasn't sure if I was relieved or annoyed that there had been no sign of Thea, Milan, or Tremor. In fact, the only slight bit of excitement the entire evening had come from the private room that Venita and Theseus were in.

I hated it when she managed to get to the library in the

evening. Tonight, she was turning Theseus into her school principal and was being called into his office for some discipline.

Venita: You're having a hard time staying behind your desk, aren't you, sir? It's hard to sit still in that big leather chair while you're getting so big and hard seeing me in my uniform. I shouldn't have worn this black lacy bra under my white blouse, and my daddy would spank me if he could see that I've folded the waist band of my kilt over twice. You can see that my kilt is wa-ay high on my thigh.

Theseus: Come here this minute. I think we need to measure the length of that kilt.

Venita: If you were to put your hand out, palm up, and I were to walk toward you, the bottom of the skirt might skim your hand . . . and if I opened my legs just a little, your hand would move right through . . .

Theseus: You're not wearing your complete uniform, Venita, are you?

Venita: Well, I was, sir, until I heard your voice over the intercom, and I just started to get so wet that it soaked right through my panties . . . so I ducked into the doorway to the Industrial Arts room and slipped them off. *wiggling on the palm of your hand* Can you feel how wet I am for you, sir?

Theseus: *groaning*

Damn, he wasn't the only one, although my moaning wasn't sexually inspired. What was it about this girl that she got such a kick out of scripting masturbation sessions for dirty old men? Where the hell were her parents while all this was happening?

If, as Alchemist said, she was only thirteen, she was learning this behavior and this language from someone.

Surely a thirteen-year-old didn't just make this up on her own.

Maybe her parents had inadvertently let her rent Atom Egoyan's *Exotica*, so that she had some inkling of how schoolgirl uniforms turned on some Viagra-swilling geezers. Or, who knows, maybe she had just been taking notes during music videos. Of course, it might be wrong to blame the parents. Oh hell, might as well blame the parents. If we didn't have lousy parents, where would Oprah be today?

I stood behind my chair, one elbow held with the other hand, leaning my lower lip and chin against the side of my coffee cup, trying to decide how to deal with Venita. Could she get prosecuted for transmitting kiddie porn, if she herself was the underaged component of the porn? It occurred to me that it might be Babel that was shut down if we tried that angle. Proving that she was consistently acting on her own wick and always within the confines of a private room could be very difficult. I was going to have to do something about her, though, if we were going to bring in the big guns to help us out with Tremor. I didn't need any police types getting so distracted by her hiked-up wet kilts that they refused to take us seriously.

So how was I going to declaw the sex kitten? I tapped my teeth against the rim of the cup. There had to be a way. If I chased Theseus away, maybe she would follow. On the other hand, maybe she would just set her sights on another regular.

I would try talking with her. Maybe she would respond to a reasoned request to clean up her act. I would approach her as Alvin and ask her to tone down her actions. The thing is, I would need to have a fallback plan in case she decided not just to stick around but also to get snarky about it. If she wouldn't respond to reason, I was going to have to have the means to get rid of her, and permanently. Banning her would only work for as long as it took to register another nickname.

So, how did one make a thirteen-year-old girl disappear? Ask her to clean her room? Take away her cellphone? Tell her there were calories in what she'd just eaten? Dangle tickets to a boy-band concert? Post a picture of her with acne?

Hmmm, now maybe that was a possibility. What the heck was a thirteen-year-old with those many coursing hormones doing lap dancing with a forty-year-old? If she was so hot, why wasn't she working her way through the basketball team in her junior high?

I set my cup down on the edge of the kitchen table and pulled the computer chair out with more purpose than I'd felt all day. After the earlier search for Thea's sign-on identity, whipping through the steps to find out who Venita really was turned out to be a snap. Maybe I was fertilizing my inner geek, after all.

It seemed that Venita had logged on as a Julie Madison from Oxnard, California. Thank the lord she didn't hail from New York. I knew it was a long shot, but I decided to Google the Oxnard public school system. I came up with five middle schools and logged in.

There are all sorts of privacy laws hovering over Canadian schools and institutions. I couldn't even post the marks attached to ID numbers of students on my office door at the college. However, it didn't seem like there was quite that amount of security involved in California schools. I cruised through the on-line yearbooks of two middle schools, searching for Madisons.

Nothing. On the third, I hit pay dirt. She was listed as a member of the glee club and the computer club. I'll just bet she was.

I clicked on the link to the computer club. There, just under the blinking banner (obviously no teacher had bothered to vet their entry), was a group photo of seven earnest-looking boys, two bored fellows who likely had to pick up the option or lose some sports benefit, and three girls. The first one had long blond braids, braces, and a vaguely equine look. She was sitting near the back of the group, and looked older than most of the boys. The name embroidered on the sleeve of her sweatshirt was Amy. The second one was Asian and was fighting her breath-taking porcelain beauty by spiking her hair and bleaching it blond. The third, I knew, had to be Julie Madison. She was sitting cross-legged on the table next to the computer. She was wearing the standard costume of the average skateboarder—clunky runners, oversized hooded sweatshirt, baggy pants. The trouble was, on Julie, none of the clothes were baggy.

Julie, as well as being clinically obese, had a terrible case of adolescent acne. Her hair was probably just lank, but in the photo it looked greasy. No wonder she had turned to the Internet for her fantasy sex life; if she didn't watch out, it was going to be the only sex life she was going to see.

I felt a moment of pity for Venita/Julie. Adolescence was a hellish time to live through, with your body play-ing all sorts of tricks on you and your frontal lobes unable to keep up. To have to go through the most self-conscious time of your life in a body that would be the butt of cruel jokes and cutting remarks would be a level of hell Dante hadn't even known about.

Well, if she was willing to behave herself, Babel would not ever have to meet the real Julie Madison. I shrugged as I took a copy of the image of the computer club, a screen capture of the full page complete with photo, and created a bookmark to the web page. I was a reasonable person.

I turned full attention back to Babel. Why couldn't Venita be frolicking in the word games, conversation, and general silliness that was the open room in Babel? Tracy was taking everyone on a psychological journey that she'd learned about in her university Introduction to Jung course. People were being told to describe what the tree looked like that they stopped beside on the path, and then to look down and pick up a key, and then describe it.

Gandalf: This is like Myst!

Kara: I think a lot of computer games are like Jungian dreamscapes. Or in some cases, nightmare scapes!

Carlin: You got something against computer games, Kara?

Kara: No shit, Sherlock. I had to get a laptop so I could log on to chat at all. Hubby plays Tomb Raider for hours at a time, and Kid is hooked on her Sims.

Gandalf: You ever try Myst? That is one freakin' weird concept.

Carlin: I spent about a month on it a year or two ago and managed to get through it. Course, I had some help from a cheat site on-line.

Kara: I couldn't get past the first four places on that island. I admit, though, I used to love those little Hugo games on DOS shareware. I think I went through three of them.

Tracy: Okay, I have three key descriptions in. Any more coming in or should I take you further down the path?

Gandalf: Further! Further!
Maia: Is it further or farther in this case?
Vixen: Why don't you ask Sanders?
Maia: Is he around?

My antennae began to quiver. Why would Vixen refer Maia to Sanders? Damn, while I was nattering with Vixen about Thea, I should have pumped her about Sanders, as well. I might have known she'd have some inside dope on everyone in this place. It was a wonder Chatgod hadn't hired her as monitor.

It seemed that Sanders wasn't around, and while Tracy talked them down the path toward a door, I decided to take another tour of the private rooms. Maybe it was time for Alvin to have his little chat with Venita.

Sure enough, Venita and Theseus were at it hot and heavy. It would have been interesting to see how Julie managed to avoid the censure of the librarian while writhing on the screen in front of her. Surely she couldn't be sitting there, stonelike, as she created her web of virtual jism and other body fluids with which to entrap Theseus.

I wrote a quick report of intent to Chatgod, detailing the offer I was about to make to Venita, and I copied the message to Alchemist. Then, under the hood of private messaging, I hailed the teen princess of priapism.

PM from Alvin to Venita: Hi there, toots. You know, we have some standards here and you're flying way off the radar of appropriate behavior.

PM from Venita to Alvin: Since when is a private room censorable? Are you reading my discussions? That's outrageous!

PM from Alvin to Venita: Who are you going to complain to? I own the boat, I say who sails in her. I'm not kidding, kiddo. If the authorities come through checking for kiddie porn, you and your virtual blow jobs could pull us off the 'Net.

PM from Venita to Alvin: So what are you saying?

PM from Alvin to Venita: I'm saying, either you and the old guys cool it here and play nice or you take your sugar daddies and go play elsewhere.

PM from Venita to Alvin: And what if we don't? There's not all that much you can do. What are you going to do, ban me?

PM from Alvin to Venita: If I have to.

PM from Venita to Alvin: Well, that is just so unfair. I'm not the only one having cyber-sex in your precious Babel, you know.

PM from Alvin to Venita: You're the only one doing it who can't get a driver's licence. Or, come to think of it, a part-time job.

PM from Venita to Alvin: Nobody else knows that, Alvin. I swear to god. I tell them I just look young for my age, but that I'm in college.

PM from Alvin to Venita: What would your parents think of your actions here?

PM from Venita to Alvin: Oh sure, tell them if you think they're going to give a damn. I promise you, I haven't told anyone I'm underage.

PM from Alvin to Venita: I'm sure you don't tell them the whole truth, honey. That's one of the wonderful things about the Internet, isn't it? The power to reinvent one's self. Thing is, I know how old you are and you can bet the police will know how old you are, and I can't afford that kind of hassle. So, you can cart old Theseus off somewhere else, or you can tell him how old you really are and start behaving yourself.

PM from Venita to Alvin: He wouldn't care. If I told him I was really thirteen he would come in his pants. I think you're being really unfair. It's not like we're hurting anybody at all.

She had a point, but I knew that if we did have a killer wandering through Babel, it would only be a matter of time before the Mounties and INTERPOL were all over the server. If they caught one whiff of Venita, we could end up looking like the bad guys instead of the victims. I had to get this Lolita to don her little heart-shaped shades and scram.

PM from Alvin to Venita: Really? And do you think Theseus would be having quite the fantasies if he were to see a picture of you with your school computer club?

PM from Venita to Alvin: You wouldn't!

PM from Alvin to Venita: You don't want to find out what I would and wouldn't do, little girl. Now, either you clean up your act, and that means *No Cyber-Sex* in Babel, or you leave Babel. That simple.

PM from Venita to Alvin: You're a prick, you know.

PM from Alvin to Venita: Sorry, honey. Them's the rules.

Idly, I clicked on the bookmark to the computer club page in another window. I was glad I'd taken a copy of the picture, because Venita/Julie hadn't wasted any time yanking it off the school web page.

PM from Alvin to Venita: I've got a copy of the photo. Don't worry, kid. Puberty isn't a terminal disease.

PM from Venita to Alvin: You win, asshole. Too much lag in this crap site anyhow.

Venita: Baby, put it back in your pants for the moment. We have to check out of here.

Theseus: *whimpering* What's that, darling?

Venita : Come on, hon. Let's take it to IM. I don't like the smell in here.

Theseus: Whaa?
Venita has left the building.
Theseus has left the building.

Okay, one problem solved. I loaded a copy of the incriminating JPEG onto the Babel server and transferred the screen capture of the site to the server as well, wrote another short report to Chatgod and Alchemist, and went back out to see where Tracy had managed to lead the crowd. They were in some sort of tunnel inside a mountain. Maia was seguing off on a story about her claustrophobia. Boy, could I relate to that. I logged in as Chimera and joined her in the discussion.

I chatted for a while, continuing to keep an eye on things, but Venita was true to her word. Who knows, maybe the library in Oxnard closed early. I was hoping for the best from her but was ready for the worst. Sanders never did pop in the entire time I was holding down the fort, and I went to bed wondering what he'd been up to, and fretting away at the continuing puzzle of who the hell he was.

Thanks to Venita, and maybe Carl Jung, I had lurid dreams involving masked men, a tree in a forest, Steve, and kilt pins. I was relieved when my alarm rang in the morning, although I didn't feel in the least bit rested. I unwound the twisted sheets from my sweaty body to escape my cocoon, and wondered at the whole concept of sexual fantasy and pornography. Any time I had ever stumbled onto a porn site, it had done nothing for me. I would rather have one solid man than all the virtual lovers in the world.

Speaking of solid men, maybe I could lure Steve out for a lunch. I shook off the bedclothes and dragged myself to the shower, whistling Ravel's *Bolero*.

CHAPTER 30

Steve was busy, but Denise was free for lunch, which would suit me just as well. I had wanted to pump her a bit about the fellows from the gala, and I figured she would be rested enough to indulge in a good gossip. We didn't call it gossip, of course. If we acknowledged it beyond conversation at all, we tended to refer to it as analysis. Sort of critiquing the performance art that is life.

Whatever you called it, I wanted to know just how much Denise knew about the crowd we'd been hanging with that night. While I had been finding out so many interesting things about other folks in Babel, I figured I might as well find out who the fellow closest in geographic proximity was. I had checked through the registration procedure for Sanders much the same way we'd traced Thea and Venita, but for some reason he had managed to sidestep some of Chatgod's security provisions. He was listed as Thomas Chatterton, from Edmonton. Either Chatterton was a reference to the faker-poet or just a pseudonym for a chat-room denizen, but it certainly wasn't his real name. I had not been introduced to anyone named Chatterton at the gala, and, if there was one thing I was positive about, it was that Sanders had been one of the crowd there.

Well, if the registration wasn't going to do it, maybe talking with Denise would. We were meeting at The Upper Crust, one of the better places near me. Their carrot soup was to die for.

It took me five minutes to get from my door to the restaurant, even allowing time to agree with my neighbor, Mr. MacGregor, that it did seem milder than this time last year. Denise was already ensconced in the corner table at the back, under one of the most amazing prairie paintings I'd ever seen. That's the thing about The Upper Crust: they act as a sort of art gallery for a few of the more interesting artists in town. This painting offered the wheat field, in its ultimate white-gold blondness, under a malevolent prairie-storm sky. This is what those camera commercials had been aiming for, but it was impossible to film something this dramatic. It was too momentous for reality-based media; it had to be painted, or sung in high opera. I checked the artist: Ian Sheldon. I checked the price and sighed. Someday.

Denise looked like a million dollars. U.S. dollars. She had on brown leather trousers, and a thickly knit cream overtop. A leather thong holding a ceramic pendant draped from her neck, and small, thick gold hoops hung in her ears. She smiled as she saw me walking to the table, and the image of the supermodel vanished. Her smile was so real and wide and wrinkle-unafraid that she managed to make everyone around her delighted with her grace and beauty rather than envious of her wardrobe and style.

"Randy! I am so glad you called. Another day and I was going to go and rout you out of your little cyber hidey-hole. We hardly had any time to talk at the gala. What did you think of it, really? It went well, I thought, no?"

I grinned, shrugged my bomber jacket off and onto the chair, and reached for the menu. "First things first, Denise."

"Yes, they have carrot soup, and I've already ordered for us. Now tell me what you thought."

"Well, first of all, I think it was splendid, and you looked fantastic, and I am thrilled to have got those opera tickets. How many people actually were there? I can never estimate a crowd."

"We sold five hundred tickets, but I have a feeling not everyone came. We made $350 at the coat check, though, so either there were some high rollers there or we had at least that many people there. Of course, some folks tip a toonie nowadays, and some double their jackets, so who knows?"

"A lot of interesting-looking men there."

"Why, Randy Craig. I think it's terrible that women on the arms of presentable and eligible men should actually be surveying the scene."

"To tell you the truth, that's about the only time I ever bother to look at anyone. If I'm totally solo, I figure it's going to translate as me being desperate and on the make. I noticed you were getting your fair share of attention, though. Has Chick Anderson called you since that night?"

Our soup and a plate of focaccia bread to dip in another swirly plate of oil and balsamic vinegar arrived just then. Maybe it was the reflected color from the soup, but I swear Denise blushed just a bit as she replied.

"Actually, Chick and I went out for dinner last night."

My eyebrow went up in the international symbol of "tell me everything."

Denise smiled. "He's very nice for a millionaire."

I almost snorted carrot soup through my nose. "I don't have that much experience with moneyed folks to know, one way or the other. I didn't know you did, either."

"Oh Randy, you know what I mean. I don't mean to get all Irwin Shaw on you, but there really is something different about the rich, isn't there? Maybe someone should do a survey on when it is that people with money forget what it was like not to have money. I know my father can't recall getting bailed out by my maternal grandparents when he was doing grad work and living in married students' quarters. My grandmother tries to remind him of that any time he begins bellyaching over the price of a university education today. But I look in his face and see that he really believes I should be able to fly home every holiday on my budget and that I am somehow just crying poor to flout him. And, of course, Chick has no idea what poverty might feel like. He was born rich, and having all the money you'd ever need to do whatever you dream up is how he knows how to live. Period."

"Wow," was all I could say. I'd never thought about it before, being so solidly middle class, but there must be a distinctly weird shift in perception for someone who never had to worry about money. Just think of never having to check the prices on a menu before ordering what you'd like to eat, never tallying up what was in the grocery basket before reaching for the bag of cookies, never heading past the new arrivals for the sales rack. I shook my head slightly. I couldn't wrap my mind around it.

"So, what does Chick do with his time? Does he work for the family business?"

"In a manner of speaking, I guess he does. He is on the board and he owns stock in the company. I think he is above what they refer to as the 'working rich' out in Riverbend and Terwillegar. He is the moneyed class and has an office and a secretary and a membership to the Centre Club." Denise smiled. "On the other hand, he is a very sweet man who obviously makes a point of making himself pleasant to whomever he wishes to be with. Do you know, he went out and bought *Life of Pi* the day after the gala and read it so that we'd have something to talk about when he called me? That is more dedication than I've seen in a graduate student trying to sign on an advisor."

I had to admit there was something very flattering about the idea of being courted with that sort of effort. Especially given the obvious pluses someone like Chick Anderson brought with him. A tiny flicker of envy tried to ignite inside me, but I had to admit that Denise really deserved a good guy. She was often pursued, but at the same time she'd had to spend an inordinate amount of time letting totally inappropriate fellows down easily. It was time she had some sugar. The fact that Chick took her work seriously enough to make an effort to understand it was a very good sign. I grinned at her, and it was as if she could read everything that had gone through my head. She grinned back, and I suppose we looked like every two women discussing an admirer have looked since time began. There really is nothing new under the sun. Except for maybe the Internet, which seemed to be what Denise wanted to talk about now.

"How is your on-line job going?"

"My distance teaching or the monitoring?" I asked, but I already knew which job she was referring to. Denise had been worried about my involvement with this job since the beginning. Maybe Chatgod's warning to tell nobody about the job was to avoid this very sort of haranguing from friends and family.

"The monitoring, of course. Are you getting paid regularly? Has anything weird happened?"

"Well, actually, there is something sort of weird going on. And it has to do with the gala, funnily enough." I told her generally about Sanders, about not letting him know where I lived, about him talking about the gala on Babel. In spite of herself, Denise was captivated.

"So tell me again why you didn't just let him know you were from Edmonton, too?"

"I value my privacy on-line. Besides, being a monitor makes me have to stand a bit beside, rather than in, the full swing of things."

"Bulltweet, Randy Craig. You are afraid of getting involved with this man because it's all of a sudden too real. When you could just flirt from a distance, it was one thing, but, if you met face to face, then you'd have to decide whether you and Steve were really serious and actually make a decision."

I opened my mouth, ready to counter her accusation, and then just looked at her. Maybe Denise was right. I was a little phobic about committing. Steve had wanted to take our relationship further last year, and I'd been so leery that we'd decided to give up on things for a while. Now he was back in my life, and I was still keeping him at arm's length. And the whole Sanders problem was just going to exacerbate things. That really was why I hadn't let Sanders know my location. It would be one step closer to learning my identity, and all of a sudden there would be two men in my life when I wasn't even sure I wanted one. I definitely didn't need one who spoke cryptically of death and assassination.

"Well, you may be right, but right now I just have to figure out which of those guys is Sanders."

"Why don't you just ask him?"

"Because it would mean a whole heck of a lot of explaining, wouldn't it?"

"Explain that you had to keep mum because of your job."

"No! I was told not to tell anyone about the job. I shouldn't even have told you. As far as everyone is concerned in there, the systems operator is Alvin, and he owns the server and runs the chat for the revenue from the advertising banners. They know nothing about me or Alchemist being paid monitors, and they have no idea about Chatgod."

"That is just too freaky, Randy. Have you mentioned any of this to Steve?"

"Of course I have. It's not freaky; it's just another universe."

Based on Denise's reaction to the secrecy aspect of my job, I certainly wasn't going to explain that Sanders might be more than just an interesting fellow in a chat community. Until I tracked down Tremor and had a better handle on what the heck was going on there, there was a chance that Sanders might be involved. He had appeared once out of the blue, just like Tremor; he had fudged his identity when registering; and he lived a little too close for comfort. If he was one of the bad guys, I didn't want him knowing exactly what block I lived on. It was enough for Denise to think I just had a salacious curiosity about Sanders.

Denise grudgingly agreed to pump Chick Anderson a bit about his involvement with the Internet and to drop a suggestive comment about Thomas Chatterton to see if he rose to the bait. "Not that I think Chick has anything to do with the Internet, you understand."

"Of course not. Just consider it an exercise in semi-otics. Discover whether there is another level of meaning to his words."

She hit me with her shoulder bag. "Your irreverence for theory is going to get you into trouble someday, Randy Craig."

CHAPTER 31

If Denise was going to concentrate on Chick, as I am sure she was all too happy to do, I would have to do my own investigating over Alex Danvers and Winston Graham. Since I had no idea where to find Graham, I picked Danvers as the next on my list.

I left Denise at The Upper Crust and crossed 109th Street to wait for a northbound bus. Within minutes, I was walking through the boxy canyons of the downtown core toward the postmodern spires of Grant MacEwan College. There is something about the city-center campus that just makes me happy, especially when approached from the 105th Street corner. The first building has wood paneling, which then morphs into sandstone, and then concrete and glass. The spires of concrete are also the air intake for the ventilation system, so they're not completely useless appendages. A huge clock hangs on a glass wall above the main doors on Building Seven. You can sit behind it in huge comfy chairs in a reading section in the Learning Resource Centre, what we pre-computer-chip types used to call a library. Each section of the campus is numbered according to the block it takes up on the city grid; business courses are mainly in Building Five, the science and arts-related courses cling around the LRC in buildings Six and Seven, and the Sports and Wellness Centre is located in Building Eight. A parkade is, I suppose, technically Building Nine, though there is talk of another building of classrooms as well as a dormitory soon to be built.

The English Department is in Building Six, on the second floor. I still wasn't sure what to say to Alex Danvers but thought I would figure out something on the spur of the moment that might sound more realistic than a rehearsed speech. Of course, I had no idea what Alex's timetable might be, or where his office was located. I technically shared an office with seven other part-timers and had a mailbox in the general office, so I decided to just wander in there for starters. I joked a bit with the secretary about being the invisible person, then riffled through the pile of paper in my mail slot.

There were two *MacEwan Today*s, the staff circular; a United Way envelope; invitations to two book rep displays, one of which I had already missed; a note from the chair reminding us to get our text selections in for the next term, which didn't apply to me since the distance course had only one choice of reader; and a note from one of my distance students who had happened to be on campus and tried to look me up. I dumped everything except the latest *MacEwan Today* into the recycle bin. What had happened to the promise of the paperless society?

I took a look at the other mailboxes. Alex Danvers's was empty. So was Valerie Bock's. I knew where Valerie's office was, so I decided to amble down to see her. I could say I was looking for Alex to discuss some distance issues with him. Or I could just say hi. She had seemed really approachable the other night at the gala. Maybe there was a friend waiting to be made there.

I nodded at several people down the hallway of offices, halfway recognizing them from the initial departmental meeting in August. Finally, just as I passed the wash-rooms and break-through hallway, I reached Valerie's office. And the door was ajar.

I knocked on the door frame, and Valerie, who had been working with her back to the door (something I could never do), turned sharply. Her smile started as soon as she saw me, originating in the eyes. Even without the sparkly dust in her hair, red highlights shone in the light from the huge window that was the fourth wall of the office. In repose, Valerie's face would be conventionally pretty, but there was nothing restful about her. Her attractiveness was in her motion, her actions and reac-tions to what was being said. She was a perpetual-motion machine, one of those people who seemingly maintain their figure by constant fidgeting. Her booted leg was crossed over the other but bounced to a beat of some salsa music she was listening to inside her head.

"Randy! How nice to see you again so soon. Isn't that the way, though? Sort of Jungian synchronicity. I find that whenever I teach Robertson Davies, there are coinci-dences bouncing out all over the place, more than I rec-ognize at other times. Do you think that is possible, or do we just see them more when we're tuned in to expecting them? Ooh, wouldn't that make a great essay topic? Hang on a tic."

She scribbled something on a notepad shaped like a penguin, and then turned the force of her personality back on me. I bet none of her students ever nodded off in her class.

"I miss being able to come up with my own essay top-ics. Distance teaching has its advantages, but some of the sacrifices, like those prefabricated learning packs, take the joy out of it all," I admitted.

Valerie nodded. "That's why I can't stand teaching distance. I need to be able to look my students in the eye to know I am getting through to them. I don't know how you and Alex stand it. At least Alex has a few face-to-face classes to keep him going."

"Does Alex not like distance teaching?" I asked. "I thought he was really the big computer whiz." This was a stab in the dark. I had no idea whether Alex was a Luddite scratching things out with a quill pen or a geek hard-wired into the computer world.

Valerie smiled, the way a mother smiles over a child's precocious comment. I had a feeling she didn't consider computers the wave of the future. "Well, he has some real concerns over the concept of community in an on-line course relationship. I think he tries to find a new path in his work, something more than just correspondence courses with high-tech delivery, you know? But it's difficult. There is resistance, on the part of the students most of all. A lot of people who benefit from the distance courses we offer are not really clued into the Internet world, you know. Sometimes they are taking the course via distance because they're so isolated from the mainstream that it's a last resort. So, as a result, the students most likely to benefit from distance courses are not the ones most likely to enrol in them."

This sounded like a discussion that Valerie and Alex had thoroughly hashed out already. It still didn't tell me whether Alex Danvers could be my Sanders, but I was beginning to wonder. Even though it sounded like Alex had both a real and philosophical interest in the concept of the Internet, I couldn't imagine him being on the flirting prowl when he was attached to someone as vibrant as Valerie.

Of course, that was a specious argument, as divorce statistics all over the continent showed. There was no telling what could trigger the dissolving of a relationship. Maybe Alex Danvers was secretly having cyber-relationships behind his lady's back. It was possible, I knew that academically, but I didn't understand it internally. I would never understand the workings of the devious mind. My modus operandi had always been to finish one thing before beginning something else. If everyone operated this way, of course, there might be less acrimony, if just as much heartache.

So who knew? And how would I find out? I was running out of things to chat with Valerie about when Alex himself popped his head around the door. He was dressed in a thick black turtleneck and black wide-waled corduroys, looking utterly professor-like even with the black leather jacket hooked over one thumb and shoulder.

Valerie lit up like a neon light. And here I thought she was intense before. He beamed back at her before he noticed me tucked into the student chair beside the door.

"Randy! Great. I was just coming by to see if I could coax Val out for lunch, and here you are. Can you come, too? I have a craving for sushi. Let's go to the Mikado and bully them into letting the three of us have a little room to ourselves."

Valerie raised her eyebrows and looked at me, with the I'm-game-if-you-are look she must have perfected in junior high.

I grinned. "Sushi sounds great."

Valerie pulled on a stunning red and black shawl with Salish-looking ravens embroidered on it. It flowed to her knees, and looked terrific. I complimented her on it as we strode down the hall to the staircase.

"Isn't it marvelous? Alex bought it for me when we went to the Learneds in Victoria last time. I was worried that it wouldn't be warm enough for our Edmonton winters, but have you noticed our Edmonton winters ain't what they used to be?"

"You, sir, have exquisite taste," I said to Alex, who was grinning at Valerie in adoration. I had a feeling that I could just sit back and enjoy my sushi. I wasn't going to find Sanders sitting with me today. This man was utterly besotted with a fabulous woman.

It was while we were crawling into the tatami room and fitting our legs under the fake low table at the Mikado that it occurred to me that I could quiz Alex more about his former student Winston Graham. That way, I could cleanse my conscience about sitting around enjoying raw fish while I should be finding a killer. I doubt if Inspector Morse ever worried about that sort of thing while he holed up with his music and booze, but I had a classic Canadian conscience. This meant that as long as I could justify an action, or the Americans were doing something even worse, I didn't feel quite so guilty. Besides, this was my second sit-down lunch of the day, when usually I noshed on a bagel and an apple. I definitely needed to avoid guilt any way I could. Guilt can go to your hips faster than chocolate.

Valerie and I each ordered a Bento Box Number One, which had sushi, tempura, teriyaki chicken, a salad, rice, and a bowl of miso soup to start with. Alex was more adventurous and ordered miso followed by a bowl of chirashi and two pieces of octopus sushi on the side.

It wasn't long before we were tucking into our food.

Alex and Valerie were good company, and it seemed like the conversation had only taken brief pauses for ordering and settling in. Otherwise, we were still on the same thread of conversation that had begun in the hallway at the college.

"Pretty soon this whole area will be swarming with walk-in traffic," Alex was commenting. "Right behind us this whole Railtown area is adding condo towers, and the dormitory across the way will be teeming with students avoiding cafeteria food. Then there are all sorts of developments around Oliver, and I have a feeling that it will carry through all the way to 107th Street."

"That's going to take some heavy regentrification, Alex, unless you think the exotic massage studios will meld into the new populace?" Valerie laughed.

"Well, since a lot of that populace is going to be perpetual students congregating around the downtown undergraduate university, I can't see Sinderella's Massage doing much to outrage. Of course, I am not so sure any of them would ever have the money to keep places like that afloat."

"Speaking of perpetual students, tell me more about that fellow we met at the gala, Winston," I suggested. "Were you serious about his lifestyle, or was that exaggerated for his entertainment?"

Alex shook his head. "Oh no, if anything, I was being way milder than the reality of the situation. He pops up on my radar every so often, mainly working in pizza joints or mowing city verges to make enough money for tuition. The man is amazing in his scope of interests. One year he will be studying classics and philosophy, and the next time I run into him he'll have switched into astrophysics. Mostly he is working in senior-level courses, too, so I am assuming his grades are good enough to allow the prerequisite courses. I understand he's an asset in every class he attends. He's up on all the reading, he speaks up in seminars, and he engages other students. All in all, the level of the discourse rises exponentially when Winston is in the room."

"Damn. They should pay him to attend classes," I said admiringly.

"No kidding. I think his goal is to take every class the university has to offer in his lifetime," laughed Alex.

"I don't know," mused Valerie. "Maybe he is like Kafka's hunger artist, only maintaining his fast because he hadn't found anything he really liked to eat. Maybe, if Winston found something he really enjoyed, he would settle in and become a specialist."

"But the Renaissance Man is what we really need now, Val. There are too many specialists. They can't talk to each other without a translator for all the jargon. When something goes wrong that is outside their direct purview, what can they do but call in another specialist? What about the jack of all trades who can see the problem from different directions at once?"

"It seems to me that you either get that sort of person with a Winston-like program, or you look to the rural farmer who has learned to make do," I said, thinking of my uncle, who could weld any broken piece of equipment back into shape, after having driven it back to the farmyard with gum and binder twine holding it together.

"Exactly what Sharon Butala says, Randy," agreed Valerie. "She says we're decimating the rural world at our own peril. And she'd be right. How many Winstons are out there, after all. And when it comes right down to it, could Winston get the furnace going again?"

"Interesting question. Could he, Alex? How handy is Winston, or is it all book-learning? Is he into computers? Or machinery?"

"Well, I know he worked on the grounds crew for the university for a few summers, so maybe he knows his way around a basic motor and engine, and I know he did some computing, because he was doing some sort of theoretical engineering with probabilities and worst-case scenarios at one point. After a conversation with him around then, I avoided walking across the High Level Bridge for almost a year," Alex laughed ruefully.

I decided I didn't want to even think about it.

So, Winston had computer experience, and he knew his way around the inner workings of probability programming. There was a chance that Winston Graham was my Sanders. From what I was learning about Alex in the meantime, I could almost write him off. His specialty in English had been Melville and Hawthorne, and, while he knew his way around computers for distance work, he professed not to like them all that much. Valerie seemed far more sympathetic to the age of silica than Alex, and I was already certain she couldn't be Sanders. I tucked into my last California roll and decided my next step would be to track down Winston Graham, professional student.

Chapter 32

Of course, that wasn't my next step at all, since I got home to find three messages from Steve on my answering machine. I dialed back his pager and then sat down at the computer to mark an essay that was sitting in my Inbox on my e-mail. If I never read another paper about the death penalty in my life, I would be immeasurably grateful. This one wasn't too bad, but the student lost points for being unable to soften up her antagonistic readers with any form of de-polarization and for waxing on with too many emotional outbursts. Emotion was no way to win an argument against someone who didn't agree with you.

I really did care about teaching rhetoric to my students, because I figured that, if you could see how words and phrases could trigger reactions and manipulate people, you could be more wary of propaganda and more purposeful in your own persuasiveness. Of course, if you didn't care about your own language and its many twisty tricks, you deserved who you voted for.

Steve called back about three minutes after I had mailed back my marked and annotated version of the essay and recorded the grade in my distance-course binder. I clicked onto my bookmarked astrology site and waited for my horoscope to load while I listened to him berate me for not owning a cell phone, for never being easy to locate, and for not having called him before lunch. The screen finally loaded and I read:

"Cancer: What to you will seem an obvious path may be less clear to others. Trying to explain your methodology will prove difficult. Smile and acquiesce, since arguing would be futile. On the plus side, you'll be considered irresistible by everyone you seek to ensnare."

Well, if the stars said to make nice with Steve, who was I to argue?

"You're right. Maybe I should get a cell phone. I went down to Grant MacEwan to get my mail and ended up having lunch with Alex and Valerie, who you met the other night, remember? So, what's on your mind?"

"It occurs to me that you're right in the middle of something again, something that I am working on. We need to talk."

"Oh, Steve, do I have to go down there? I just got in."

"No, I can come there. But I mean it, Randy. This is official stuff."

"Does that mean I can't make you coffee?"

I could hear the smile crawl into his voice. "No, it means we have to keep our clothes on while we drink it. Put the coffee on now." And then he hung up.

I went to put on the coffee. And some lip gloss.

CHAPTER 33

Steve was at my door within twenty minutes, even without a cruiser at his disposal. I had a feeling I wasn't going to like whatever it was he had to say, but I really had no idea what that could be. It's not as if I even jaywalk.

"Randy, thank goodness. We really do have to get you a cell phone. I have been calling you since nine in the morning, and what if something were to happen to you? Who would know where you were heading?"

I nodded. That was the joy and problem of the single life, no one to watch your back. Maybe I should start making a note of where I was heading to leave on my kitchen table whenever I went anywhere.

I handed Steve a mug of coffee and sat on the edge of my old chesterfield, motioning for him to sit beside me. Instead he sat across from me in my sturdy bent-willow chair. This wasn't a good sign. Whatever it was, it was going to be serious.

"There's a visiting specialist in town, a computer-crimes specialist. He's been here since yesterday and spoke at a station assembly. He's here tracking an on-line killer."

Steve was watching me very carefully. "His name is Ray Lopez and he's from Austin, Texas."

"And he's tracking Theresa Banyon's husband's killer," I said.

"Shit." Steve's shoulders sagged. "I was hoping against hope that you had no idea what any of this was about, but the more he talked about chat rooms and the international scope of his investigation, the more my gut began to twist. Randy, I think you have to talk to this guy."

"I agree. In fact, I was hoping that the owner of Babel would have got in touch with the police a lot sooner, but he was hoping that it could be cleared up without involving our chat community. And, you know, he's right in a way. I don't think it has anything to do with the underpinnings of Babel. It's just a coincidence, like the murder happening in a certain apartment building or nightclub. It's not the location that's to blame."

"Any time you have some knowledge of a crime and neglect to report it, you are in contravention of the law. Now, we have a bit of slack for you because you are a Canadian citizen potentially unaware of an American crime having been committed. They just determined a couple of days ago that this guy's computer was tampered with to create a circuit when he touched a certain key and moved the mouse at the same time. So, like I said, it wasn't a crime officially till yesterday or so, but there is only so much I can do to protect you. I think you should speak to this Ray Lopez. He seems like a pretty good guy."

Ray Lopez indeed was a pretty good guy. Steve called him up, and we met for an early supper at the restaurant in his Holiday Inn. It seemed as if this was my day to eat out. He was a trim fellow but looked imposing because of his very broad shoulders. His face, too, was broad, but so was his smile, and his eyes were twinkling as he spoke. I had a feeling a laugh wasn't far away from anything he said. After our obligatory remarks about how damned cold it was here, and how did we stand it, he and Steve got into a detailed discussion about grain-fed beef over corn-fed beef. The upshot was that Ray was obliged to order a steak, and Steve looked jubilant when Ray announced after the first couple of bites that, yes, he could taste the difference and that, yes, it was delicious.

Steak sticks in my teeth, so I was working through a chicken Caesar salad as we began the serious part of our discussion. I told Ray about Babel and my duties there. Steve looked a bit shocked at my matter-of-fact discussion about cyber-sex and porn, but Ray nodded with an understanding of the ways of chat rooms. I described the relationship between Thea and Milan, Thea's disappearance, and Milan's distraction. I also tried to paint a description of how Tremor behaved in relation to the rest of the chat, to let Ray know that he wasn't the norm, and he certainly wasn't a regular, but he seemed to be able to appear and disappear at will. Ray, like Alchemist, was pretty sure that Tremor had to be a hacker with the ability to find a back door into the program.

"It was just by chance that I happened to be reading an Austin paper and read about the electrocution of the fellow there, and that his wife was Theresa Banyon. Otherwise, there would be nothing from Babel to have alerted me to that crime connection."

"Truth to tell, we still don't know if there is a connection. We're following up on the files we managed to save from Theresa Banyon's computer, one of which is her on-line bookmarks. There is a strong Canadian presence in Babel, so my supervisor sent me up here to suss out the activity."

"A strong Canadian connection? As far as I know, aside

from a woman in Halifax and a few teenagers in Winnipeg and Brandon, and me and another fellow here, I am not aware of any Canadians."

"Who is the other fellow here? Have you two met?"

I could feel Steve's curiosity as well.

"Well, no, he doesn't know I am from here. I didn't think it was a good idea, given my role as a monitor, to let out too much personal information. The thing is, I think I might have figured out who he is, well, within a circle of three, but I'm a bit leery of him, too, because his registration information seems to be fudged."

Ray laughed. "You would be astonished at how many registrations get judiciously altered, and not for nefarious reasons, either. Mostly, it's to guard against spam, since so many spammers use webcrawlers to harvest addresses for e-mail sales lists. It's like knowing it's a telephone solicitor if he asks to speak to the 'man of the house' when you answer the phone. If you get e-mail for Harvey Foomph, then you know you can delete it immediately. Some e-mail programs even allow you to list the only names allowed through, and block the rest."

"Harvey Foomph?" Steve laughed.

Ray laughed, too. "You'd prefer Tungsten Phoobie?"

I was impressed by Ray's easy knowledge of on-line activities. It turned out that he was subcontracted by the Austin police to deal with computer issues but that his main job was as a troubleshooter for major computer companies integrating systems and upgrading around the world. He had been one of the front-line community builders and counted people like Howard Rheingold among his good friends. If this weren't such a serious situation, I would love to have discussed on-line community concepts with him all night.

"So, not using your proper name isn't a sure sign of subterfuge. I can see that. It just gives me a bit of a jolt in a place like Babel where it is requested only as a safeguard to ensure that people respect the place. Most of the people there have given correct information. In fact, that's how we found Thea. You'd think if she had been planning to have her husband killed, she wouldn't have given out her name and address quite so easily, right?"

"Well, maybe when she signed up, she had no idea she'd be plotting to remove him from her life," mused Ray.

Steve nodded, too. That's what I loved about Steve, his amazing ability to get up to speed on practically any topic. Until this evening, his grasp of computers was really utilitarian, with a dose of general cyber-porn regulations. Still, he was already understanding the scope of Ray's investigation and starting to see the parameters of my job.

Being cops, they had to check out the dessert cart. Since this was my fourth meal of the day, I couldn't even finish all the romaine in my bowl. Steve regretfully declined a decadent-looking piece of cheesecake, and Ray looked longingly at a chocolate éclair but refused it. It turned out that his wife was a Weight Watchers leader back at home, and he didn't dare go over his points too badly on road trips, or there would be no sympathy on that front.

We shook hands in the lobby, and I promised to meet up with Ray the next day to show him around the university. Steve dropped me off at home after a nice long goodbye in the car. There is nothing like kissing in a car to make a person feel youthful. I walked down the hallway to my apartment door with a spring in my step. I'd have even more spring if I hadn't eaten out so many times that day. I made a silent vow to go for a power walk the next morning before anything else. For good measure, I laid out my sweats at the end of the bed before making the coffee and logging into Babel for my shift. The Internet could put ten pounds on your rear end, and I didn't need to go helping it along.

CHAPTER 34

I'd set my alarm for the first time in ages, since I wanted to get an early start to the day. There was no way I could get up before noon without external aid when I was routinely heading to bed at three in the morning. Today, though, I planned to power walk around the entire campus, get home to shower, and then be ready to meet up with Ray Lopez at the front of HUB Mall at noon.

I braided my hair and put on a polar fleece headband that covered my ears. I put on my gray hoodie and sweatpants, but all I had underneath were panties and a sports bra, and there was no way that would be enough insulation at this time of year. I added a fleece vest, mittens, and knee-high sports socks, then laced up my runners and tucked my apartment key into the little zipper pocket on my vest. I checked the time as I pulled the door closed behind me. Nine-fifteen. I should be home by 10:00.

I headed down 87th Avenue toward the campus. By the time I was passing the Education Building, I had got into my groove. I had a rocking gait that was not quite race walking but easier on my knees than a flat-out slow jog. Some folks used earphones and music to speed them along, but instead, I sang. Under my breath, though, so that no one could hear and report me to the looney-bin catchers. Show tunes, old Neil Diamond songs, bizarre novelty songs from the 1970s, as long as it had a snappy beat to it, it was fair game. It was also my fail-safe for monitoring my heart rate. As long as I could puff out a song, I was still within an aerobic workout.

I was halfway through "Longfellow Serenade" as I passed the Faculty Club, on Saskatchewan Drive. I could feel a steady stream of sweat running down between my shoulder blades. This was where I tried to put on a bit of a burn. If I could get to The House, the building where part-time English lecturers had offices, before I had finished "The Wreck of the Mary Ellen Carter," I knew I had worked off at least 150 calories, which was just about one quarter of any one of yesterday's meals. I tried not to think that way. Checks and balances tended to make me despair of ever coming out ahead, whether it was my budget or my waistline. Instead I tried to focus on how healthy I was feeling, burning high-octane fuel instead of sludge, moving like a well-oiled machine.

I was puffing by the time I reached the Human Ecology Ecohouse, but it was too cold to stop for a rest. Any piece of grass I trod on was crunchy underfoot. If I didn't keep moving, the sweat on my forehead and down my back would become icicles. It took two extra choruses of "I Enjoy Being a Girl" to get me down the alley to the back door of my apartment building. My face felt wind-burned, and I could hardly bend over to unlace my runners. I really had to make a concerted effort to get out and moving more often.

After a ten-minute shower and kiwi-flavored gel scenting the air, I felt better. I squinted toward the alarm clock by my bed as I was toweling off. Ten-twenty. Hah! There was no excuse for not scheduling some workout time into my day.

Dressed in black cords and a deep green turtleneck, I wandered into my office area while braiding back my hair. I still had an hour and a half before I had to meet up with Ray Lopez. I had left a message for Chatgod and Alchemist about the meeting, mainly because I didn't want to be acting behind anyone's back. There was an e-mail message from Chatgod. Thank goodness it wasn't requesting a discussion. He seemed resigned to the police connecting Thea's problems with us and asked that I keep him up to date with anything I discussed with Detective Lopez.

I was planning on letting Ray Lopez know about Sanders today, too. At least he was going to get my theories about Sanders. I had heard back from Denise by e-mail the night before. She claimed that Chick barely knew his way around e-mail, let alone Internet chat rooms, and that he seemed completely bemused when she made some allusions to Chatterton, asking whether that wasn't the name of a geology prof he had had classes from in the late 1970s. So, on that basis, I was letting Chick off the hook. Sanders, for my money, had to be Winston Graham. The profile fit. He knew about computers, he was a loner, and he had a wide range of knowledge from all the various courses he had been taking over the last twelve to fifteen years.

I wasn't totally sure where we might find Winston Graham, or even if we could find him. There were several listings for W. Graham in the phone directory. Steve could certainly access any unlisted numbers in the ex-directory file, but I wasn't sure whether he should even bother looking. It cost a lot to get an unlisted number, and why would Winston hide his phone number if he was so willing to let people on-line know what city he lived in?

Of course, what did I really know about him? Aside from the fact that he was literate, well-read, and had been at the gala, nothing. Still, while I was worried about revealing too much to him and I wasn't too sure about his cryptic commentary, I didn't really have a sense of his being a bad guy. I popped some sugar-free gum into my mouth as I left my apartment, once more heading to the university. Of course, I wasn't so sure I really knew what a bad guy seemed like. I had had some pretty close shaves in the past and hadn't seen them coming. Maybe I was naïve and gullible when it came to the secret workings of the human heart. On the other hand, maybe I had a strong belief in finding the good side of people. I needed to hang on to that attitude, in order to keep teaching freshmen who didn't want to be taking my classes in the first place.

I made it to HUB Mall about ten minutes before noon. I wanted to be visible for Ray, since he had said he'd be coming from downtown by the light rail transit subway. I had told him to come out on the ground level, so he should be popping out either here at the HUB entry or perhaps down the road, if he'd exited at the wrong end of the platform. Whatever the case, it wouldn't be too hard for him to spot me.

Right at noon, he stepped out of the LRT entrance. I waved and walked toward him.

"I thought I'd take you on a brief tour, because everyone will be racing to the lunch spots right now. This is an on-the-hour day for class schedules. By 1:15 we can take our pick of where to eat."

"Sounds good to me," Ray said, and we fell into a companionable walking speed. I noticed that he had on a good thick melton jacket and gloves, along with high-tech around-the-back-of-the-head earmuffs. I commented on his preparedness.

He laughed. "For a Texan? I did a degree at MIT, and whenever I think winter, I think Boston winters. This really isn't bad at all."

"No, I agree. If you can block out the wind and stay layered, you can keep ahead of the cold. That's the advantage to the 'dry cold' concept."

We talked about various places we had studied and how we'd been drawn to computers. Ray had gone the engineering route, while I'd been attracted to the ease of word processing and to the early bulletin boards and Usenet as an exploration in communication. Both of us were fascinated with the changing concepts of community, and he told me some great stories about Howard Rheingold's shoe-painting parties.

I gave him a brief rundown on Babel. He told me that it sounded a lot classier than most AOL or Yahoo Chats and less distinguished than much of the Well or Brainstorms. Of course, of those latter two, one was a paid subscription site and the other was by invitation only. I told him that, while we might not have an international brain trust in Babel, we did have a fairly interesting composite and variety of life skills and temperaments.

"It makes discussion worthwhile, because no groove ever seems to wear into a rut, if you know what I mean."

"Do I ever," he laughed. "With some of the older communities, you can already sense what the response of twelve or twenty regulars will be to any topic, and so sometimes you don't even bother. On the other hand, that's really closer to true community, isn't it? The really close-knit kind, like the old church social group, or lunchroom crowd, or small-town service organization. The sort of place where everyone knows everyone."

"The *Cheers* mentality?" I suggested.

"Exactly! Norm!" Ray laughed, and then commented on the sculpture on the side of the Student Union Building. He was a good tourist. He made appreciative comments about the older buildings and the newer features, and seemed impressed with the layout of the campus. I told him he and Stella should consider vacationing up here in the summer when all the festivals were on.

"You'd be surprised. It always seems as if they've planted two or three hundred new trees on campus, when the deciduous trees come into leaf."

"But you end up losing that great view of the river valley, I'm betting," Ray said, pointing across the road from where we were standing. We were on Saskatchewan Drive, near the Tory Turtle, the lecture theatre that was linked to the Tory building by means of an underground walkway.

I pointed across the drive to Rutherford House, the historical home of the founder of the university and former premier of the province. "I know you must have a lot of historic sites in Austin, too, but I'm wondering if you'd like to go there for lunch. They have fantastic soups and salads. The solarium has been made into a tearoom."

"Wow, beats the food courts all hollow. You bet."

We were seated pretty quickly, and soon we had ordered and been given our own personal teapots with cozies.

"You know," said Ray, "this sounds crazy, I suppose, but Edmonton feels an awful lot like Austin."

"Yeah, with that minus-fifteen-degrees wind blowing, I'll bet it does."

"Well, if you don't count the weather. But we can get

our cold winters, too, you know. What I mean, though, is the feel of the cities themselves. Follow me on this one. They're both the capitals of really rich states—excuse me, provinces—where the money comes from cattle and oil. They are the university towns, rather than the head-office towns, and there is also a strong blue-collar feel to both, which you don't get from either Dallas or Calgary. There is a big arts scene in Austin, and the whole theater and festival thing in Edmonton is sort of the same. See what I mean?"

"Sounds like the same sort of idea, all right. It sounds like I might be pretty comfy in Austin."

"Oh, you'd like Austin, and you'd love San Antonio, and you'd probably be interested in Houston, but you'd hate Dallas. That is, what do you think of Calgary?"

I grimaced, and Ray laughed.

"You look just like an Austinite thinking about Dallas. I tell you, the Texas/Alberta parallels are there."

"What about the computer scene in Texas? Is it as strong as here?"

Ray chewed on his cranberry and brie sandwich. "There is about the same usage coming out of Texas in the way of personal computers as Alberta, which is wildly skewed because of population density."

"What do you mean?"

"Well, we have about five times your population and almost the same number of users logging in for personal use, gauging after-business-hours usage."

"Wow. I knew that there was a lot of Internet usage up here, but that is amazing. Maybe it's because of our relative isolation. I think Albertans have always had this need to connect to the rest of the world and keep abreast of things. There have been a symphony and an opera company and several theaters going for years, way more arts per capita in Edmonton alone than anywhere else in the country. Maybe that's why the computer usage, too."

"Maybe. I know a couple of old classmates who live near the mountains around here who telecommute for Motorola. They live to ski, so they work from home and ski as much as they can. You have to admit, the Internet does appeal to that hermit type."

"Marshall McLuhan was born in Edmonton, you know. Maybe the whole idea of the global village being accessible from way up here was what appealed to him in the first place."

Ray laughed. "Maybe. This sandwich is great. So, I think we'd better get down to work, or my boss is going to wonder why I toured the university for two hours on the APD's dime. Tell me about Babel, and more about this Tremor guy."

I filled Ray in the best I could, giving him an idea of how Tremor seemed to be really intent on connecting with Milan. His discussion with me about Thea had given me the creeps, even if Alchemist had tried to blow it off as innocuous. Ray agreed with me. It sounded to him as if Tremor was the one we were after.

"You said there was someone else up here who logs into Babel as a regular. Who is it?"

"His handle is Sanders, which I think refers to Winnie the Pooh. He registered, as I mentioned yesterday, as a Thomas Chatterton, who, if you remember your literary history, was the poet who faked the ancient monk's poetry on some old paper he found in the attic of a church. He committed suicide shortly after being found out."

"What does that have to do with Winnie the Pooh?"

"Well, that doesn't. You see, there was a writer-in-residence fundraiser last week." I tried to explain the whole blue-suit business, the opera tickets, and the possibilities of who could be Sanders. "Denise says that Chick Anderson doesn't seem to have the required skills on a computer, and I wouldn't think Alex Danvers would be flirting on-line. Besides, I'm pretty sure Sanders was on-line talking at the same time as Alex and Valerie were at a movie they told me about. So, it has to be Winston Graham."

"Who chats under the name of Sanders," supplied Ray.

"Exactly." I smiled. "It sounds a bit lame now that I try to explain it to someone else."

"I don't know. I'd say someone who would make a play on a plagiarizing poet for his registration, also making a reference to children's literature, is more likely than to think that there'd be two people doing the same thing in the same chat room at the same time. I would put money on Winston Graham, given what you've explained. So where do we find him?"

"I'm not sure, although from the sounds of things he is doing an art history class and some comparative religion courses. Why do we need to find him, anyhow?" The weird conversation I'd seen about killing people echoed in my memory, but I felt odd about offering something so ambiguous to the police. There was likely a very plausible explanation for that entire discussion.

"Well, I will admit, we focused on Edmonton because there was so much activity coming out of here on Babel. Part of that, of course, we now know, comes from your monitoring work. It doesn't explain all the activity, though. We're getting log-ins from all over town. Now, either your Sanders logs in from libraries and computer labs and Internet cafés, picking a different place each day, or you have way more than just Sanders for neighbors."

I stared at Ray. More people than Sanders on Babel? That was too weird to contemplate.

Ray insisted on picking up the lunch bill. I walked him back to the LRT entrance, promising to send him Chatgod's e-mail address and a list of registrations for Babel. I told him I'd have to okay it with Chatgod, and he smiled and nodded. Since Chatgod had already pretty much agreed to my cooperating with the police, I didn't think it would be problematic, either. He suggested that Steve and I have lunch with him the next day. I told him it would be our treat, and I'd have Steve call him at his hotel later if it was a go for him.

After he'd disappeared down the stairs to his train, I walked home, a lot slower than I'd power-walked earlier in the morning. I had a lot to think about. More than two Edmontonians in Babel? Who were they? And why weren't they admitting it when Sanders talked about his hometown? Was it something about Sanders's style? Maybe nobody wanted to meet up with him for coffee. Or maybe there was something a lot weirder than that going on.

CHAPTER 35

The first thing I did after logging into Babel was call up the registration file and demand a print on the entire list. Since it listed people who were no longer current members, it took a while of churning out page after page, but that was okay by me. If there were more Edmontonians in Babel, I wanted to know who they were.

I stood in the middle of my office-slash-dining room and stared at the general chat room moving along on my computer screen. Every night I was drawn into this world of language perpetrated by people I didn't know, would never meet, and might not like at all if I were to meet them in different contexts. However, I had stopped watching television, I had taken on a job devoting myself to keeping this area relatively free from the creeping uglies, and I was connected by shared experience to many of these people. Even I, who had tried to maintain a carapace of anonymity, was part of the community. I had been there when Vicky had left her abusive husband, I had been there when Vixen's son had been in the car accident and it was touch and go for thirty-six hours, I had been there when Andreas had finally asked Jennifer to come visit him in Holland for the summer holidays. The people of Babel were my community, and in among them were folks who were not who they seemed to be.

That, of course, was bad enough. But the real capper was that someone pretending to be someone else might actually turn out to be a hired killer.

Finally the list was finished. I read through Alchemist's notes on the general activity of the previous eight hours and traded a few jokes before he signed off.

PM from Alchemist to Chimera: A. My neighbor's guard dog turned on her. B. Doberman pinscher? A. No, Doberman bit her!

PM from Chimera to Alchemist: Ouch! That one is so bad it's good.

PM from Alchemist to Chimera: That's what I thought, too. Okay, sweetie, I'm outta here! Have a good, crime-free night. Hope nobody hires a hit on your shift.

PM from Chimera to Alchemist: Don't be so dang flip about it, sonny. You're not the one having to talk with the policemen.

PM from Alchemist to Chimera: Careful, chicky-wicky. Don't forget the original agreement. You weren't to discuss your job with anyone. If you hadn't let your policeman boyfriend know about it, you wouldn't be having these conversations with the law, now, would you?

PM from Chimera to Alchemist: Well, they were noticing a big spike of activity from Edmonton. They would likely have been knocking on my door once they'd gone through the service provider. I just wish I knew who else was pinging in from here. Besides, don't get owly. I might need you to help out.

PM from Alchemist to Chimera: Just yanking your chain, sweetums. You know I'm in your corner.

PM from Chimera to Alchemist: BTW, any luck tracing Tremor-the-mild-mannered-hacker?

PM from Alchemist to Chimera: Well, I figured out how

he could get in and out without being seen, but I haven't heard anything about this guy from any of the general hacking circles.

PM from Chimera to Alchemist: You know hackers?

PM from Alchemist to Chimera: Most of them are pretty good people who test security of various programs to bring weaknesses to light, not to take advantage of those weaknesses.

PM from Chimera to Alchemist: I guess I can see that.

PM from Alchemist to Chimera: I really do have to boo-gie, kiddo. Have a good night. See y'all tomorrow, okay?

PM from Chimera to Alchemist: Sure thing, hon. Sleep well!

And I was on my own. I set the main chat room in a large window, and opened the three private rooms that had action in them in smaller screens, just enough to keep track of the names of the participants and whether they were passing URLs or photos. Meanwhile, I spread the typed lists of registration information in front of me, on the surface of my desk. I slid the keyboard tray under and leaned on the desk, pencil in hand.

What I was looking for were recognizable e-mail hosts or suffixes denoting countries. Anything that was international I could strike through, but the anonymous on-line hosts were the troublesome ones. Anyone could join Hotmail or Bigfoot or several other mail companies offering ease of delivery from any access computer, since they were Internet portal mail sites. Most professionals knew enough not to use Hotmail, since, when it began, it reeked of cheating spouses sneaking around on-line, and that was a hard reputation to expunge. However, there were enough other subscription e-mail services that didn't bespeak a set location to make my expurgated list still at least half the size of the original.

I decided to work through on the basis of who I knew anything about. I was surprised at how much I did know about my fellow Babelites. I managed to remove another sixty-seven names based on information I possessed about their backgrounds from chatting with them that seemed to tally with their registration information. If it looked the least bit ambivalent I left the name on the list. If I had never seen the person in Babel, I circled the name and considered it removed from primary consideration. People tend to come and go in chat; sometimes they'll hang around for several months, and sometimes they just flit in from day to day, trying out new people each time they went for the experience. I was looking for the regulars; people who were guaranteed to have been logging in and posting every day or every second day for the previous few weeks. Long enough to cause a spike in Edmonton usage.

In the end, I had twelve names that were possibilities. I had seen five or six of them, but I decided to run it past Alchemist, too, since the others might be daytime users. If they were, chances were they were from Europe and not my problem anyway.

I typed up the list of twelve for Alchemist, made a copy for Ray Lopez, and turned my full attention back to the room. Two of the private rooms had closed down, and the action wasn't all that great in the main room, either. Even webbies occasionally managed to go out on a Friday night, it seemed. Actually, given the authority with which so many of them discussed newly released movies, I figured a lot of them went out a lot.

I made a pot of decaf and watched the action without

interacting at all. Sometimes you feel like a chat. Sometimes you don't. The only person I really felt like talking with was Steve, if talking had to be done. Of course, I was open to other forms of communication as well. He'd sounded distracted, though, when I had called about meeting Ray the next day for lunch, so I didn't suggest he come over after his workday, which I had been half planning. We were still in that edgy period, not sure if we were totally back to where we'd been before or if we were creating a new sort of relationship. Neither of us seemed to want to stick out our neck because both of us had been hurt by the separation. Then, I had been positive I didn't want a major commitment. Now, I wasn't so sure. And I wasn't so sure what the heck Steve wanted, anymore, either. Maybe he had decided that we would be better off just seeing each other casually ad infinitum. Relationships. If only there were an owner's manual for them. With my luck, of course, if there was one, it would be badly translated from the original Korean.

My shift was done for another evening. Things had slowed down to nearly nothing, anyhow. Either Far Eastern folks didn't on the whole care for chatting, or, more likely, they had found sites that were configured with greater ease to their own languages. At any rate, Chatgod's continuous demographic chartings showed that Babel stayed dormant from 3:00 a.m. till close on 10:00 a.m. I certainly wasn't about to argue. I shut down Babel and then my computer and went to bed.

CHAPTER 36

Another day of being woken by the alarm was not what I had signed up for. I grumbled my way into the shower, but, after several minutes under the pounding water, I was feeling a little more human. By the time I was dried off and clothed, I was feeling myself again. A grumpy self, mind you, but recognizable.

Steve was going to pick up Ray downtown and bring him over to the High Level Diner for lunch. I would walk over to meet them there about 11:30, before the big lunch crush. This gave me time to log in to the Grant MacEwan site to record the marks of the two students in my distance course who had barrelhoused through and finished the entire course in four weeks instead of the four months allotted.

That was one of the real pluses of distance teaching. The students who tended to get into it were often strong and highly motivated. I occasionally dreamed of having an entire classroom filled with students all equally motivated. Unfortunately, a good class was usually filled with eight motivated learners, ten time-markers, and twelve or more people with chips on their shoulders who were annoyed they had to pay money to take this particular class. You thanked the stars for those eight and suffered the rest.

I filed the marks, sent a heads-up e-mail to both the students, and sent copies to the distance classes coordinator, who liked to have a running tally of who had completed the courses. By 10:30 I had finished my Grant MacEwan duties for the day. I read my on-line horoscope, swept the kitchen and office area, dusted the bookcases and the venetian blinds, and washed up the few dishes that were sitting in the dishpan. I rubbed some hand cream into my knuckles, pulled on my leather jacket, and grabbed the list for Ray on my way out.

My luncheon companions were already at a table by the window, and they waved as I crossed the street toward the restaurant. I managed to wiggle past the lineup of six or seven people at the doorway and headed straight for them, nodding to the waiter watching the door. Ray was poring over the menu, while Steve was describing various dishes. The High Level Diner was one of our favorite restaurants, and Steve could probably explain exactly how each dish on the menu was made and served. Even so, they changed their menus with annoying regularity and had recently removed one of my favorite dishes, their curried chicken. I made do with their chicken enchiladas but reminisced about the curry every time I went there.

Both the men looked expectantly at me, as if I was bringing the Price Waterhouse Academy Award results with me instead of a list of possible Edmonton chatters. I handed over the list, explaining how I had come to winnow it down to these ones. Ray nodded approvingly as I listed my parameters, and I felt as if I'd accomplished something rather special. To celebrate, I ordered the bowl of café latte instead of just a cup of regular coffee.

"It should be easy enough to get addresses on these people if they're here in town," said Steve.

"I can get you a copy after lunch, if you'd like one," I offered.

"The trouble is, figuring out who is from Edmonton and who isn't won't be easy. We'll have to track down some of the service providers and lean on them for disclosure. My colleague Kate is good at that," added Ray. "I can tell you right away, though, that four of these chatters are from Silicon Valley. That e-mail program is a Stanford think-tank exclusive."

"Well, that is what I call winnowing down. Already we have fewer people to deal with." I pointed out Sanders's registration information. "This is the fellow I was talking about before. I think his real name is Winston Graham, and I jotted down the phone book information for all the W. Grahams listed. Of course, that doesn't really mean much, does it? I have a friend who lists himself in phone books as Earl Grey. Winston Graham might be Chatterton or Winnie the Pooh in the phone book for all I know."

"We'll find him, even if we have to check all the Orange Pekoes in the book, too," Steve assured us. He looked a little more determined than usual.

"I am certainly not saying that I think there's anything particularly fishy about him, except for the fact that I came across one fairly ambiguous discussion about assassinations. By the way, there is no registration for Tremor, which I can't really understand. To enter Babel, he would have had to register at one time. I'll ask Alchemist about it tonight, but I'm pretty sure of that, at least."

"Is there any way of changing your handle once you're registered in the system?" asked Ray, making notes in his Palm Pilot.

"No, I don't think so. I think you'd have to let your

registration expire and then reregister with another nickname." I promised I would ask Alchemist about that, too.

"Have you thought about logging in to Babel yourself?" I asked Ray. "Maybe you might see some of the possibilities for hacking better if you looked around yourself."

He smiled at me. "Oh, don't worry, we're all over that. On the whole, it's not a bad little joint. It's a lot more hospitable than a lot of chat sites I've been to. I think you and your co-worker do a very good job of being unnoticeable, too. There is a seamlessness to it that works."

I smiled, a bit nervously. I wasn't sure I liked the idea of Ray and his peers having already been through Babel. I felt a bit violated, to be honest, even if they were the good guys.

"How long have you been in Babel?"

"Well, I've been in there ever since we recovered Thea's bookmarks. I went in as Emilio Lizardo, and the Austin homicide detective I'm working with is Perfect Tommy."

"Ha! And there's a Buckaroo in there, too. Is he one of yours?"

"She. That's my cohort, Kate Brouder, who is maintaining a connection between us and the hacking world. Actually the whole *Buckaroo Banzai* theme was her idea. She's a fan of weird cult movies. I'm lucky we're not all *Rocky Horror Picture Show* characters."

"Does Chatgod know who you all are?"

Ray's face lost some of its good humor. "That boss of yours is not someone I'd want to divulge all to. He's above-board as far as we can tell, but he isn't very forthcoming. Kate thinks he might be a little too good to be true."

"Meaning?"

"Meaning porn."

"But there isn't any porn allowed on Babel. That's one of Chatgod's main reasons for putting Alchemist and me in place—to guard against that sort of thing."

"There might not be any porn allowed on Babel, but who's to say what else is on Chatgod's server? I have a feeling that Babel is a front for something, and the only thing that actually makes any money on-line is porn, so what else could it be?"

"Makes a certain amount of sense," agreed Steve.

I wasn't so sure. "You don't think Tremor is actually connected to Babel officially, do you? What if the whole thing is a front for hired killers? No wonder they can afford to hire monitors."

Ray held up a hand in a stop signal. "Hold on, Randy. I wouldn't worry too much. I think Babel is pretty much what it appears to be, a chat site that makes money by selling banner ads to advertisers. I think Chatgod very likely sells e-mail subscription lists and that people who log into Babel get a trifle more spam than other folks, but that is par for the course in most on-line interactions. I just think most entrepreneurs have a certain lack of ethical safety guards, is all. If Chatgod saw a way to make an easy buck, I think he might take it. By the way, do you know what his real name is?"

I shook my head. "Not unless it really is Alvin."

"You nailed it." Ray laughed. "The server is registered to an Alvin Epstein in Coral Gables, Florida. He runs a mail-order coupon business and houses the server for Babel in the front room of his duplex. His wife runs a daycare in the other side of the house. Kate's been down to see them and is keeping an eye on things at that end."

"Florida or Alberta. Did you toss a coin or something?" Steve asked, jokingly.

Ray shook his head vigorously as he answered. "No, you know, I twisted arms to get this. I have always wanted to see the north, especially at this time of the year. I am hoping to catch the northern lights. That would be worth seeing."

We agreed that the aurora borealis was a spectacular light show but warned him that he might not catch much of them at this time of year, or located in the middle of the downtown core, with all its ambient light.

"The best thing to do is head out of town and hope they last until you get past the city-light bleed," Steve explained, and launched into a story about us heading out of the city to catch the Persiads meteor shower at three in the morning last winter. We had almost frozen because we couldn't keep the car engine on without having the running lights on, too. Instead, we bundled up and stretched out on the hood of the car, hoping to gather in some engine heat. Then we stared up at the sky where meteors flew over us. One exploded like a roman candle right above us, lighting up everything around for miles in silvery shadows. It had been neat, seeing a carload or two of people in every lay-by, and we drove home tired but pleased to have seen them. Apparently they wouldn't be that bright again in our lifetimes.

Ray looked envious. I promised him I would call, no matter what time it was, if I saw any northern light activity. Meanwhile, we turned our thoughts back to the situation at hand. It felt as if I was putting two ten-pound weights back onto my shoulders. Ever since finding out that Thea's husband had really been murdered, the joy had somehow gone out of the whole chat-room experience, and, I had to admit, it had become a large part of my life.

If Tremor was a hired killer, then he was still out there and unidentified. If Thea had arranged to have her own husband murdered, then I had spent months talking with a woman who would take another's life. It is scary when you realize how little you know about people, people you see every day, let alone people whom you know only as little blips on the screen.

What about that waitress there? I had seen her working in this restaurant for at least ten years. I didn't even know her name. Did she have a husband she loved? Did she have children she worried about?

I also had to admit that this wasn't just existential angst over humanity's inability to interrelate. I was a bit nervous, to tell the truth. What if there really was a hired killer on Babel? What if he was hired to kill again? What if someone disliked me enough to have me killed? I knew that the likelihood was slim, since I didn't know many people well enough to piss them off that much, but, still, the thought was enough to make me shiver. Steve, whose arm was draped across the back of my chair, must have felt it, because he squeezed my shoulder.

"Goose walk over your computer terminal?"

"Oh God, don't use the word *terminal*, okay?"

Both of them laughed, and after a minute I did, too. Easy for them, of course. They thought in terms of crime and mayhem every day. They could compartmentalize it into their jobs. This had nothing to do with their personal worlds. They weren't members of Babel. And, for whatever it was worth, I was.

CHAPTER 37

Steve and I walked Ray to the downtown bus stop across the street and up the block, and then he followed me to my place, ostensibly to pick up another copy of the list. I opened the file with him standing behind me, kneading my shoulders. I was in a real quandary. I adore backrubs but absolutely detest people looking over my shoulder. I opted for letting the backrub continue and kept my own council. I eliminated the names of the people Ray had said were from Stanford, and hit print. Then I leaned back into Steve and looked up to see him squinting at some of my recipe cards on the cork wall surrounding the window behind my desk.

"Steve?"

"Uh-huhn?"

"I know that I am just peripherally involved in this and that you can't discuss police business and all that, but just why is someone like Ray Lopez up here?"

"What do you mean?"

"Well, if the murder happened in Austin, Texas, why did they send one computer expert to Florida and another to Edmonton? Do they think that Tremor lives here? Or that he's going to do some work here? Or both?"

"Randy, I am pretty much in the dark here, too. I know

that most everything Ray does is handled on a need-to-know basis, but I have to think it's something big, like you say. I was told to aid in his inquiries. You, of course, are acting out of sheer good will. As a Canadian citizen, you don't have much responsibility to get involved. On the other hand, as a person receiving international money transfers for salary, you're probably wise to do as asked, or I'm betting your taxes will get a whole lot harder to do."

"Yeah, but are we talking danger here? I'm allergic to danger, I think. It makes me break out in cold sweats, and sometimes in blood."

"I know, and believe me I don't want you in danger. Frankly, I don't think there is anything. From what I can gather, Ray is here because you work for Babel and there is what he calls an inordinate amount of activity from here. But that could be due to you and this Sanders guy, I figure. Doesn't have to mean anyone else. After all, you're on constant log-in. That has to be something they hadn't counted on. If Sanders is always on, too, like with a cable modem, then that could explain the spikes, right?"

"Right," I said. I wasn't so sure, though. I had a feeling, now that I knew that Ray and his hacker-pals were in Babel, that Ray had all sorts of reasons to be up here in the land of snow and honey. I'd feel a whole lot safer if I only knew what they were.

Steve ran his hands down my back and touched my ribs lightly, causing me to jolt up.

"Damn it, Randy, you nearly knocked my jaw out of kilter with your skull!"

"Well, tickling doesn't count as foreplay, Browning." I stood up and turned toward him, nudging the chair out of the way. "Now, why don't you tell me just what it was you had in mind?"

CHAPTER 38

Steve showered and left about 3:00, humming "Afternoon Delight," to my blushing amusement. I didn't feel quite so nervous about hired killers anymore, but that was likely the endorphins running through my system. I might not be too sure about the forever and ever bit but I was all in favor of other aspects of committed relationships. Before long, I was humming the same tune myself as I danced around the kitchen, making myself a bowl of tuna salad. I chopped two pieces of celery into the mixture of tuna and light mayonnaise, doused it all with garlic powder and stirred. I debated dumping it on bread for tuna melts but then decided to just eat it out of the bowl.

I cleaned the bowl and the rest of the dishes sitting in the dishpan and then decided to clean the entire counter area, pulling out the toaster, the blender, and the coffee maker. I couldn't do too much with the countertops, which were contemporary with the building itself, but at least I knew they were clean after I had scrubbed their dark surfaces. I swept the floor and washed the kitchen tiles. Then I hauled out the dishes from the cupboards and yanked out the shelf paper. I measured and laid out new paper from the drawer and put my dishes back. I did the same for the food cupboard, realizing that I hadn't shopped for staples in quite a while. Maybe Steve would be up for chauffeuring me to one of the mega-stores.

Finally, the afterglow wore off, and I went to shower and get ready for a night of Babel monitoring. It occurred to me that I had cleaned the kitchen with the same intention I usually had when starting a big writing project. If there was any way to put off the work, I knew I could find it, and being a good Canadian girl, housework would always present itself as a justifiable alternative to whatever it was I was supposed to be doing. To counter that, I would always jump into a fury of housecleaning prior to starting a project, or I would eventually find myself over my deadline with a beautifully defrosted freezer compartment.

The thing was, I had no writing project on the go. What was it I was trying to clear the runway for? Obviously there was something I had already unconsciously identified as something I would rather not be doing. I sat down at the desk, where the computer screen was still lit. I looked at my little cyber-world. One desk, half a wall of recipe cards, and lists of names. A chair. A goosenecked lamp with a scooped-out area for pens and paper clips at its base. A filing cabinet in the corner, tucked in beside the small kitchen table. What I wouldn't give for a staff room right now, a place filled with like-minded people who could discuss what was going on around me. Instead, the only thing I could do was log in to Babel and send Alchemist a private message. So I did.

CHAPTER 39

PM from Chimera to Alchemist: Hi hon. How are things going? Got time for a private room?

PM from Alchemist to Chimera: Sure thing. It's a morgue here. Meet you in Lanai.

I punched in the name on the location grid and laughed when the screen changed. Someone, probably Alchemist, had put up a wallpaper of palm trees and hula girls in pastel colors. I remembered what Ray had said about Chatgod really being someone in Florida named Alvin as I looked at the Miami-colored motifs. I wondered where Alchemist was from. Actually, what did I know about him, anyhow? He had a great talent for seeming to offer a great deal of personal information while really not offering any at all.

Here in a private room we didn't have to make our postings private. No one else could come in without an invite, and even then they wouldn't be able to see anything previously posted.

Alchemist: So what's shaking, chicky-wicky?

Chimera: Oh, you wouldn't believe what's happening here.

I filled him in on the things that Ray had been discussing. I told him about the police folks who were registered in Babel as Buckaroo Banzai's Hong Kong Cavaliers, and he didn't seem too bothered by it.

Alchemist: Well, at least they're the good guys, right?

Chimera: Yeah. The thing that bothers me, though, is that obviously they think there is something wrong with Babel, or they wouldn't be all over us, right? If they thought Tremor was a killer and Thea had hired him, or Thea and Milan, then that wouldn't really have anything to do with Babel, right? But their focus seems to be Babel, rather than the murder site in Austin. So . . .

Alchemist: So?

Chimera: So, either Tremor is working out of Babel full time, or someone else in Babel is on his hit list.

Alchemist: Yikes.

Chimera: Well, can you think of any other reasons?

Alchemist: And they say that there is all sorts of action coming out of Edmonton?

Chimera: That's what Ray says. How would he be able to know that, anyhow?

Alchemist: Honey, if they're hacking their way through here, they've probably got a constant pinging device wired onto the program itself. The thing is, I can't believe that you and Sanders can be conjuring up that much of a presence for them to take much action. I think they're right to be looking for other names.

Chimera: I gave them a list of eight that I couldn't track a source for. I think they're going to track down Sanders, too.

Alchemist: So you're sure of who it is?

Chimera: It has to be Winston Graham.

Alchemist: Are you sure?

Chimera: Well, I am hoping it is. I can't stand the thought of the other two possibilities being cyber-

Casanovas while working on actual real-time relationships. I suppose that sort of thing happens all the time, but I just don't like to think about it.

Even as I typed it, I thought about Sanders sending suggestive private messages to Vixen and me at the same time. Maybe it still was one of the other two blue-suited boys. I made a note to call Steve and ask him to keep the other two men in mind when considering Sanders.

Alchemist: Maybe we should create some sort of diversion to make Tremor surface.

Chimera: I dunno. I have played bait before. It's not fun when you have no idea how the other person is going to react.

Alchemist: But you said there are policemen crawling all over Babel. What's the harm?

Chimera: Maybe we should talk it over with Ray.

Alchemist: Sure, who did you say he was? Emilio Lizardo?

Chimera: Yep, from *The Adventures of Buckaroo Banzai: Across the Eighth Dimension.*

Alchemist: "Wherever you go, there you are."

Chimera: It's not my planet, monkeyboy!

Alchemist: *ROFLMAO* Great movie.

Chimera: Truly bizarre.

Alchemist: Well, why don't we talk to Dr. Lizardo and see if he doesn't think some deployment techniques might hasten a conclusion?

Chimera: Say what?

Alchemist: First strike.

Chimera: You're scaring me, kiddo. So, who would the target be?

Alchemist: I would volunteer, but you seem to have a glut of police coverage right with you.

Chimera: I also apparently have a glut of Internet activity coming from this area. That might mean that Tremor wouldn't even have to catch a bus to do the hit.

Alchemist: I think you're overreacting to some very generalized statements. We don't really know why the police are targeting Edmonton, except that they wanted to talk with you. We don't know that Tremor really is a hired killer. We don't know that he is even in Canada, let alone under your bed.

Chimera: Ooh, thanks for that one. Hang on while I poke a broom under the bed.

Alchemist: LOL. Anyhow, what I'm suggesting is a sort of modified I-know-what-you-did-last-summer sort of thing. Just leave a PM for Tremor saying that you have talked with Milan and might be able to send some more work his way. Then if and when he surfaces you can sound him out, with your policeman sitting right beside you.

Chimera: I can't even sound out a regular chatter enough to know who he is. How am I supposed to find out who a killer is?

Alchemist: When you put it that way, I can see your problem. You are obviously not forceful enough. Do you want me to hire the hit?

Chimera: On who? Me? No thank you.

Alchemist: All right, then why not have me killed?

Chimera: Bite your tongue. I don't even like thinking about this sort of thing in the abstract. What if someone took you seriously? I don't think you can un-hire that sort of thing.

Alchemist: Maybe not.

Chimera: I will talk with Ray and Steve and see what they think. I don't think we should be playing games with people like Tremor, though. We don't know what he is liable to do.

Alchemist: On the contrary. We think he is liable to kill. What we don't know is where he is liable to be. That's why it's so important to flush him out in the open. Off-line.

Chimera: Yeah. Well, maybe I should start small, and see if I can flush Sanders out first. If he is a bad guy, then we've done something. If he isn't, then we might have one more good guy on our side.

Alchemist: Not a bad idea. Whatever the case, honey, it's your shift starting, and I really have to get going.

We said our goodbyes and I closed Lanai after Alchemist had signed out. I joined the general room as Chimera, opened up the private message line to Alvin, and checked for any newly created private rooms. There wasn't too much going on. Several people in the room were discussing the US role in global peacekeeping. For the most part, it was a leftist slant on things, although I was surprised to see a general view that two-year armed forces conscription should be considered in every country. The Israelis and Germans were being invoked as good models to follow. I wondered how those governments would feel being lumped together.

I marvel at how many left-wing thinkers I have run across on-line, given the general tendency for technological geeks to lean to the right. Think Bill Gates, after all. But more and more I was finding a tendency to see the Internet being used as a space for organizing activists and setting up manifestos. Whether it was searching for intelligent life in the rest of the universe or trying to feed the multitudes, the web was right there.

I tossed my two bits into the army discussion, which

was that I didn't look all that great in camouflage, and sat back to watch. I was trying to puzzle through how I could flush out Sanders. I looked at the copy of the list of names and e-mail addresses I'd made, first for Ray and then for Steve. Sanders's information was at the top of the shortened form I'd printed off for Steve and myself. Thomas Chatterton, chatter@clapham.com. How was I going to figure out who he was? Maybe I could just e-mail him and ask him outright. I did a mental double take. Why not? In the hubbub of the gala, how many e-mail addresses and phone numbers had been exchanged? Why couldn't I just e-mail him as Randy Craig and ask him out for coffee? He would assume I'd got the e-mail address from him at the gala or from one of our mutual friends. Then whichever of the three men met me, in a very public place, would be my Sanders. I could decide then whether to let out my alter identity as Chimera.

Maybe this chatter e-mail was only for his on-line world, but then again, maybe not. I couldn't see what harm it could do to try. I clicked open my Eudora e-mail program, and hit the button for new messages.

```
To: chatter@clapham.com
From: rcraig@uofalberta.com
Subject: coffee sometime?

Hi there,

I was wondering if we could meet for coffee to
discuss some mutual acquaintances. Would Java
Jive in HUB tomorrow at 2 be convenient?

Thanks,

Randy Craig
```

I read the message over several times, trying to see it from all angles. If it was Winston Graham, he might think I was referring to Alex and Valerie. If it was Alex, he would probably think I meant someone at Grant MacEwan. If it was Chick Anderson, he might think I meant Steve, but more than likely would figure I meant Denise. Whatever the case, I was pretty sure whoever got the message would recall me from the gala, if he had been focused enough to report to complete strangers that I'd bid and won the opera tickets.

I hit Send and went back to monitoring the action in Babel. It could be ten minutes or several hours before Sanders checked his e-mail. I wasn't counting on a reply right away.

CHAPTER 40

The corner of my screen began flashing its little mail indicator about an hour after I'd sent the e-mail to Sanders.

```
To: rcraig@uofalberta.com
From: chatter@clapham.com
Subject: Re: coffee sometime?

Hello!

Coffee at Java Jive is always a welcome idea.
Tomorrow at two would be grand. See you then!

>Hi there,

>I was wondering if we could meet for coffee to
>discuss some mutual acquaintances. Would Java
>Jive in HUB tomorrow at 2 be convenient?

>Thanks,

>Randy Craig
```

Damn, he hadn't signed his name, which would have made things so much easier. I had a feeling he was toying with me, and that I had somehow laid myself open to being spotted as a Babel chatter by using this particular e-mail address, but what the heck. I would just bluff my way through and claim he'd given me that address when we'd met at the gala. Anyhow, if I felt I could trust him, I would likely tell him my chat identity. I didn't need to let him in on the whole monitoring job, after all. One layer of secrecy at a time would do.

The rest of the evening wasn't a dead loss. Sanders showed up in Babel shortly after I read his e-mail answer to me, but Chimera had logged out by then, and I was monitoring invisibly. He flirted quite generally with Vixen and Maia, and joined in a discussion of which 1970s and 1980s television shows promoted a distorted view of North American life to the Third World.

Maia: We jumped from *The Waltons* to *Dynasty.* I am not sure people don't think we all live in mansions.

Vixen: Or with roommates we get along with in enormous New York apartments, which we somehow pay for on waitressing wages.

Sanders: And then we wonder why people flood Immigration Services.

Gandalf: Heck, maybe we should all move to TV Land. Sounds like that is the place to live.

Maia: But you can't blame people for assuming that is the status quo, now, can you?

Sanders: When has fantasy ever been anything like reality?

Vixen: But TV is all about reality these days.

Sanders: But that is these days, dearheart. You were just making references to the '70s and '80s, which I'm not sure I'm not too young to remember.

Vixen: *snort*

Maia: *sugared* Well, you could always catch them

on *Nick at Night* like the rest of us precocious spring chickens, honey!

Sanders: *LOL*

Gandalf: What the heck does it matter what people think of how we live? They're going to hate us no matter how we live, right?

Vixen: I don't think so, Gandalf. If we could all see each other a bit clearer, I am sure that we'd be that much closer to harmony.

Sanders: I am not so sure that if my child was dying of starvation in my arms, I would be more understanding of someone whose greatest worry was whether she could afford orthodontia for both of her perfectly healthy children.

Maia: *sigh* When you put it that way, we might as well all just slit our wrists and get the guilt over with.

Vixen: Oh Sanders, Maia. This is getting too heavy for me. I can take only so much imperialist guilt per day. Besides, tomorrow is my day to work at the food bank, so I feel I'm entitled to a nightmare-free night of it. Ciao, bambinos!

Sanders: Sweet dreams, heavenly creature.

Maia: Nighty-night, Vixie.

Gandalf: See ya!

Dilly: *hugs* G'night, Vixen!

There was more of the same when Maia left ten minutes later. Sanders stayed to discuss some chess concepts with Gandalf, but pretty soon the evening regulars were packing it in. The Australians weren't up yet, and Tracy from Singapore was chatting with Flora from Malaysia before heading to the hospital where she worked. Once again, my shift in Babel was coming to an end.

Of course, tomorrow would open up a whole new door to the chatting concept. Tomorrow I was going to have a face-to-face meet.

CHAPTER 41

I recall several long on-line thrashes about whether to call face-to-face meetings between on-line friends meets or meats, since cyber-space was considered a distinct world from where flesh and blood, ergo meat, walked about and interacted. Something about referring to human beings as meat just felt wrong to me. I resolutely thought of face-to-face meetings as meets, and I was almost as highly strung as I had been in school before track meets. I changed outfits three or four times getting ready for my date with Sanders, and when I finally decided that I was wearing the right sweater with my clean dark jeans, I slobbered toothpaste down the front and had to start over again. Finally, I managed to get out of the house wearing a sand turtleneck, jeans, and my leather jacket. I had to go back for a hat as soon as I hit the back door. It was definitely winter, even though this year the ground was staying obstinately brown. I think it feels colder when there is no snow, although, given it was January, it was allowed to be cold just on principle.

I was really cold by the time I hit campus, so I decided to deke into the Law Building and take the walkways through to HUB. I passed through the edge of the Fine Arts Building and crossed the pedway over the same place

I'd waited for Ray Lopez just a couple of days earlier. I really was expanding my horizons, meeting all sorts of new people. Denise would be impressed. She was always after me to make more connections, to network my way into a full-time position somewhere. The networking I'd done lately might not lead to any full-time jobs, but it certainly had expanded my social calendar.

I was fifteen minutes early, so I decided to buy a coffee and sit at one of the small tables located down the middle of the mall. Whoever he was, Sanders had replied to Randy Craig. He knew who I was. I would just let him come to me.

I wasn't completely surprised to see Winston Graham slide into the modular chair across from me. In fact, I was pleased that neither Denise nor Valerie needed to worry about philandering men. Of course, it didn't mean I was any less nervous about things. I wasn't sure I was going to be able to manage this conversation without giving too much away. While I was planning to admit to being in Babel, I didn't want to give away my level of involvement. Chatgod and Alchemist both had been very specific about the need to maintain discretion about how much overseeing and control might be involved in the community. No one, after all, wants to think that Big Brother, or in this case Big Sister, might be watching them.

"Hi there, Randy! I was intrigued to hear from you. Do you need another coffee? Dark or mild?" He waved away my attempt to offer him some money with which to buy our coffees and swirled off into line, all overcoat and scarf. In many ways, he was exactly how I had imagined Sanders to be. He had to be slightly older than I, maybe even in his late forties. His hair was beginning to get a a salt-and-pepperish look at the temples and sides, but he still had plenty of hair, and it was slightly over-grown out of what had probably been a very good style. My bet was that some stylist at a discount hair salon or even a beauty school had a soft spot for this guy and gave him a hundred-dollar haircut for six bucks whenever he bothered to come by.

He was smiling as he came back toward the table and it occurred to me that he might even get those haircuts for free. There was a real charm in his smile, a high-wattage interest in whomever it was directed to. He placed the coffees on the table and then hung his book-bag over the back of his chair and sat down, shucking his coat off behind him, covering the bookbag.

"There we go, comfortable seats, good company, and coffee. What more could a man ask for?"

"Thanks for meeting me on short notice."

"No problem. One of my greatest strengths and/or weaknesses is my eternal curiosity. It's what has pushed me into the life I lead, and, if my mother is to be believed, may eventually be the death of me."

"Oh, I hope not. I'm really impressed by your drive toward the whole Renaissance-man thing."

"My mother wasn't. She thought I should settle into one field and discover happiness through repetition." He grinned. "What she was really campaigning for, of course, was grandchildren. Oh well."

"Well, to satisfy your curiosity on one point, I asked to meet with you to discuss some mutual acquaintances."

"Right."

"On-line mutual acquaintances." I paused. "I feel somehow as if I've been deceiving you, though it's cer-tainly not personal and there has been no malice in my motive. The thing is, though, we know each other from Babel. My handle in there is—"

"Chimera."

Okay, so I had got it wrong. It wasn't Sanders who would be the one shocked by the revelation. It would be me. Had he known all along?

As if he could read my thoughts, which possibly he could, given what Steve called my anti-poker face, he hurriedly continued. "I didn't know before, but it all fell into place just now as you were talking." His face registered pleasure and a little bit of extra concentration, as he readjusted all his previous on-line conversations with me to fit the picture he now had of me. It was much the same thing I had been doing while he had been putting milk in our coffee cups. "So, the mystery lady was closer than I might have imagined. I can understand your desire for anonymity, of course. That's one of the great freeing things about on-line discourse, the idea that you may never have to meet whoever it is you're talking to. You can be utterly vulnerable or, alternately, utterly false. It cramps things if someone shows up at your shoulder who is too close for comfort, doesn't it?"

"I don't know. How do you feel about it?"

"How do I feel? I think it's great. I'm all for face-to-face conversations. Most of the reason I went on-line was experimental, and to find the lost art of conversation. Maybe I am just getting too old for the average person here on campus, but it seems more and more difficult to engage in an argument about philosophy or ethics or even the superiority of one writer over another. Unless I'm willing to discuss hockey or *The Sopranos*, I haven't a hope of an interesting conversation around here. Now it may just be that we review our past with the proverbial rose-colored glasses, but I am sure discussions were more spirited and interesting about fifteen or twenty years ago."

"You may be right," I grinned. "I know that it is almost impossible to engender an argument in class anymore, and I recall some real doozies when I was a student."

"Yep. Ennui sweeps the world. So, that is why I decided to explore the on-line world of chat and community. I'd read *Wired* and, of course, *Virtual Community* and figured that I might find like-minded people in the cyber-world. And for the most part, I was right."

"Not completely satisfying, though?"

"No, not for someone like me, of limited resources. There are some folks in various communities who have face-to-face get-togethers all the time. That augmentation, for me, is where the real thing would come from. This disembodied community is very dissatisfying. Like a peep show when you really want contact." He looked straight at me quickly, maybe to see if he'd offended me with his simile.

"I guess you never bought into the telephone campaign of 'reaching out to touch somebody,' eh?"

He laughed. "Exactly. However, while for me it would have been far more interesting to have met up with you for a pizza shortly after we'd met on-line, this is better late than never, and I can certainly understand why a woman on-line would want to maintain anonymity."

"Thank you. I have to admit, it was a decision I had a lot of problems with. Part of me has been very, very curious about you. Part of me has been worried that a meeting like this will change the dynamics of Babel for me."

Sanders (I still couldn't think of him as Winston)

shrugged. "I doubt things will change all that much. After all, look at all the people in Babel who have met face to face. Vixen and Maia. Vixen and Lane. Diane and Trudy are sisters, I think. And Thea and Milan, of course. Nothing seems to change once they're back on-line."

"Well, actually, it's Thea and Milan I needed to talk to you about," I admitted. He looked surprised by that. I wondered briefly whom he expected we'd be talking about. "I've been contacted by the police because of my involvement in Babel. Apparently, Thea's husband was murdered in Austin, and the police think that the killer came from Babel, or that Thea met with him to conspire there, or something. All I knew to tell them was that Thea hadn't been around in weeks, and that Milan was looking for her and Tremor was looking for Milan. It occurred to me that they might have talked with you, too. So, I thought I'd get hold of you and see what you knew, or if they'd talked with you."

Even as I said it, it sounded sort of lame. I wondered if I was managing to pull it off.

"No, the police haven't contacted me, but that's probably because I input a false name and address in the registration field. Why would they track a murder in Austin to Edmonton, though? It's not as if Babel is routed here."

"They said something about a high density of action from here in Edmonton. I have a feeling it's more than just you and me logging in from here."

"Did you tell them about me?" He asked it casually, but I felt the hairs on the back of my neck rise ever so slightly.

"I mentioned that you had said you were from Edmonton but that I didn't know who you were. I figured I owed it to you to track you down and let you know they would likely be looking to talk with you, too." He nodded, and I think he seemed satisfied with my answer.

"Well, do you have a name of whom I should contact at the police station?"

"Actually, he's probably not at the police station, but he's police. His name is Ray Lopez and I do have his phone number." I took Ray's card out of my bag and was hunting for a scrap of paper, but Sanders already had his datebook out of his pocket and a pen. I passed him Ray's card, and he noted down the penciled-in number on the back as well as the Austin police number, which I had noted but never bothered to phone for confirmation. Of course, Sanders didn't have a policeman boyfriend to introduce Ray, and I was rather impressed by his thoroughness and foresight.

Just thinking of Steve must have been infectious. The next thing Sanders said was, "So, I suspect the fellow with you at the writer-in-residence festivities was your significant other?"

"I'm not quite sure how one describes our relationship at the moment, but it is significant, yes."

Sanders shrugged. "So, I never stood a chance in the first place. I couldn't figure out how my gold-plated flirtations were getting great reception with everyone except you. Of course, you knew me to be nearby, and you were otherwise engaged."

"A lot of folks on-line are 'otherwise engaged,' though. Do you mean to say that you can flirt with married women and make conquests? Is everyone on-line unhappily married?"

"On the contrary, I think a lot of people on-line are very well grounded in their own realities. Cyber-space is a different animal, though. I don't think it counts as much in people's minds, or perhaps there is an edge of danger and excitement that is akin to Mardi Gras where everyone can wear masks. People at masquerades are able to explore their fantasies with impunity. Shy people can speak out without fear. Besides, no one can tell they are shy because they can begin again, brand new, in a brand-new world. It's my theory that marriages are stronger as a result of on-line chat rooms. Couples don't need to receive all their validation from the other anymore."

"I'm not sure what you mean."

"Well, this is mostly cobbled together from some old courses in family dynamics and personal relationships, but look at the demographics from when there was only one job per family. The man leaves for the day and connects with people of both sexes, receiving commentary on his performance, and even compliments on his tie. By the end of the workday, he has received all the strokes to his ego that he requires. He then returns home to discover that his wife has been without that sort of feedback. It's somehow up to him alone to give her that validation for her efforts in keeping house and nurturing the children and shopping wisely for provisions. What took seven or eight people to stroke him, he has to do on his own for his wife. What do you suppose the likelihood of that is?"

"But what about working women?" I asked.

"There you have the 1970s and beyond starting to happen. It doesn't happen overnight, but soon and definitely by the 1990s, you have the need for two-income families occurring more and more. So you would assume that each person is receiving an adequate amount of strokes from outside sources to be equal, right?"

I nodded, thinking he would make a good lecturer.

"Well, the sad truth is that men still tend to get more

validation in the workplace than their female counter-parts, and to cap that off, with cutbacks and more telecommuting, people are becoming even more isolated than the 1960s housewife ever was, men and women alike. So, my thesis is that to go on-line and relate to a variety of strangers who are offering appreciative flirting, some affirmation of comments you make to the general room, and the offering of friendly conversation, goes a long way to providing all the validation that anyone requires. Healthy individuals equal healthy relationships. Ergo, the Internet will help save, not destroy, marriages."

"Bravo. Well argued, I must say. You're going to get a lot of backtalk from all the people who believe that the Internet is the work of the devil, you know. But I can see your point. Are you planning to write this all up in suit-able academic language for a sociology periodical? Hey, is Babel your laboratory?"

"Oh, I'd just rather discuss it with like-minded indi-viduals for the nonce." He smiled at me, perhaps just a tad too ingenuously, which made me think I might have nailed it. Sanders was using his on-line discourse for soci-ological experiments. And I was willing to bet he hadn't cleared it with any of his subjects. "Which brings me back to my initial statement, which is that real-life con-versations like the one we're having at the moment hap-pen too seldom anymore."

I knew what he meant, and I could remember having longings fulfilled as I went on-line. What had happened to our ability to talk to each other, anyhow? Were there still groups of earnest people somewhere with candles stuck in Chianti bottles arguing whether Descartes had sold out, like Beckett seemed to imply? Was I just too old to be invited to the scrum? Or were they all talking about music videos and whether the latest pop idol had had breast enlargements?

Winston "Sanders" Graham coughed politely, bringing me back to the table. I was glad we'd met, although I wasn't sure I was any further ahead with the whole business of Ray Lopez and Thea the widow. Sanders had managed to very quickly deflect our conversation into a philosophical rant about chat in general, rather than anything personal. I was, in fact, more curious about his overview attitude on chat than anything else. I was betting he really was using us all as his guinea pigs for some sociology paper.

"What about the assassin talk I overheard you making the other day?" I was going to play that I'd just wandered in behind their discussion if need be, but I had to know what he was up to in Babel. "Was that some sort of ploy to see how people react to outrageous commentary?"

"What do you mean?" His face, just moments ago animated, was closing like a metal bank-vault door.

"Well, I can see that you're documenting all of this somehow, right? Now, whether or not I think that is moral, or even admissible evidence for a thesis, is beside the point. I want to know what sort of games you're playing on Babel before the police close us all down."

Sanders spoke tersely. "It's not a game on Babel. It's a game here on campus, called Assassin. We sign up, and are given a target to douse with shaving cream. Someone else is given our name at the same time. You score points for 'killing' as many targets as you can before you are smeared in shaving cream yourself."

"You're kidding." I couldn't fathom it. It sounded so sophomoric, even more so when being explained by someone older than I. Sanders looked a bit abashed as he admitted it. "And the fellows you were talking to on Babel are playing it, too? Are they from here, too?"

"They're thinking of signing on to play at their own campuses. There are Assassin games all over the world, though it's a mainly North American phenomenon, I believe." He shrugged, and then began to make a big show of looking at his watch and putting on his coat. For some reason, he was done talking with me, although I wasn't too sure what subject had triggered the reaction. If this assassin game was so innocent, why the sudden lockdown on charm?

"One thing that Detective Lopez mentioned has me puzzled." I would give it one last try. "Why would there be so much Babel action coming from Edmonton? Do you know of anyone else besides ourselves who logs in?"

Sanders's smile was genial, but I am not sure whether it reached his eyes at all. He shrugged his shoulders as he pulled his scarf up toward his neck from behind, like a back-drying towel motion.

"Until today, I didn't even know you were from Edmonton. I'm not sure I really will have all that much to add for Detective Lopez."

"Please give him a call, anyhow, okay?" I hoped he would do it as some sort of chivalric gesture for me, if nothing else. "I'm not sure he thinks any of the information I've given him is worth much. At least if he hears it from the both of us, he'll know it's on the up and up."

Since I still didn't have a phone number for him, although I was sure the police could retrieve that easily enough from the university administration, I figured it was worth doing the figurative eyelash batting. If Ray was right about there being a lot of Edmonton action on Babel, and Sanders was right about it being just the two of us, then one or the other of us was on there a lot more than we were willing to admit. I'd already admitted my undercover behavior, at least to Ray. Was Sanders hiding something equally shadowy?

CHAPTER 42

I wasn't satisfied with Sanders's blithe excuse for dis-
cussing assassinations on-line. I had heard of murder-
mystery parties and even dinner clubs, but this seemed a
bit far-fetched. As soon as I got home, I logged into
Google and searched "assassin game." It was amazing.
Over 120,000 hits came up, and the first ten included
MIT, Harvard, Dalhousie, University of Manitoba, and
Texas A & M.

It sounded like a really complex game of tag, played
with shaving cream. Everyone who signed into the game
apparently was assigned a target to "kill." Each killing
had to be done in a public place, with a witness. The
killings were not to be done during class. Aside from that,
it was up to the killer. The only problem was that, at the
same time as the assassin was stalking, he or she was also
some other assassin's intended victim.

Having been the real intended victim a time or two in
my life, I couldn't see the glamor of the game, but
Sanders had insisted it was a lark, played by a lot of university students to let off steam.

I made note of the URLs that best described the game
so I could give everything to Ray and Steve when I saw
them next. I still wasn't completely satisfied that

Winston/Sanders was being straight with me, but I couldn't dispute that the game really did exist and was played ferociously on many university campuses. I just couldn't visualize a man Sanders's age sneaking up on a coed with a can of shaving cream in his hand. There was something a little too *Animal House* about it all, and Sanders had chosen the Internet precisely to get away from that sort of behavior, or so he had said. For what it was worth, that part of his conversation I believed totally.

There was something almost unreal about this whole business of Thea's husband's murder, and Ray's chase for the faceless killer on the Internet. Somehow it still didn't gel for me why there was such a strong police interest in Babel. Of course, I knew as well as anyone who watched TV that the police didn't release all the information to the media. Maybe the murder had larger implications, or maybe it was the sign of a longer trail of killings. I had no real feel for the murder, of course. Maybe it was because I didn't actually know anything about Thea's husband. It wasn't as if it was someone I'd chatted with. If other people were able to consign on-line personalities to mere blips on the screen they could turn off at will, I had a similar ability to consign fictional status to people I heard about on the news or read about in the paper. If they didn't actually intersect with my life, they didn't actually take shape. In fact, fictional characters I'd spent any amount of time with were allotted more credence than strange names or descriptions in the news.

I usually saw this as a blessing, in that it gave me a stronger link with the materials of my profession, but at the moment I could see it for the failing it was. I wasn't some Ray Lopez, able to throw himself into the minds and problems of people all over the place whom he'd never met. I was having a hard time drumming up any sympathy for Thea for getting me into all this, let alone her poor fried husband, for whom I should be feeling the most pity. Instead, I think the real emotion that kept rising up in me was resentment. I was pretty ticked at Thea and Milan for starting an affair before Thea had rid herself of her impediments, and I was appalled at the way they'd decided to rid themselves of the impediment. They had muddied up my play area with their unethical actions, and if I was honest with myself, that was worse to me than the actual killing of her husband.

I couldn't help feeling a bit sorry for Milan, left high and dry with all of this happening. I was pretty sure that Ray's crew were circling around him, if they hadn't already tracked him down in Milwaukee. If he wasn't acting some really Byzantine double-blind, Thea had disappeared from him, too. It had to be something like that. If he was involved in the hiring and execution of the killing, then why on earth was he calling so much attention to himself?

And were we really sure the killing had been committed by Tremor? Or was Thea more involved than she had let on? What if she had done it all herself, but created a smokescreen of a hired killer? Was she adept enough for that? I made a note to ask both Ray and Alchemist about what they figured. That reminded me that Alchemist was going to be setting up his scam with Tremor to draw him out, and I was supposed to log on an hour early to get brought up to date. I had things to tell him about Sanders as well. All in all, I was rather proud of myself for tracking Sanders down, even if it had been a best-out-of-three proposition.

Alchemist was suitably impressed that I had found

Sanders, and he accepted the assassin-game excuse a lot quicker than I did.

Alchemist: Well, we know that Tremor is up to something. The odds of two hired killers working the same chat room have to be extraordinarily high. I can crunch the numbers if you want, if I look up the statistics on murders in North America as a mean. So, since we know that Tremor was up to something, I am willing to believe that Sanders is, statistically speaking, innocent.

Chimera: Yes, well, you can take your lies, damned lies, and statistics, and put them in your pipe and smoke them. I still think there is something fishy about him. Besides, what about this extra action all over Edmonton that Ray Lopez was referring to? I honestly can't see this guy Sanders wandering through Internet cafes; and the university computer labs all have dedicated IP addresses. So, who is logging in all over the place?

Alchemist: Well, if it's not you, and it's not Sanders, the logical answer is . . . someone else.

Chimera: Good God, Holmes!

Alchemist: Scoff if you want, Watson. Eliminate the impossible, and whatever remains, however improbable, is your answer.

Chimera: Meaning what? That Tremor is a giant hound? That everyone on Babel lives in Edmonton? That Sanders moves around a lot? Maybe we should get Chatgod to let us access the server logs and just sort through for IP address usage.

Alchcemist: Do you have any idea how long that would take? Not to mention the printout? Besides, I still think we should keep as low a profile about this to Chatgod as possible. He may have given the nod to you discussing this with the task force investigating the murder, but I don't think he likes it one bit. Remember that non-disclosure form you signed when you joined up? That explicitly says no discussion about what happens on Babel.

Chimera: But this is the police we're talking about! This is a little bit different.

Alchemist: Not entirely. Remember, one of those policemen is a personal friend of yours. That constitutes a little blurring of the lines, don't you think? Well, no matter what you think, I just think it's advisable to look into this with the resources at our disposal. If the task force decides to impound the server down in Florida, that's fine. It's not our headache. But when all this is done and dusted, we've still got to work here, Randy. Looking out for number one!

Chimera: I never took you for a Randy Bachman fan.

Alchemist: Say what? Oh. Well, you know what I mean. The thing is, does it matter why they decided to target you in Edmonton? The real likelihood is that your monitoring duties skewed the numbers as far as they could determine, and they're now just covering their bases by saying there were other IP addresses being bandied about.

Chimera: Maybe.

Alchemist: The thing to concentrate on is getting Tremor out in the open. If we can isolate him, and determine where he is coming from and that he is indeed a hired killer, then we've solved everything.

Chimera: So why don't we log back through to find discussions with Tremor and Milan or Tremor and Thea?

Alchemist: Chances are they did all their talking in private rooms, or in some form of Instant Messenger program. We don't have any logs of private rooms in Babel.

Chimera: What? I thought it all had to be logged in order to have a licence.

Alchemist: Technically. If you have a monitoring system in place, you can forego the private logging. Babel got really big a lot sooner than Chatgod expected. The server has only so much room, even for zipped material, and the regulations are that records have to be kept for six years. That's why he decided to hire monitors. With us to monitor the content of the private rooms and chase people back into the general area, Chatgod can keep costs down. Our salaries are nothing compared to the upgraded system he'd have to instal to keep the authorities satisfied. And for what? I don't recall ever being asked for records in the time I've been on Babel staff.

Chimera: I suppose. It would be handy right now, though.

Alchemist: Well, right now we have a handle on who to watch, and a pretty good idea of what we are looking for. How would having a record of their conversations help us? Thea's husband would still be dead. We would still be only as close as their latest IP addresses, which we do have. You see, this is what comes of talking to the police—the methods take over from the logic of the matter.

Chimera: All right, already. So, I keep pillow talk to a minimum. I understand. Meanwhile, what are we going to be doing about Tremor?

Alchemist: Well, so far, I've sent him an e-mail asking to meet up with him in Babel tonight to discuss a business transaction.

Chimera: Tonight?

Alchemist: Strike quickly and decisively.

Chimera: And who is supposed to be meeting with him?

Alchemist: The two of us. We're conspiring to kill your husband.

Chimera: I don't have a husband. And besides, why did you decide on us?

Alchemist: Well, from what we've seen of his activity, Tremor has to be at least a bit of a hacker. If he has the ability to come in a back door and disappear at will, and switch IP addresses while he's at it, then chances are he can also monitor to a degree what is going on in Babel. Likely he can't get into ghosting through the private rooms and hovering like we can, but I wouldn't put it past him to be able to track who is logging in and when. Since we meet daily and talk privately, it would make sense to him that we're intimate and up to something. I was just aiming for being as transparent as possible. The more truth in your fabrication, the more strength.

So, if Alchemist's plan worked, I would be dickering with a hired killer tonight about the cost of offing my husband. I wouldn't have a chance to discuss this with Steve or Ray, but maybe that is why Alchemist sprang it on me the way he had. I had the distinct feeling that he was warning me about Chatgod's mood vis-à-vis the police investigation.

Well, I'd been hired to monitor and shepherd. I really believed that a good shepherd knows when to call in the reinforcements, which is what I had done. Well, not exactly; they'd found me. But, all in all, it amounted to the same thing. We had a whole group of people watching out for the innocent members of Babel, and that had to be in Babel's best interests, right? Which is what Chatgod wanted, right? So why did I have the gnawing feeling that he was really irate about my connection to the constabulary?

There was no real point in arguing with Alchemist about his plans. As far as they went, they made sense. We'd try to flush out Tremor with a decoy. If he went for it, there would be plenty of time to create a trap.

Oh yeah, listen to me, I know so much. If I had all the answers, I'd have bought Amazon early and sold Lycos stock at $178.

CHAPTER 43

There was no message from Tremor when I went into the main area of Babel, but Alchemist had told me to signal him by e-mail if Tremor showed up. He had also promised to come back in if he received a private e-mail back from Tremor. It was the best I could hope for, but I still felt extremely vulnerable. I didn't spend much time in the main room. Instead, I created a private room and logged Chimera in there, then spent the rest of the time hovering up in the rafters of the main room, watching the action. I was in no mood to discuss anything with anyone on-line.

Maybe it was just my mood, but the conversation seemed to veer between the edgy and the banal all evening. Sometimes it feels as if people go on-line just to pick fights, as if they avoid confrontations in real life if they beat up on some ether people. Meanwhile, the rest of them seemed to have been dipped in Prozac.

Maybe this was how policemen doing surveillance felt, but there was a sense of boredom tinged with an edge of panic. Bizarre. I thought of the word *petrified* and how it applied in both its definitions in this situation. The last thing I wanted was the upcoming confrontation with an alleged assassin, but if it had to happen, why couldn't I just get it over with?

I took a look at the clock on the wall. It was almost 10:00, way too late to call even close friends, but maybe I could squeak a call in to Steve, given that his police genes might extend the etiquette time. What if Alchemist was right about Chatgod being upset about me talking with the police, though? If I lost the job with Babel, my resources would get frighteningly slim. There was still no mention of any spring classes nor any talk of more distance courses at Grant MacEwan, and I wasn't sure how to broach the possibility of other assignments.

Of course, if the police believed a killer was haunting Babel, it wouldn't be too long before they just closed the place down anyhow, and I'd still be out of a job. The flip side was that the killer might make me permanently redundant.

Instead of calling Steve and possibly jeopardizing my job, I opted to make more coffee. When I got back to the computer with a steaming cup of mocha roast in my hand, there was a flashing note at the top of my screen telling me to check my e-mail. Alchemist, true to his word, was letting me know of his response from Tremor.

```
To: rcraig@uofalberta.com
From: alchemist@babel.com
Subject: An Answer Came

Hey kiddo,

He bit. We're supposed to meet him in Babel in
a private room called Lair tomorrow evening at
seven. I'm game. The line is, we want to off
```

your husband. Come prepared to discuss his
habits and whereabouts. It's going to cost
$10,000. And we thought life was cheap.

A.

To: alchemist@babel.com
From: rcraig@uofalberta.com
Subject: What the heck

Wow.

So, do you think I should alert the task force?
This is the sort of thing they'd likely want to
monitor, right? I don't think we can handle this
alone.

R.

To: rcraig@uofalberta.com
From: alchemist@babel.com
Subject: The boss won't like it

Randy,

I am not sure what to say. My instinct says that
Chatgod will get really upset if we haul in the
feds, but that doesn't mean it's not the best
thing to do. What matters is that you feel safe
throughout this, and if that means bringing in
the police at your end, I can understand that.
I would appreciate it if it became your decision, though, rather than our decision. I don't
want to influence you either way.

A.

To: alchemist@babel.com
From: rcraig@uofalberta.com
Subject: lonely

Yeah,

I know what you're saying. I agree. If Chatgod
gets annoyed, it might as well be just one of
us who gets canned. I don't suppose you could
see your way clear to coming up here to protect
me, eh?

R.

To: rcraig@uofalberta.com
From: alchemist@babel.com
Subject: You'll never walk alone

Hon,

If I could I would in a second, but it's just
not possible. Sorry.

Things are going to be okay, though. After all,
there is no actual target for him to kill,
right? You don't have a husband you're not
telling me about, do you? So, even if he takes
the bait, nobody's going to get hurt.

Don't panic. See you tomorrow.

A.

There it was. Alchemist wasn't going to help me with
my moral quandary, after all. He had laid it neatly back in
my lap. If I wanted to get Chatgod's dander up and possibly get fired from the only steady work I had at present, it
would have to be my decision and mine alone. Of course,
if I wanted to have some back-up while a hired killer
roamed the streets, trying to find my mythical, irritating
husband, I had to make that decision on my own, too.

After three more cups of coffee and a long game of
Spiderette in the corner of my screen, I decided to call

Steve. After all, if a killer really did come to town looking for a man associated with me, Steve himself might be a target and in some danger. He had a right to know what foolishness I was cooking up. I had no misconceptions about my own strength or judgment as it related to the capacity for the police to do their job. I wasn't some sort of one-woman vigilante clean-up squad.

I had finally talked myself into calling Steve when the phone rang, startling me out of my socks. Who the heck would call at midnight? I picked up the phone and wiped up my spilled coffee with my sleeve.

"Are you okay?" Steve's voice sounded a little strained, as if there was someone with him, listening to his side of the conversation.

"Sort of, although phones ringing at this time of night scare me, even when I'm still up working."

"Yeah, sorry about that. You are still up though, right? Mind if I pop over? I think we need to talk."

"I'd like that. I have something I want to talk to you about, too."

"I can be there in fifteen minutes."

"I'll make tea."

"Great, Randy. See you then."

I wondered what Steve had to say to me that needed to be said at this time of the night. Maybe that was the way with great relationships; each partner knew when the other needed to talk. On the other hand, maybe that was more the situation of people who worked odd shifts; any time they could find to connect was a good time to talk.

Babel was closing down for the evening. Tracy and Dion were spooning in private messages to each other. They were separated by an ocean and still seemed to manage a strong relationship. Maybe there was hope for

Steve and me yet, separated by nothing more than a few quibbles about levels of commitment. Of course, that was provided neither of us was killed in the next few days. It's always the little things like that that make or break a relationship, I find.

CHAPTER 44

Things couldn't be too bad. Steve had stopped off to pick up doughnuts at Tim Hortons on the way to my place. I bit into my Canadian Maple while Steve inhaled his two honey glazed. Every once in a while sugar and lard is what is required, I don't care what Dr. Andrew Weil says.

The doughnut-induced smile on his face disappeared as I began to inform him of what Alchemist and I had set in motion.

"Oh God, Randy, you don't do things by halves, do you?"

"So I take it you think it's not a great idea?"

"I wouldn't say that. No, I'd say seriously insane idea. How's that?"

"Well, we needed to do something, Steve. I need to keep this Babel job. Once the last of my distance students check in for their exams, I might be out of a teaching job. I have no idea whether there's any more work from Grant MacEwan on the horizon. If Ray and his crowd decide to close Chatgod down, then there goes my livelihood. On the other hand, if we managed to corral the killer so that you and Ray could nab him, then we would be heroes, and we'd keep Babel going, and Chatgod wouldn't can me for insubordination, maybe."

"When were you planning on telling me about this plan? When the killer was knocking on your apartment door?"

"Well, actually, I was just about to call you when you phoned. Why did you phone so late, anyhow?"

Steve stretched back and set his feet on the edge of the coffee table. "Maybe I just wanted to see a smiling face before I went to sleep."

"And maybe you're full of manure, too. Tell me, why did you call? I know you were with someone when you were on the phone. Was it Ray Lopez?"

"No, it wasn't. It was my chief, who is, as you can imagine, not in the least happy that you are involved in this."

I cringed as I recalled my last run-in with Steve's boss, Staff Superintendent Keller. He had been condescendingly officious about the need to keep civilian personnel out of the middle of an investigation. I had inadvertently found myself up to my neck in a serious police matter, and Steve had felt caught in the middle of things. One of the main reasons we had called it quits at the end of the summer had been a residual effect of this man's attitude, as far as I was concerned.

"Oh Lord, I will bet Keller thinks I invented the Internet just to vex him and get in your hair."

Steve laughed. "I don't think he's gone as far as crediting you with the Internet, but let's say he wasn't altogether surprised when your name came up in conjunction with this joint task-force investigation."

"There's more going on than just the murder of Thea's husband, isn't there?" This was just a sudden guess on my part, but from the way Steve stiffened beside me, I figured I'd hit the mark.

"Honestly, Randy, the murder is way more than you

should be involved in, anyhow, so why don't we leave it at that?"

"Fine. I don't care in the least. This is my livelihood we're tromping all over, though. I do have an interest that is more than just prurient."

"That is one of the myriad things I love about you, Randy Craig. You are the only person I know who would use the word *prurient* in a conversation. I have no idea what half the words in the English language would do without you around to take them out for an airing once in a while."

Teasing me was Steve's way of deflecting my annoyance at his superiors. I could think of better ways to get my mind off police restrictions. Of course, with a potential killer aiming at me, the thought of being caught in the altogether wasn't altogether appealing. That reminded me of something I had been meaning to ask Steve.

"Do you wear your Kevlar vest all the time?" Okay, so maybe that was blurting it out a bit, but it occurred to me that Tremor looking for a husband to off might see Steve and not bother to check for wedding bands. The last thing I wanted was for Steve to walk into a bullet based on all of this.

"It's regulation. You know that." Steve looked at me, and I could see the gears turning. "I'm thinking I should requisition one for you for the time being, too. I'm not too sure that this guy isn't going to smell a rat and drill everyone he holds responsible."

"Nonsense, there are no rats in Alberta." I didn't sound as secure as I wanted to, though. Maybe a bulletproof vest would do something for my sense of security. I wondered if it would make me look fat.

"He's not going to know that unless he's already an

Albertan, though. Right? That's the trouble with all of this. I don't know how much stock to put in Ray Lopez's usage reports pointing out Edmonton as a hot spot. I don't know how much I want to trust your instincts on whether this Sanders guy is on the level, either. After all, I've heard of assassin games, but he's pretty long in the tooth to be playing games, isn't he? Maybe it's all a cover."

"Everything is a maybe at this point, aside from the fact that Thea's husband was electrocuted by his computer and a suspected killer is going to be contacting us tomorrow night in Babel. Aside from that, the only other certainty I know is that you are standing right here. And I love you."

I hadn't been meaning to say that out loud, so it came out as much a surprise to me as it did to Steve. His face seemed to lose an outer layer of stern solidity, as if a veneer was shattering off in little quarter-sized pieces. Underneath was a shining look that turned into a broad smile very quickly. About as quickly as it took him to close the space between us.

"Well, I'd say learning something like that is worth having a hired killer on your trail. Randy Craig, I love you, too."

CHAPTER 45

We decided to pop into Tremor's private room before we closed things up for the night. If Tremor was going to be stalking my man, I wanted to know everything I could about the guy.

The appropriately named Lair had been created quite some time ago, and there were a few signs of it. The background wallpaper was the same blobby purple that had been all over Babel when I first joined, before Alchemist had taken it upon himself to do a complete make-over of the place. If Tremor had created this private room before that changeover, then it had to be three or four months old, at least.

I couldn't figure out why either Alchemist or I hadn't tripped over it if it had been in Babel this long. Maybe Tremor had a way of keeping it current by not logging off, and that was how he seemed to be able to appear without logging in. Maybe he was continually changing the name of the room from inside. If that was the case, then maybe his IP address was either a low-grade constant buzz or recorded so long ago that it didn't show up on the daily lists.

Whatever the case, Tremor wasn't there now, and he hadn't left anything incriminating on the screen. Unless I worked through a process of digging into the logs, which would involve Chatgod, I would never know what had ever been discussed in that room. There might be no record of it at all, seeing as it was a private room.

I decided to leave myself connected to Babel through Lair, just as I suspected Tremor of doing, and check back in the morning for any activity. It would be a drain on the electricity, but no greater than someone leaving a store sign on all night. I put my Sierra Club conscience on hold for the night.

Steve stayed the night. Aside from the glow we had wrapped ourselves in with our—okay, *my*—admissions of vulnerability, I was feeling a lot more secure having him by my side through that night. We had determined that we'd call Steve's boss and Ray in the morning. Steve was going to organize a task-force meeting at my apartment, and we would run the operation like a sting, hoping to draw Tremor to us. All I could think was that I didn't want bullet holes over my mantelpiece. However, I was keeping my own council on that one. I was just relieved that Steve was taking this seriously and keeping me in the loop throughout it all.

We showered and dressed, ready for a long day—comfortable but presentable. Lord knew how many people were going to gather in my tiny apartment by the end of the day. Because of that, I raced about dusting and cleaning and putting away items too personal for casual eyes while Steve whipped up a couple of omelets in the kitchen. Our efficiency as a couple amazed me. The place was sparkling, we were fed and watered and nodding to each other that the day had better begin, and the clock hadn't yet hit 8:00 a.m. Man, this was going to be a long day. I poured myself another cup of coffee while Steve took the phone and his clipboard into the living room and started the ball rolling.

While he was calling Ray Lopez and his detachment, I got on-line and e-mailed Alchemist. I wanted to let him know I had called in the cavalry. In the first draft I spelled it *calvary*. I was uneasy about the Freudian slip. Did I really think I was heading toward self-sacrifice with this exercise?

Alchemist e-mailed back, saying not to worry, he would keep things on track in Babel through the day. He also mentioned that Chatgod had been in the chat room already, which was unusual in itself, and that there was an overwhelming number of private messages to Alvin for what reason he couldn't imagine, since none of them sounded particularly worried about anything.

That was odd. Aside from the women who seemed to fantasize about the mysterious host of Babel, the only people who usually contacted Alvin were folks who wanted to complain about someone else in the room or some function, like lag, which bothered most people more than traffic jams in real life. Apparently, these messages were all personal, like, "Haven't seen you around in a while, are you feeling okay, buddy?" I put it down to the social pulse of the room. The participants weren't sure what was up, but they felt something out of whack, and they felt it viscerally. Interesting psycho-sociological phenomenon.

I e-mailed him back, telling him I'd checked out Lair and was ready and able to jump into things at 5:00 p.m. my time, which was Tremor's appointed hour. In the meantime, I had work to do in the real world. Steve was now off the phone and making lists. He stopped long enough to tell me that Ray and one of his teammates was heading over, and that two of Steve's colleagues who worked predominantly in the computer-crime field were coming over, as well. One of them would be bringing Kevlar for everyone, as well as some sort of plastic wrap for the windows that would undercut the possibility of shattering glass everywhere. Boy, that made me feel all warm and cozy.

Ray and Kate Brouder, who had flown in from Florida the day before, showed up with four large cups of Tim Hortons coffee and a box of Timbits. Kate was an interesting study in contrasts. She was a very attractive woman in her mid-forties, who obviously knew how to pack for international travel. At present she was wearing an emerald green big sweater and brown suede pants. Behind that stylish façade, though, she had the demeanor of a departmental secretary, that sort of efficient but comforting presence who could whip up a Thanksgiving dinner for twenty just as easily as sort out class size problems with one or two well-placed phone calls. She seemed like someone who would be a terrific grandmother when the time came. When she spoke, however, everything was so precise and pointed that you had the feeling you were listening to the CEO of a Fortune 500 company. I was betting that people underestimated Kate Brouder all the time, to their eternal chagrin, and that Kate knowingly used that as part of her arsenal. She and Ray seemed to get along very well, and that—coupled with the fact that she didn't turn up her nose at my apartment—made me willing to give her a chance.

I wasn't as sure of the folks from Edmonton's Finest. Steve didn't know them all that well, and they seemed to be a team unto themselves. Detective Scott Lewis was a slender, nervous type, who pulled on his mustache as he spoke. Detective Iain McCorquodale, on the other hand, had a booming laugh and didn't seem to be taking things seriously enough. Of course, these guys were normally on the hunt for money launderers and child pornographers, but surely a hired killer warranted a little bit of decorum? Maybe it was just that he seemed a bit blasé when handing me a bulletproof vest, as if we were all overreacting a tad, that made me rankle.

My apartment, which was already tiny, was getting a little on the crowded side. It didn't help that we were all middling to large people, not a single one of us under five-eight, and Steve skewing the averages from his lofty six-three. I decided to perch on a corner of the sofa to make room. Kate took the willow chair, and Ray sat at the computer desk, tinkering with a program that was supposed to duplicate the events on my computer onto his laptop without letting outsiders know, a sort of high-tech phone tap.

Lewis and McCorquodale were taping the windows and making me realize I should dust my venetian blinds more often. Steve was on the phone once again.

"Randy," called Ray. "Would you mind coming here for a minute? I want to see if we're okay now." I headed over to the desk, and Ray moved to his laptop, which he had set up on the kitchen table. "Okay, you're still logged in to Babel. Open a new window, though, and let's see how that works for my mirror site."

I opened a new window and brought up the Edmonton weather page, which was sort of depressing. The next five days were going to be really cold. I looked over at Ray, who put up a thumb in response, indicating that it had shown up on his screen. I looked beyond him to Detective McCorquodale, who was taping the kitchen window. Tremor had better not shoot out my kitchen window if the temperature was intending to plummet to minus 25°C by tomorrow night.

Steve then called me into the living room and we went over the biography of coupleness he and I had been working up to fool Tremor. We had to muck into the Alberta Stats site and salt the record of a wedding some ten years ago in order to cover our tracks. If Tremor was any kind of self-preservationist, he would research his subjects. Steve was being turned into an insurance broker and I was left as a sessional lecturer, just in case bits of my background had leeched out into the general discussions in Babel over the past while.

According to our fiction, Steve was disinterested and distant, and I thought he might be having an affair with a woman in his office. Alchemist and I had linked up because of my feelings of despair for my marriage. Now it seemed as if Steve was unwilling to grant me a divorce. We weren't sure yet whether it was because he was just a dogmatic bastard who insisted on keeping what was his, or whether it was because he was intending to hide our mutual assets and leave me broke. I was leaning to the latter because I figured that might tempt Tremor into thinking there would be more money. Steve didn't like being painted as materialistic, even in hypothetical situations, so he was holding out for the tenacious bastard persona. We canvased the others. Kate just shrugged and said one was as good as the other, while Ray was voting with me. Lewis liked the idea of Steve being a bastard, and McCorquodale dug into his pocket for a loonie to toss. I called heads, mainly because I've always been a Tom Stoppard fan, and Steve won.

Okay, I wanted to have my husband whacked because he wouldn't sign divorce papers. Maybe I was just as guilty as Steve of not wanting to seem the nasty one in our scenario. I shrugged and tried to think my way through this melodrama. It was such a weird twist to be trying to create a vision of Steve as someone I was so sick of being tied to that I was willing to pay to get rid of him. How ironic that this should happen on the same day that I had actually decided I wanted to spend the rest of my life with him. Of course, if I didn't get this right and it didn't work exactly as planned, that time frame could be very short indeed. I shook my head and tried to concentrate anew.

The phone rang at the same time as the computer peeped to let me know there was more mail for me. Ray could read my mail once I'd opened it on my screen, but I still had to be at my computer to initiate the opening. Steve moved to get the phone, and I headed back to the desk in the dining room.

The e-mail was from Alchemist. He wanted me to know that Sanders had been in Babel looking for me. Right now he was flirting with Vixen, who seemed to be spending the better part of the day holding court in there, but Alchemist had thought I should be warned that he was barely veiling the fact that we'd had a face-to-face meet. Of course, Alchemist knew that we had, so he might be reading things into Sanders's postings that others wouldn't see, but still. I wrote back to thank him for the heads-up. It was just as well we'd decided not to monkey with my bio too much for Tremor if Sanders was in there spreading innuendo.

Of course, Sanders also knew that Steve was a cop. A whole lot depended on Sanders not spilling the beans at an inopportune time. Part of me wondered if we should have taken Sanders into our confidence during the planning of this sting. I had almost e-mailed him, and then the whole assassin discussion returned to my mind. I still couldn't equate the fellow I'd had coffee with, with that sort of adolescent game. There had been something a little too self-aware and cynical about Winston Graham. Yes, he had no qualms about signing up for junior-level courses in new fields, but he came across as a middle-aged man aiming at filling his mind with new experiences and ideas—a last gasp at becoming a Renaissance man. I just couldn't see him indulging in this level of horseplay.

On the other hand, I could see him exploring the possibilities of murder as an esoteric exercise. What if Sanders was Tremor? Had Ray and Steve and I come up with enough reasons for that not being a scenario? I couldn't remember, and there were too many people in my apartment for me to think clearly.

If only we had a really clear idea of who Tremor was. All we knew was that he was someone who knew his way around Babel so well that he could create and maintain a private room for some length of time. It could be Sanders. It could be Vixen. It could be Milan himself or Thea. It could be Alchemist. It could be Ray Lopez, for that matter. I knew it wasn't me. That was about all I was certain of.

Why would I think it was Sanders? Well, aside from the assassin talk I'd caught him at, there was that comment by Ray that had so much activity out of Edmonton. If Tremor was keeping a room going all the time in Babel, maybe he was located in Edmonton.

Oh, that was a nice thought. What if the killer was less than twenty minutes away? When we called him up and set him on target, we might have way less time than we thought. Of course, maybe that was why there were so many people in my apartment. Perhaps I was the last person in the group to realize the possibility that the killer was from here.

If it wasn't Sanders, then who? A faceless stranger named Tremor or a faceless colleague named Alchemist? Well, if it was Alchemist behind all this, he wouldn't be showing up guns blazing since he would know this was all a scam. On the other hand, he would also know we were after him and that Steve wasn't an unwanted husband but my boyfriend, and a very necessary part of my life. It couldn't be Alchemist.

As if he were reading my thoughts, Ray cleared his throat beside me. "Do we have any actual biographical info on this pal Alchemist of yours?"

I turned to him, wondering how much of my thoughts he had read.

"His name is Tim Ross. He's a freelance IT guy. He lives in Elburn, Illinois. He has worked for Chatgod and Babel for about six months longer than I have. Up until I was hired, he was the sole monitor for the site. That's about all I know. Why?"

"Well, according to the Whois? database, the Elburn phone book, and the US Taxation Roll, there is no such person as Tim Ross at that location."

CHAPTER 46

When I was in grad school, a friend of mine used to play a game she called "worst case scenario," where she would think up all sorts of wondrously gruesome outcomes to any particular situation. Her theory was that, since what happens is never what we expect, if we think up horrific outcomes, they will be eliminated as possibilities. It had seemed to make sense at the time, although that could have been the beer talking, so at various times since then I have indulged in the game. Of all the possibilities I had been able to conjure about this sting operation to catch Tremor, the idea that Alchemist wasn't true blue had never occurred to me. Damn.

If he wasn't who he said he was, then who was he? If he was the killer, then I was completely sunk. Either he would keep totally away from us, knowing our every move, or he might be hiding in the laundry room of the apartment right now, ready to kill us all and wipe our hard drives of any clue about his identity.

As if I didn't have enough to worry about. I looked at my apartment, overflowing with law-enforcement officers. Was I some sort of magnet for hassle, drawing danger and fearfulness to me the way other people collect stamps?

It was as if Steve could read my mind. He put a hand on the back of my neck, and started massaging the tension out of my shoulders.

"You are not the Typhoid Mary of the Internet, Randy. This is all going to work out, and Babel should thank you for clearing things up. Trust me."

I was just trying to trust that we were both going to come out of this alive. I leaned back into Steve's hand, thinking just how strong he was, when Ray called to me from his perch at the kitchen table.

"Things are starting to happen, Randy. I think you'd better get over here."

I sat down with a sort of fatalistic knowledge that whatever happened, this was the Rubicon. The moment I typed anything, we were going to just have to go with the flow. I looked at the screen. I had both the main room in Babel and Lair open on my screen. Alchemist was in Lair, greeting Tremor, who had just arrived.

"It's showtime," I overheard Detective McCorquodale muttering, in a Bob Fosse homage. I took a deep breath and logged in to Lair.

Chimera: Hi there.

Alchemist: *kiss* Hi hon.

Tremor: Evening. So, time is money. What can I do for you folks?

CHAPTER 47

For some reason, I had Marlon Brando in his Stanley Kowalski persona in mind as I read Tremor's words. He tended to affect a working-class dialect in his writing, which I knew wasn't necessarily how he might actually talk. Few of us do write exactly as we talk, after all. Each medium requires its own stylistics.

However, I could almost hear him scratching himself and chewing gum while he watched Alchemist and my little pseudo-courtship rituals. It was awkward to begin with, trying to act all lovey-dovey with Steve and the rest of the Happy Gang looking over my shoulder. It was even worse because I was trying to adjust my thinking about Alchemist. If I couldn't trust him on-line, who could I look to for support? Well, given him as an unknown and Tremor as the probable killer, I decided my chances were better kissing up to Alchemist.

Chimera: Am I late, sweetheart? I tried to get here on time. Nice to see you, Tremor. So, what have you been talking about already?

Alchemist: We were basically waiting for you, love.

PM from Alchemist to Chimera: Tell him you were just at the bank, and that you can have five thousand dollars ready by the end of the weekend.

PM from Chimera to Alchemist: Five thousand? How do we know that's the price? I thought you said you two hadn't started talking?

Alchemist: Did you get to the bank, hon?

So he was going to force it. Fine. If I could pretend I had a dud husband housed somewhere about, I could manage a meager five thousand imaginary dollars.

Chimera: You bet! In fact, I have five thousand dollars in my purse as we type.

PM from Alchemist to Chimera: You don't have to tell him you have the money on you. That might be too dangerous.

PM from Chimera to Alchemist: Whatever it takes to push this thing to closure, doncha know? Are we sure five thousand is the magic number?

Tremor: Well, that sounds like you're playing my song. I gather you folks would like to hire my expertise?

Alchemist: Indeed. You come highly recommended.

Tremor: By whom?

Alarm bells were ringing for me. I didn't want to get Milan into the soup, in case Tremor had told him not to say anything, but we had to tell him something he'd believe. The other thing was, I couldn't imagine Stanley Kowalski saying *whom*.

Alchemist and I had decided we would use Milan's name rather than Thea's, since presumably Tremor already had Thea's address but might not be as readily able to attack Milan. This was all presuming that Thea and Milan hadn't been stupid enough to tell Tremor everything about themselves. Since these were people who had allegedly hired an on-line killer, one couldn't be too sure.

I was going to leave it to Alchemist to shop Milan, though. I couldn't bring myself to do it.

Alchemist: Well, he was the soul of discretion, but it was Milan.

Tremor: I see.

I could feel the weight of every person in my apartment leaning over my shoulder, waiting to see what was about to happen. I was beginning to feel a headache starting right behind my left eye.

Chimera: So, we were wondering if you could do for us what you did for him and Thea.

Tremor: I take it you have a nuisance problem?

Chimera: Yes, my problem. We were wondering if you could take care of it.

Tremor: Well, before I do I'll need to know a little something about your general life and activities. And your husband's schedule and activities, as well. My services depend a great deal on understanding the habits of my customers.

There was nothing he had said yet that could pinpoint him as a killer. I wondered if he had a script to keep him from divulging anything incriminating on the screen. If he was good enough to come and go as he pleased in the chat room, he was smart enough to understand screen captures and logged conversations. Hell, he might even be canny enough to suspect I had an apartment full of Internet task-force personnel. The latter was still beyond me, and I could see them actually surrounding me.

Alchemist: Well, we're not quite sure what you will need to know. Maybe you should ask us some questions and we can answer them for you.

Chimera: We also need to know a few things, like costs and guarantees and times, and all that.

Tremor: Plenty of time for that, ma'am. But you're right. Maybe I should ask you some questions. First off,

I should warn you that, if you haven't already got life insurance in place, purchasing it in the near future will seem rather suspicious to both insurance investigators and law-enforcement officers. The object, of course, is to be as easygoing as possible. Accidents happen, after all, and no one can deny that. Anything that makes a tragic accident appear to be anything other than what it is would be unfortunate and might lead to a lot of unnecessary questions being asked.

Chimera: Our insurance is relatively minor and purchased to cover the mortgage, that's all.

Maybe that was what had triggered the investigations concerning Thea's husband's death. I wished all of a sudden that I could remember his name. It seemed awful to think that he had died horribly, and no one was mourning him or even considering him, except in relation to his murderous wife. I wonder if Thea had taken out a recent insurance policy on him. I turned toward the room behind me.

"What was Thea's husband's name, again?" I asked Ray and Kate.

"Why do you need to know that?" asked Kate, peering at the mirror screen over Ray's shoulder. Maybe she thought I would screw things up on-screen, because I saw her squeeze Ray's shoulder, warningly.

"Don't worry, Randy. I know this all seems impersonal and weird. I'll tell you his name later, though. We don't need it slipping out in front of Tremor. You're doing a great job." Ray was smiling encouragingly, like a swim coach leaning over the gunnel of the boat, luring me across Lake Erie.

Tremor: That's fine, then. I like to hear that sort of thing. Greedy people are not my favorite sort. I myself carry only enough insurance to cover litigation in case of accidents.

This guy was definitely no longer sounding like Stanley Kowalski. Maybe Dick Cavett had taken up contract killing in his dotage.

Alchemist: So what else do you need to know? I can assure you we will not be doing anything to call attention to ourselves. We have no intention of becoming the center of any untoward investigation.

Maybe it was catching. Alchemist was beginning to sound like Lloyd Robertson. I tried to calm myself by rationalizing that people do tend to take on each other's style when conversing, but it was spooking me. What if Tremor and Alchemist were the same person, and this was all some sort of show being put on for all the folks wedged into my apartment? I didn't dare call him on it, though, in case I was wrong. This was the closest we were likely to get to Tremor. That is, unless Tremor got a whole lot closer to us. That didn't bear thinking about. I accepted a fresh cup of coffee from Detective Lewis and turned my full attention back to what was happening in Lair. I noticed in passing that the main room was starting to fill up. What would happen if Chatgod popped in and discovered both Alchemist and me hidden away in Lair? What if Chatgod was Tremor? I just hoped Geoff L and his heavy-metal lyrics stayed off-line tonight. I wasn't in any mood or position to multitask any more than I was already.

Tremor: Glad to hear it. Okay. So here's what happens. I ask some questions. You put some money in a bus station locker and the key to the locker somewhere I tell you, and then you just go about your regular business. Pretty soon, you don't have any troubles any more. Easy as that.

Chimera: How soon is pretty soon?

Tremor: You can't rush perfection, ma'am. However, within forty-eight hours of drop-off at the bus station, you should be breathing a bit easier.

Alchemist: Sounds fine to me.

Chimera: Okay by me. So, shoot.

Yikes. Talk about your basic Freudian slip.

Tremor: What is it that your husband does for a living?

I blanked. I couldn't for the life of me remember what Steve and I had been working on earlier in the day for our cover story. I leaned back and whispered to Steve, as if somehow Tremor would overhear me if I spoke out loud.

"What is it that you do? I can't remember any of this. I can hardly type, let alone think."

"Don't sweat it, babe, I've got it all right here. A cheat sheet. I'm an insurance broker."

"You're what? Isn't that going to look odd now that I've said we hardly have any insurance?"

"Nah," Iain McCorquodale tossed into the mix. "It's like the shoemaker's children going barefoot."

"I thought that was his elves who went barefoot," mused Ray Lopez. "Or is that a different story?"

"Okay," I muttered, scanning the rest of the paper Steve had handed me, and typing "He's an insurance broker" onto the screen, waiting to see what Tremor's response was going to be to that.

Tremor: Ha. Sort of like the shoemaker's children, right?

There was a snort over my left shoulder from McCorquodale.

Chimera: I guess so.

Tremor: Does he keep business hours or what?

Chimera: He is in the office half days, usually mornings,

and in the afternoons and evenings he goes on calls, or takes meetings with corporate clients.

To me, this sounded like way too much detail for a wife to know about her husband's work, but Tremor seemed to be buying it. Who knows, maybe husbands and wives shared all the minutiae and butt-ends of their days. Maybe that's what Steve and I really had to look forward to, talk over dinner of police paperwork and workable classroom techniques. Of course, that didn't sound too bad. I was just hoping there were going to be some days to share when this was all over.

Tremor: Sounds like a nice predictable life. Does he have his own office where he works?

We hadn't worked this out. I looked over to Steve, who shrugged, so I turned toward Ray, who nodded.

Chimera: Yes. A corner office. Probably things would have been different if getting that office hadn't been so important.

Alchemist: That's long ago and far away, sugar. Things are going to get a whole lot better real soon.

Tremor: You can bank on that. Speaking of, where will this bus station be located?

Chimera: You mean what city?

Tremor: Yes.

Chimera: It's downtown Edmonton. Canada.

Tremor: Ah, the Great White North.

Chimera: Is that a problem?

Tremor: Nothing is a problem, ma'am. I am in the business of alleviating problems, right?

Alchemist: Right.

Tremor: Okay. The down payment goes into a sports bag and is left in the bus station. The key goes in a Fed Ex envelope addressed to L. Cranston at the YMCA,

Edmonton. Nothing will happen until the initial fee has been processed, of course. Then, once my end of the bargain has been fulfilled, you will be contacted for the remainder. Agreed?

Chimera: Agreed.

Alchemist: Agreed.

Tremor: Okay. What is your husband's name, and what are your names?

Here it was. The moment when we could cut and run. Nothing had actually been said, besides the fact that I had told an ax-murderer what city I lived in, the one cautionary step I had always tried to avoid on-line to this point. I craned my neck to check the folks behind me. It was as if everyone was holding their breath. I reached out to the keyboard with both hands shaking.

Chimera: His name is Steve Browning and my name is Randy Craig.

Our names hung there on that purple blobby screen, and I wished desperately to haul them back. There was such a feeling of invasion and vulnerability, knowing that a murderer was seeing the real me. And then, of course, as if that wasn't bad enough, I saw what went up on the screen after that.

Alchemist: My name is Tim Ross and I live just outside Chicago.

What a rat.

Tremor: You'll be hearing from me. G'night.

He logged out, or at least it said he had. I wasn't so sure he hadn't just created that appearance. His IP address hadn't yet dropped off the upper screen, so I wasn't taking any chances. I stuck to private messages with Alchemist.

PM from Chimera to Alchemist: Do you think he's really gone?

PM from Alchemist to Chimera: Not sure, but it's best to be safe. So, I guess the money stuff is going to happen at your end?

PM from Chimera to Alchemist: I think it's already happening.

Kate and Steve nodded to confirm my theory. There were three cell phones and my land line all working at once. Ray was still following things from my screen on his, but he was also transmitting something, probably a log of the conversation and the pertinent screen captures.

If Tremor was as adept at the Internet as we thought he was, it wouldn't take him long to have tracked down this address. If, God forbid, he was already in Edmonton, it wouldn't take him long to get to the Y. I could hear Lewis requisitioning undercover cops to go and register into the Y immediately so they could be on-site in the lobby when Tremor came to get his mail.

Suddenly I didn't want to be on-line anymore. I couldn't stand the thought of chatting with Alchemist. Dealing with Tremor had exhausted me. I knew I could probably bow out of talking with Alchemist, and he wouldn't suspect a thing. He knew I was scared silly by all of this. The thing was, I still had several hours of monitoring to sit through. Besides, it's not as if I could have signed off and flaked out. My apartment was still full of law enforcement officers. I slumped down in my chair, and yawned.

More coffee appeared at my elbow. So not everything about having an infestation of cops was to be sneezed at. However, it was my party and I'd kvetch if I wanted.

CHAPTER 48

I am not sure how I made it through the night. Every time I heard a movement in the hallway my heart jumped and raced. And boy, was there a lot of movement in the hall. Ray and Steve had commandeered what seemed like an army, and my apartment was mission control. If Tremor was already in Edmonton, casing the joint, he wouldn't stick around long, I figured.

Ray was sure he wasn't here yet, though. There was someone watching the airport and someone else covering the train station, the bus station, and the Red Arrow express bus to Calgary. I had a hard time envisioning a hired gun riding in on the Greyhound, but I supposed stranger things had happened. Arriving at the bus depot would make him good and close to pick up the money.

Several cops were already tenanted in the downtown Y, and my neighbors, including Mr. MacGregor, had been moved out of their apartments to stay in the campus apartment hotel down the street. I was torn between being happy that my neighbors were apprised of the situation and out of danger, and being worried that they all now knew my business and were going to be annoyed with me.

My monitoring duties were finally done for the night, and I tried to sleep, with no real luck. Steve and Ray tried to shoo the extraneous bodies out of the apartment, but there was a constant undercurrent of movement and muttering in the outside room. I finally got up, got a clean pair of jeans, a fresh sweatshirt, and underwear out of my chest of drawers and went into the bathroom to take a shower and dress.

When I came out, everyone looked up with astonishment, as if they couldn't imagine why I wasn't sleeping like a baby. I shrugged, and went to pour myself some more coffee.

"Randy, you look great," Ray enthused, "and you're just in time to see what's up. We've got the money in the bus-station locker and the Fed Ex envelope is on its way to the Y. We were going to just deliver it there ourselves, and then we determined that he might be tracing the package number on-line, so we figured normal channels were the best route there. So, now we wait. Steve's address is covered everywhere and should lead to here. Now, it might give Tremor pause when he arrives here to find an insurance broker in a small university apartment, but we decided to add a condo sign to the front of the building and create a locked door front." He noticed my shock, and hurried on, "Don't worry, it's a very tasteful small brass sign just under the numbers. No one will even see it, and it will be gone before the rest of the tenants come back. This way, he'll think you two are some sort of urban yuppies. After all, it's impossible to tell how big the apartments are from the outside of the building, and once he's inside, we've got him."

"So, we just sit and wait for him to come and kill Steve?"

"It's a little bit more complex than that. We figure he'll case the joint first, and we can nab him then. We don't want him actually doing any damage."

"I would hope not."

"Randy, don't worry. I am not going to get killed."

"I don't know. It all feels just slightly off. Maybe one of the things is that I just don't know where Alchemist stands in all this. And what about all the Edmonton spikes on the system that Ray was talking about before? Has anyone managed to explain that one yet? And is anyone keeping an eye on Sanders? There are just too many loose ends, and meanwhile we're sitting here with a spotlight on us and a killer coming for us." I had a hard time clamping my jaw shut, although I knew I had to stop babbling.

Steve put his arm around my shoulders and squeezed me to him. "The sooner all of this goes down, the sooner everything can get back to normal. Don't worry, hon. There is nobody who can get through to us. The chances of him figuring out it's a trap and running are way higher than of him getting through and doing the job."

There is nothing worse than being a sitting duck. I wasn't allowed to go anywhere, because I had to be ready to take any e-mails from Tremor or Alchemist, or, indeed, anyone, to indicate I was still on the up and up. Since I didn't have to be in Babel till 7:00, it was decided I shouldn't go near it. Instead, I watched as Ray logged in as Emilio Lizardo.

Detectives Lewis and McCorquodale had left for the night, but Kate Brouder returned about 8:00 a.m., just as I was noticing the sun rise. She had brought a bag of Egg McMuffins, which smelled divine. I wolfed down two of them and found myself looking longingly at a third. She laughed and urged me on.

"They're no good once they're cold. Go for it!" Danger obviously makes me hungry. I wondered how many people ever had to learn that about themselves, as I bit into another McMuffin. Kate was full of information about the rest of the Banzais, as she referred to the Austin task force.

"We're trying to cross-reference all the airline manifests into Austin for three days prior to Charlie Banyon's death, to compare them to reservations and entries at the Edmonton International. You'd think, with all the Homeland Security happening, that this wouldn't be a problem. To hear the airlines tell it, though, we're asking for the moon."

Ray nodded as he helped himself to breakfast. He excused himself to go back to the hotel for a shower while I tuned into the little nugget of information Kate had slipped in there. Thea's husband's name had been Charlie. There. I didn't have to think of him in the abstract anymore. Well, technically, since he was dead, I supposed that's all I could do—but that would be splitting hairs. I walked through mission control into the living room, bumping my hip against the edge of the kitchen table as I passed it.

Steve noticed me rubbing my hip.

"Careful, Randy. Your reactions will likely be slower and your dexterity limited. You've been up more than twenty-four hours and your body doesn't like that sort of thing. You have to know to ease back on expectations, and conserve the energy you do have."

"What about if something dreadful happens while you're tired and slowed down?"

"Never underestimate the power of adrenalin, kiddo," he grinned. "You just have to trust that it will be there when you need it."

I was going to trust Steve on that one and hoped it held true for the both of us. What had I got us into? I knew that most of the reason I was so upset was that I no longer felt I could trust Alchemist, and he had been the one to really get me into this whole plan. Was it all a trap? Who the heck was Alchemist, anyway? Was he the killer? Was he in on it with Tremor? What role in all of this was he playing?

Suddenly, it came to me. It had never dawned on me before that Alchemist and Alvin shared the first two letters of their names. What if Alchemist was actually Chatgod in disguise?

I moved toward my computer, trying to puzzle it out as I drew closer. Why would Chatgod hire me to be a monitor if he already was monitoring things? Of course, Alchemist took a different shift from mine, but he was around an awful lot to cover for me, and he would often make it feel covert, as if we were pulling one over on the boss. Would the actual boss play with an employee that way?

He might if he were testing my loyalty. I ripped backward through my memory, trying to remember if I'd said anything horrible about Chatgod and his weird ways. I couldn't recall any particular gaffes, but who knew what I'd said in passing that might have been construed as an insult?

There was a sort of validation of Alchemist's being Chatgod, if I thought of him as Henry V wandering disguised among his troops. He was evangelical enough about chatting and community to be ever-watching. Maybe he just hired one person to watch while he slept and merely invented the Alchemist persona to make me feel as if I was joining some sort of corporation rather than a one-man operation. Of course, if that were the case, why invent a mythical Illinois alter-ego?

"Kate?" I asked, coming into the kitchen. "You met with Chatgod, didn't you, when you were down in Florida?"

Kate looked up from her mapping of the area around my apartment building.

"Yes. His name is Alvin Epstein, and he runs the server out of his home in Coral Gables. He funds the chat-room through advertising banners and uses the chat room figures to demonstrate his demographics on the pulse of the Internet. Our supervisors were initially concerned that he might be fronting porn; but I think his master plan is to sell the chat software, since he has done some interesting tweaks on the program, or maybe to see if he can be bought out by one of the community sites to run the chat as a sort of town square forum."

"What did you think of him as a person?"

"He seems quite nice, in a computer geeky sort of way. He's better-looking than many of the fellows I went through computer science with, and slightly older. He's tall, and sort of monkish."

"Would you ever think of him as a smart aleck, or a joker?"

"Alvin? No. Definitely not. I don't think the man has a sense of humor. At least not about Babel. It's his baby, there's no doubt about that."

I told her about my theory of Alchemist being Chatgod. It was interesting that our supposedly fictional persona, Alvin, was really Chatgod's name. From the sound of things, though, there was no way that Alvin Epstein could joke and tease every night on-line as Alchemist. I trusted Kate's judgment. She was connected to the computer world and knew the temperaments of the folks who inhabited it. If she said Alvin Epstein didn't have a sense of humor, I wouldn't even bother assuming he could turn it on and off in his presentation of Alchemist. So, who was Alchemist?

Steve and Kate sat and listened to my worries, which was really good of them, since I think they both wanted to be involved in some other, more concrete, element of planning for the siege.

"Why don't we get him to come clean?" suggested Steve.

"How, though?" I still wasn't sure that Alchemist wasn't up to his nipples in this whole scheme. Lie to me once, and I can never be sure you aren't lying about everything.

"Why don't we pull him in physically? Tell him that the task force needs him here. We can authorize transportation from anywhere. You get on to him and plead with him to get up here to help you out in person. Who knows? It might not be a bad idea, especially if Tremor intends to case out the whole set-up. If he thinks your lover is coming into town, things might head to a boil even quicker."

"I have a feeling Tremor would suggest against this," I said, slowly. "Remember that whole warning against extra insurance. This is a guy who wants to keep it very low profile. I think he wants his kills to look like accidents. In fact, who knows how many disappearances in Babel might not actually have been Tremor's doing?"

It was Steve's turn to question Kate's take on Chatgod. "This Alvin guy. You don't think contract killing is his real reason for setting up Babel, do you?"

"That's the twenty-four-thousand-dollar question, Steve. Ray still isn't sure. My take on it is no, Alvin Epstein is just a minor-league chat guru whose place is being used without his knowledge. I am pushing to get chat logs from him dating back to the beginning of Babel in 1995, though, because I think Randy is right—Tremor has been working his schtick from Babel for a lot longer than just the last few months. It's too smooth to be a new operation. I want to look through the logs for names that are seen regularly, and then drop out. I am betting anything that Tremor suggests to his clients that they resume their chatting habits in another venue."

I told Kate about Maia and Vixen, and suggested she get in touch with them to discuss regulars who were no longer regulars. If anyone kept track of the Babel community, it would be those two. Meanwhile, I was still working on the problem of uncovering Alchemist.

"So, suppose I e-mail him and ask him to fly in here. He knows you all are here, and that Steve is completely in the loop. He knows that Tremor is on his way. Why would he come?"

"Because he's your friend, your compatriot?"

"Puhleese. This is a chat room, not a sorority."

"Maybe he would like to be in on all the excitement."

"Maybe he should be monitoring our use of the software."

"Ooh, that's a good one. What if he is the only one who could coordinate the on-line activities, and the task force wants to second him to their team while this operation is *in situ*?" The two of them looked at me. I shrugged. So I read a lot of spy novels. It's not as if either of them needed a dictionary to understand me. I poured my ninety-seventh cup of coffee and tried to see the problem from all sides.

I ask Alchemist to join us, with the blessing and request of Ray and the team. He has to tell us where to send the ticket, and he arrives. We discover, when we are face to face, who the heck he really is and why he is using an alias to register in Babel. An alternate possibility would be that I ask him to join us, and he bursts out of the laundry room with an Uzi and kills us all for discovering that he is really the hired killer of Babel.

What was it about the laundry room that was spooking me, anyway? All that was there were the boiler, three washing machines, three corresponding dryers, a set of drying racks, one table for folding towels, and the recycling bins. The doors had been locked ever since we'd found a homeless fellow bunking down in the corner. It wasn't so much that he was frightening (although he was a big, shambling sort of guy who didn't seem all that reasonable) as the fact that he had been urinating in the corner of the room, giving the air a decidedly feral reek to it. That had been several years ago, but I still opened the door wide and hit the light switch before descending the two steps into the room.

So, Alchemist was likely not in my laundry room. Right. He either showed up and everything had a logical explanation, or he showed up and killed us all. There had to be some other possibilities, but I couldn't really think any up on the spot.

Steve urged me to write to Alchemist. Kate had been on the phone to Ray at the hotel, and he had okayed the idea of inviting Alchemist to mission control at their expense.

I sat down to the computer and hit the Eudora icon on my desktop. The e-mail program opened right away and dumped two or three pieces of spam into my Inbox. I hit the New Mail button, and typed:

```
To: alchemist@babel.com
From: rcraig@uofalberta.com
Subject: invitation
```

Hi Hon,

Things are heating up here, as you might expect. One of the things is that Ray and his team would like to invite you to come here and coordinate the on-line operations so that we're all running 100% smoothly. I would sure feel better if you were here. They will pay the plane ticket and hotel. Please? It's really spooky here, just sitting and waiting.

What do you say?
Love,
Randy

I had Steve and Kate look over the e-mail before I sent it. Ray showed up with lunch before there was a reply. A few more days of this and, if I wasn't a corpse, then I was at least going to be corpulent. I couldn't figure out why policemen weren't all pasty-faced and doughy, with all the takeout crap they ate during these stakeouts. Kate assured me that stakeouts weren't the norm and that they usually did eat much better. Not that I was complaining. The mandarin chicken salad was delicious, and the bread-sticks were still warm. I was just polishing off the last few slivered almonds in the bottom of the plastic bowl when I heard the telltale ping from my computer.

I had mail.

CHAPTER 49

To: rcraig@uofalberta.com
From: alchemist@babel.com
Subject: Re: invitation

Hey Randy,

Let everyone know I am more than willing to help,
but I can't get away at the moment. We could link
up with the same sort of ISEE program that Ray
linked to your monitor if that would help, though
I don't think I could make much difference from
my end of operations. Of course, I will be available to Ray for any questions he might have. In
fact, if you want to hang around in Babel, I can
give Ray the same sort of powers that you and I
have to be invisible. I am not sure that it would
fool a Tremor, though. The more I think about it,
the more I think he really has infiltrated right
into the guts of the program.

Sorry, chica, I can't come hold your hand, as
much as I would like to. However, you have Steve
for that, right?

Courage, ma brave.
Alchemist

Well, that was that. He was just point-blank refusing
to come. So much for that possible scenario.

"Maybe he can be ordered to come," Kate spoke over my shoulder, reading Alchemist's response for herself. Damn, I hate people reading over my shoulder. Alchemist ordered here? By whom? The president of the United States? I admit that I didn't know all that much about American day-to-day operations, but wasn't there something in all that declaring of independence that made people rebel against being told what to do?

Ray and Kate laughed when I voiced some of what I'd been thinking.

"I wasn't thinking of the POTUS," Kate explained. "I was thinking of Alchemist's boss—Chatgod. Maybe we can have him order Alchemist to get his butt on a plane, wherever he happens to be, and join us. After all, Chatgod is in no position to avoid helping the investigation. If it gets out that Babel is the office of a contract killer, there would go all the good will he has been building and hoping to sell to Amazon or Pharmacia or whichever big site he wants to peddle his town-hall project to. I think he might be very motivated to push Alchemist our way."

We decided that Kate would be the best suited to tackle Chatgod, and she took out her Palm Pilot and whipped off an e-mail to my illusive bossman.

We didn't have to wait quite as long for a reply from him as we had from Alchemist. The reply was a stunner, though. Kate bounced it to Ray's and my respective e-mail programs so we could see his words for ourselves. I could hardly believe them, even reading them for myself. I swear as I read it, I could feel the plate tectonics of my world shifting below my feet.

To: kbrouder@callisto.com
From: chatgod@babel.com
Subject: Re: my employee

Dear Ms. Brouder:

I am afraid that, as much as I wish to comply
with all your needs in this unfortunate business, I cannot order my employee Alchemist, aka
Tim Ross, to your side.

I hate to admit this, but Alchemist is not an
actual person. He is a self-replenishing, evolv-
ing artificial intelligence. He absorbs information delivered, has a constant search program
running behind his interface, and relates to
each person in a manner which he or she will
most easily respond to.

To put it crudely, Alchemist is a bot. He may
well be my greatest creation, although I am not
sure of his practical monetary value. He is at
your disposal on-line, but he will be of no mus-
cular use to you.

Yours sincerely,
Alvin Epstein
Babel, Inc.

"Holy cipher, Batman," Steve whispered, "and to
think I was getting jealous of that guy."

"No wonder you'd be jealous, Steve," Ray said. "The
Alchemist who was responding to Randy would be
absorbing her style and values and responding in kind.
Like-mind reacting to like-mind. Brilliant concept.
Chatgod sets Alchemist going to keep track of things and
give Randy abridged reports of the day's activities, and in
the meantime, Alchemist expands based on his interaction with Randy. If she makes a literary comment, the bot

is automatically reading the whole text in the background, which is then part of his world view."

"So, the more I talked with Alchemist, the more like me he became? Did he act like me to other people? Would he have sounded like me when talking with Kate, for instance?"

"Chances are he would absorb quite a bit of Kate and determine, based on intersections and common factors, which parts of your vision were also privileged by Kate, and which parts might be better left dormant. However, I think he might have had incredible empathy if given enough people to respond to. As it was, he was mostly working off your input. Not a bad thing, in my opinion, but not as entirely heterogeneous as Chatgod might have envisioned. This Chatgod shouldn't be underestimated. If he can imagine and create an Alchemist, who knows where he might go with his vision of worldwide community." Ray sounded grudgingly respectful. I knew that he also thought Chatgod an irritating catalyst for this whole mess, creating a world in which a Tremor could take hold.

I wasn't so sure I was willing to dump all the blame on Chatgod, even though I was still reeling from his rather cavalier use of me in his experiments in artificial intelligence. After all, you can't blame the architect for the tenants he attracts. I thought then of some of the tenement towers in bigger cities around the globe and paused. Maybe he did have to share some of the blame, I amended, but it was still Tremor we were after.

I felt a surge of revitalizing energy. I realized it came from knowing that my pal Alchemist wasn't a bad guy. He wasn't a guy at all, but he wasn't the enemy. One less thing to worry about, and it made me happy to know my instincts to trust him hadn't been misguided.

Life felt a whole lot better. Sure, I was stuck in my teensy apartment with a continuous flow of police personnel coming and going. Sure, there was a hired killer purported to be on his way to kill Steve—and likely me, too, if he discovered he was being set up. There were a whole lot of unanswered questions still hanging there, and my job future was muddy. The weather was predicted to drop fifteen degrees before the night was over. But still, life felt pretty darned good.

After all, I wasn't being lied to deliberately by my fellow monitor. My best friend was dating a millionaire, and I had declared my love for a glorious man who reciprocated my feelings. On the whole, things looked a whole lot brighter than they'd felt the evening before.

Of course, the feeling didn't last, because just then the power went out.

CHAPTER 50

I had been looking straight at Steve when the room went dark, so I knew where he was, and I crossed the room to be able to touch him. Kate was operating her Palm Pilot with one hand and holding her cell phone to her ear with the other, barking out orders for generators to be brought to us. I looked out the blurry living-room window and realized that the whole area was dark. There were no street lights, no neon store signs, no other houses lit up. The whole grid must be down. At five-thirty on a winter afternoon in Edmonton, that can make things look pretty dark indeed.

In a way, it was a relief, because I couldn't imagine anything of this magnitude being attributable to Tremor. Had it just been our power, I'd be fixating on the laundry room again. This, I was willing to believe, was a huge, irritating coincidence.

Ray and Kate didn't seem to think so, though. Iain McCorquodale came through the apartment door with a huge flashlight, announcing that everyone was in place and ready. Steve suggested I get in the bathtub and lie down, since the metal and porcelain would keep stray bullets from finding a home in my flesh.

While I am not afraid of the dark, I am intensely

claustrophobic, and the last place I wanted to be was my tiny bathroom in the dark. I suggested I crouch between the fireplace and the sofa, which was on an interior wall. I would be out of everyone's way and still able to breathe.

Steve was about to argue when Ray settled things by saying it might be better all 'round if I just got encased in a Kevlar jacket under my biggest sweatshirt and settled in by the computer. We needed to keep a connection to the world of Babel and catch any messages that might be coming our way from Tremor. They'd managed to set a generator going, which was operating the two computers, a trouble light and—I almost laughed but was afraid of drifting into hysteria—the coffee pot. Ray had his priorities.

Lucky for us, my service provider was cable. As long as we had power to operate the modem and the computer, we were in business. I let Steve help me into the vest while the computer was booting up.

"Do you think he's responsible for this power failure?" I whispered to Steve.

"I have a feeling there are things about Tremor we haven't been made privy to, Randy. If they're willing to believe it, I guess I would rather go along with it than feel too complacent. Is that too tight?" He touched my cheek as I pulled the sweatshirt down over the bulletproof vest.

The drill was that I was to sit by the computer, and Ray was on the floor under the kitchen table so as not to be seen by anyone from outside. I didn't bother to point out that I was going to look odd having computer access when all the rest of the city was in darkness. By the time Tremor got to me, if he got to me, he'd have figured out that things were not what they seemed.

Steve, in full SWAT-styled gear, was sitting in the tub, with his service revolver trained on the door. The idea was that while I was working, Steve would be in the apartment, having an after-work bath. The whole thing seemed fishy to me, but I'm neither a computer genius nor a killer. What I wanted was for the policemen staked out through the building to nab Tremor before he made it halfway down the Persian hall runner. Surely they would grab anyone who appeared; all those who would have a reason to be in the building had already been moved to the hotel.

Kate was sitting on a kitchen chair pulled into the food-prep area, blocked from the rest of us by the glassed-in cupboard containing my good china, what there was of it. She was having yet another conversation on her cell phone, this time with the people at the airport. Flights had come in from Denver, Chicago, San Francisco, and Toronto in the past twelve hours, and Kate's team back in Austin was trying to find some commonalities between the names on the manifests and those from flights into Austin around the time of the earlier death. So far, no luck, but they were still at it, trying anagrams of names, and synonyms.

I logged into Babel because I honestly couldn't think of anything better to do. If Tremor was in town making the lights go out, the chances of him being logged into a chat room were minimal. And if he was logged in some-where else, the chances he knew about the power failure in Edmonton were negligible. It felt bizarre to have the regulars stop their flow of chat to say hello to Chimera, as they did every evening. I checked the chat list and saw that most of the regulars were there, even those like Carlin and Evangeline and Lea, who were intermittent at best.

The one person I had half expected to see, though,

wasn't there. I hadn't had a chance to spar with Sanders on-line since we'd met for coffee, and I realized I had been missing that. Even with Steve sitting in my bathtub, and Ray wedged in beside my house slippers, I would have felt a bit easier if I could have made contact with Sanders. Why? Maybe because then I would know where he was. Of course, he could be living somewhere within the parameters of this power failure.

Chimera: Has anyone seen Sanders lately?

Vixen: He's been making himself scarce, I think. Who knows, maybe he's under some snowbank up there in the Great White North!

PM *from Buckaroo to Chimera:* Having him here wouldn't help us place him, though. (I'm logged in through my Palm in the kitchen.)

"Ack!" I yelped, and Kate chuckled from behind the glass cupboard. "It's bad enough you're all over my apartment, now you can read my mind!"

"I just thought I would see what the drain was on the Palm Pilot. You know, it's not too strong a drag. With lots of batteries, Sanders could have been logging into Babel from all over the town. Might that account for Ray's tracking of Edmonton usage?"

Ray muttered from his spot on the floor, but I thought Kate might have a point, although I wasn't sure Sanders could afford a Palm Pilot. It didn't make me feel any easier, though. If Sanders wasn't on Babel when he could usually be depended on to be logged in, then where was he?

I don't normally get answers as quickly or as powerfully as this one was. However, there was a hammering on the door, and Iain McCorquodale pushed it open.

"Would you come out here in the hall a minute, Ms

Craig? There's someone we'd like you to identify." He looked at my face and amended immediately, "Verify his identity. He's alive."

Indeed he was alive. He was spread-eagled on the hallway floor, with three police guns trained on him and one black leather brogue placed between his shoulder blades, but he was alive.

"Sanders! I was just wondering where you were."

CHAPTER 51

Sanders, or I guess I should say Winston, although it just didn't come easily for me, was frisked and finally allowed to stand up. His story was that he was coming to apologize for being a jerk when I was trying to talk to him about the assassins game. Apparently there had been some journalist nosing around the U of A game asking questions, which had him worried, because Sanders had been doing primary research in order to write the whole thing up in a sociology paper. When I had started talking to him about it, he had assumed that I was the journalist he'd been told about. When he discovered it was another woman, he had come to apologize.

I wondered briefly how he'd known where to find me, but my address was listed in the Edmonton phone book, so it wasn't really rocket science. As a matter of fact, Winston had been taking courses in rocket science the year before, so looking up my name in the phone book was likely a piece of cake for him.

I looked at Lewis and McCorquodale to see if they thought we should bring him into the loop. McCorquodale shrugged and said they'd hang on to him while I went in to talk to Ray.

Ray and Kate decided that we couldn't afford to let

Sanders out of our field of vision. He had seen too much that was odd to allow him free access to the 'Net. He was invited in and offered a Kevlar vest and a cup of coffee.

"You are verifiably the 'hostess with the mostest'," Sanders laughed as he buckled himself in. He seemed rather pleased to meet Ray, since he had spent an enjoyable evening discussing Corvette Stingrays with Emilio Lizardo in Babel. Kate mentioned that she had spotted him there without revealing her handle, and he didn't ask. Sanders seemed to cotton on to Kate's command a lot sooner than most people I'd seen. Perhaps those psychology courses had done the trick.

"Sorry you've been pulled into this. I've been told that the likelihood of danger is pretty minimal. It's a lot more likely that Tremor will be trapped on his way into the neighborhood."

"I wouldn't be so sure about that tonight," Sanders pondered. "With the power outage, a couple of electric trolley buses are stalled in the middle of the High Level Bridge, and since all the traffic lights are out, there are a lot of snafus. I would say there is gridlock throughout the area. Are you sure all your forces are in place?"

"We can account for everyone except those detailed to trail suspects. We're trying to stay off cell phone connectivity with them, because we can't be sure Tremor doesn't have the technology to intercept," Kate allowed. It was probably satisfying to talk about things to an outsider who seemed bright enough to be asking the right questions.

"So you think he caused the power failure?" I asked.

"Well, as much as we'd like to, I doubt that we could attribute this to privatization," drawled Winston. "There is a localized outage through the university and downtown area, and it flows along three main access routes—

from downtown across the bridge through to the Grandin Station of the LRT is all dark. So is the line down 109th Street all the way to 62nd Avenue, meaning that police cars from the south side would be unable to get through the gridlock. The 114th Street access through to the Neil Crawford Centre at Belgravia Road is also down, so cars coming from the Whitemud are at a crawl, too. There is one egress, down the Groat Bridge, through to Stony Plain Road, which is the last place you'd think to look for a getaway, unless of course you're thinking of a ski vacation in Jasper. So, that, I figure, would be the way a clever baddie would think. Always aim for the least likely, because it will be the least obvious. I am betting whoever it is has a fast car and a map of the Coquihalla Highway to Vancouver."

Kate looked at him with something like admiration. Ray was nodding. Steve, who had come out of the bathroom and was leaning in the bedroom doorway, was nodding, too.

I wasn't so sure. "How do you know where the power outages are localized to?" I demanded.

"I live on the twenty-fifth floor of the Strathcona Tower. From my kitchen window, I can see west and south; from my balcony I can look northwest and catch a glimpse of downtown. When I was leaving via the stairwell, I saw lights beyond to the southeast out of my neighbor's window. May I recommend you never move into a highrise if you worry about power outages."

It sounded reasonable, but then again, why was Winston Graham all of a sudden showing up in my apartment building tonight of all nights? I looked over at Kate, who was punching something into her Palm Pilot and nodding.

"Well, your address checks out, Winston. Sit down a spell and tell us again what your interest in all this is."

"I'm not sure I know what you're talking about, Detective," Winston/Sanders drawled. "I came to apologize for being so curt to Randy when she was asking me about the U of A Assassins and discover that she has her own militia. Most people would settle for a building with an intercom, you know."

Kate looked as if she was about to say something when Ray broke in.

"Looks like Sanders here is in the clear. The alarm on the locker in the bus depot just went off."

"Have they got the guy?"

"I don't know about that. All I know is that the locker has been touched somehow. I'm monitoring it through my computer."

"So it could be Tremor, or it could be some diversionary tactic. It could even be some drunk falling into the side of the locker, for all we know. I'll let you know when the bus-depot crew report in," Kate replied.

I was still wondering if Sanders wasn't some diversionary tactic on this end of things when Steve decided that I was too much of a target in the living room and herded us back into the kitchen/dining-room area. Sanders took a seat on the stepstool I keep by the garbage bin so that I can reach my highest shelves. With his knees up around his chest, he looked like an overgrown schoolboy eager to be part of a wild adventure. All he lacked was a school scarf and scabs on his knees.

I might have mustered up a full head of antagonistic steam toward anyone else, but somehow Sanders managed to diffuse my edginess and make things feel rather exciting, but controllable, like a glorious Enid Blyton book. I expected Kiki the parrot to show up, rhyming words, any minute. In spite of myself, I grinned. Maybe it was transference, putting all the friendship I'd forged with Alchemist over onto a human person from Babel, but I felt very close to Sanders at that moment. I sure hoped he didn't have anything to do with Tremor.

The fact that he was so much at ease in a situation that he wasn't supposed to know anything about didn't make him seem all that innocent to me. Of course, he was nattering on about assassin games and societies for creative anachronisms, and other similar affiliations. Apparently he had even once been part of a Dungeons and Dragons game where the participants had dressed the part and had badges similar to the Scouts to sew on the sleeves of their gowns. I wasn't sure if there was anything that could faze Sanders. Trying to find out was probably what made me blurt out more information than I should have.

"You see, there's a hired killer working out of Babel," I said, waving my hand around as if this should explain everything he saw—the task force, the Kevlar, the weirdly taped windows, the computers and laptops everywhere you looked.

"Oh, you mean Tremor?" he asked casually, and you could almost hear jaws dropping open all over the room. Kate leaned forward, straining toward information the way sunflowers reach for the sun. Steve had his hand on his holster.

"How do you know about that?" I squeaked, thinking my whole transference was in jeopardy. I couldn't trust anyone.

"A few weeks ago in Babel, Maia was running a game of Truth or Dare. Tremor was there, and he got a truth, which was 'What do you do for a living?' and he answered that he was a hired killer." Sanders was still smiling, but it was just beginning to dawn on him that his answer was a revelation to those of us in the room. He looked at all of us, one by one, as if for some sign we were collectively pulling his leg. "You mean this is real? He really is a hired killer? He's coming to kill us? That's what this is all about? I thought you were joking."

"You thought we were joking, or he was joking?" I wasn't following things too clearly.

"Well, both. So let's backtrack here. Tremor is a real contract killer and he has a target here. You get the wagons in a circle and leave some money somewhere for him, and he in turn puts out the lights for about a six-mile radius, leaving you scrambling. So he's got the money, he knows where you live, and you've lost track of him? And I happen to be sitting in the kitchen of the target site of the hit? Oh goodie."

"That's about the extent of it, yes," said Kate, somewhat drily. I had a feeling she hated sitting around and waiting about as much as I did. At least I was in my own place, even though it felt, at the moment, like Grand Central Station.

"I can't believe that Tremor actually told the world that he was a hired killer. What is it about on-line discourse that makes people so blasé about their intimacies?"

"Well, for one thing, no one but folks wanting to hire him would really believe him when he said it, right? And people joke about that sort of thing all the time. I saw a fellow the other day walking down HUB Mall in a tee-shirt that said, 'Don't recognize me—I'm in the Witness Protection Program.' I said to myself, Wouldn't that be a great idea for real? So that if a loved one did spot you, they could read what everyone else saw as a joke tee-shirt, and be warned not to give you away to the mobsters waiting to rub you out. It's what my dad used to call 'kidding on the square.'"

"You've been reading too many thrillers."

He looked abashed. "I know I have. Time to get back into a senior-level English class. It's a toss-up between a seminar on Virginia Woolf and a Restoration drama survey."

Kate was starting to grin, and Ray was shaking his head. Sanders just seemed to have that sort of effect on people, I guess. I was wondering who was teaching the Woolf course and was just about to ask when the phone rang.

All eyes were on me as I reached for the phone.

"Hello?"

"Let there be light." I was assuming this was Tremor's voice, rather high with a mid-western twang to it. As he spoke, all the lights in the apartment clicked on, making me drop the phone. I grabbed for it.

"What's your game? Why did you turn out the lights?"

"Why do you think, pretty lady? I see everything so much clearer in the dark. Stay by your phone." And he clicked off.

CHAPTER 52

The phone call had been recorded and played back several times. Sanders was taken to the laundry room, which I found an interesting irony, so that the team could talk in peace. At this point, we couldn't be sure whether his happening by had more design to it than he was admitting. If he was a confederate of Tremor, the last thing we needed was for him to be listening in to our plans and reactions.

According to Kate, Tremor was moving into a cat-and-mouse play where he intended to make me jump through some hoops. We still weren't clear whether he was just being cautious prior to moving in on the intended kill, or whether he had figured out that this was a sting and he was going to exact some sort of retribution on me. One thing, I didn't have to worry about him tracking down and killing Alchemist. Now, there was a load off my mind.

We decided that if Tremor was going to be phoning, we might as well make it possible to get away from the phone without him knowing it. Steve made a quick call and created a forwarding from my land line phone number to a cell phone. Kate made me slip another charged battery into my jeans pocket, just in case I ended up on the run with the cell phone.

I didn't like the sound of that, but she assured me that if I was made to move, I would be tracked closely. To that end, she asked to see a pair of my shoes. She inserted a small disc about the size of a loonie under the insole, around the arch. She asked me if I understood GPS tracking systems. I replied, of course, in the negative.

"Well, your shoes are now emitting a signal that we can track by satellite and pinpoint to the nth degree. I'd suggest you put them on now and forget the quaint Canadian way you all have of taking your shoes off at the door for the next little while." I obediently tied my laces and clicked my heels together for good measure. Ray smiled. Steve looked worried. I wasn't sure what I was thinking. It was about 8:00 in the evening, and I hadn't had much more than three hours or so of sleep in the previous thirty-six hours. The lights were on again. There was a hired killer out there somewhere with five thousand dollars and my phone number in his pocket. A forty-something-year-old perpetual student was being held under police guard in my laundry room, and my feet were being tracked in space. Just another day in the life of Randy Craig.

Tremor called back at 8:51.

"So, are you all ready to go for a little walkabout?"

"Tell me, is this to get me out of your way, or am I meeting you for some reason?"

"Now, now, do I tell you how to teach college students? Why don't you just listen to what you're going to do and this will go much more efficiently."

There was nothing of the Marlon Brando in Tremor's voice. I was hearing much more James Woods, and if that isn't scary, then I don't know what is. The folks in my kitchen were nodding at me to agree with him and get on with things, but this felt like standing at the edge of the bungie-jump platform. Once I started into this conversation with the killer, the results were entirely unclear, but I couldn't see them being overwhelmingly in my favor. I was in no hurry.

"Are you still there, Ms Craig?" He seemed to be flaunting the information. Although I knew that it was very easy to access everything he had and that I had even given him some of it, it felt like a violation for this professional murderer to be running his fingers through my private life.

"Yep. I'm here."

"Well, that's not where I want you. Take the LRT to the Bay Station and exit to the second-floor walkway. It's a cold night. Bring along a cell phone with this number forwarded to it. I'll be getting back to you."

He rang off before I had a chance to say anything else.

It was agreed that I would do as he said, with a couple of detectives tailing me and others moving into place in pre-designated areas downtown. Steve wouldn't be one of them, just in case the whole scheme was in fact a way to get me away from the scene of the supposed crime. Ray and Kate would continue to monitor from my kitchen, which I doubt was Kate's idea of a good time, since my kitchen chairs are none too comfy. Detective Lewis was staying with Winston Graham in the laundry room. They had my Scrabble game and more coffee, and they seemed reasonably content.

Detective Iain McCorquodale was going to trail me, so he set out first and headed toward a condo a couple of blocks between my apartment and the university LRT station. From my apartment it was usually easier to take the bus downtown, but Tremor had specified the Light Rail

Transit system, so I would have to walk five blocks to take the train instead of crossing the street to catch the bus.

Officer Armstrong, who had been one of the people in the front hall, pulled on her toque and mittens and deked out the back door of the apartment and through a fraternity back yard to appear on the street at the front of my building as I went out the front door. To anyone watching, it appeared that I was coincidentally running into an acquaintance on the street. She and I walked to the university, talking about nothing in particular and everything in general. I had a wild urge to confide in her, tell her my deepest secrets and my favorite colors. She, in turn, told me to call her Michele and filled in awkward gaps with proud stories about her two exemplary children.

She came with me on the subway but said goodbye and got off at the Corona Station just before the Bay Station where I was supposed to leave the train. I wasn't sure if she was going to race the four blocks above ground to be somewhere near where I got off, or whether I was being handed off to someone else.

I was assuming Iain McCorquodale was somewhere on the train, but I hadn't seen him since I left my apartment. It spoke volumes of his talent as a policeman, I suppose, that someone with that large a presence and bluster could efface himself into the woodwork, or, in this case, the trainwork. Either that, or he was off having a beer while I waltzed off to meet a killer. I was hoping he was supercop.

I got out of the train at the pretty blue ceramic station that was the Bay. Of course, the station was still called Bay Station because above ground the original Hudson's Bay Company building still stood, but the store itself had since bounced all over the city, and a television station had taken up residence in the building. The second floor of the Bay building led into a series of pedways that linked several blocks of downtown buildings, making it possible to walk indoors from the corner of 104th Street and Jasper Avenue to the Hilton on 101th Street and 103rd Avenue. Or, in fact, it hit me, as I heard the cell phone ringing the opening bars to "Oh Suzanna" in my pocket, the YMCA on 100th Street.

"Have a nice train ride?"

"Are you watching me?"

"Now, what do you think?"

I turned around, continuing to head northward to the pedway entrance. I always felt awkward speaking into cell phones in public, never sure how far my voice was carrying.

Tremor laughed into my ear. "You're going to make yourself dizzy doing that."

I was standing in a windowless hallway with absolutely nobody in view either ahead of me or behind me. This was freakier than I wanted to admit, even to myself. I didn't particularly like being downtown at night anyhow, but to be downtown, by myself at 9:30 at night, with a killer chuckling into my ear, was a little too much to bear. I'm sure he could hear the mounting hysteria in my voice.

"Where are you?"

"That's irrelevant, don't you think? It's completely irrelevant since you don't have a redundant husband, do you? You aren't actually hoping I turn up anywhere any-time soon, right? This is all about keeping Babel shiny clean, right? That's your job, right? Or is Alvin just coin-cidentally dropping weekly allowance checks into your bank account? Believe me, you can't keep secrets from me, Chimera. What is relevant is that you've been dick-ing around with my livelihood, and I don't take to that very much at all."

"What do you mean? You could be accused of the same thing, Bucky. Right now the police are swarming all over Babel. What do you think it will take for Alvin to shut it all down on me, and there will go my job." I was getting angry with his high-handed attitude. After all, he could kill anywhere he pleased. Where was I going to get another monitoring job that fit my schedule so beautifully?

"Oh, come now. You got into this because you wanted to play Nancy Drew, not out of some misguided loyalty to your job. Well, you're lucky I didn't pop your boyfriend, missy."

"So why did you haul me out here if you have it all figured out?"

"Simple. With the whole gang focused on keeping you safe, I can get out of this end-of-beyond without sacrificing the bride price."

"I thought you already had the money."

"That's what you were meant to think."

"So how will making me come to meet you help?"

"Don't worry your pretty head overmuch. Ciao for now." Click.

By this time, I had managed to make my way over 103rd Street into the Manulife II building, and was getting closer to the Holt Renfrew corner of Manulife Plaza. Since he hadn't given me any further directions, I was following instincts that were taking me toward the Y, the last place I'd had him in my mind. For all I knew he was on the street below me in an idling car, but I didn't think so. I had a vision of him marching toward me from the far end of the pedway system, and meeting me somewhere in the middle. According to my calculations, the middle should be the pedway from Manulife into the City

Centre West section of the downtown shopping mall, but the only people I could see were on the escalators probably coming from the cinemas on the third floor. I turned away from them, heading east toward Edmonton City Centre, the original section of the mall sprawl.

A janitor was washing the faux marble pedway across 101st Street. This was a double-decker pedway. Tremor might be above me on the third floor, heading in the other direction. I felt very vulnerable, all alone in this huge, well-lit glass tunnel in the air.

Where were the police, anyhow? Kate had told me that they would know my exact location at all times. But what good was knowing my longitude and latitude if it took half an hour to get to me? Tremor had managed to acclimatize to this city very well, instinctively finding the easiest way to make me feel safe enough to get vulnerable. Here I was, out in the open, with no way of getting out of the loop, but it would take several minutes for anyone not already in the maze of pedways to get to me. If I couldn't see someone, it meant they were too far away to do me any good. I stomped my GPS shoe a little extra hard, just to punish someone's ear somewhere.

And what about the phone monitoring? If tabloid journalists were constantly tracking Prince Charles's conversations, then presumably the police were managing to keep a tap on this line even though it had been forwarded to the cell phone. So where was Iain McCorquodale? Where was Michele Armstrong? Where were all the policemen posing as indigents hanging out at the Y? Where were some real indigents? I would settle for anyone. Why was it that I felt as if I were walking through one of those science-fiction movies where all the other people on earth except two Valley girls had been vaporized?

I passed a framing shop and a leather shop on my way to the walkway over the YMCA. It was quintessentially Edmontonian to have a pedway to the fanciest hotel in the city cutting across a corner of the downtown YMCA, which had stood there several dozen years longer than the hotel. I figured that this had to be the final step for Tremor. I noticed that from halfway across the pedway, one could spot the bus station. I slowed down, calculating the distance between the front door of the Y and the main doors of the bus depot, given that there was an open parking lot between the two, making it possible to go directly cross-country.

Just then the phone rang, startling me, even though I'd been expecting it.

"Are you thinking I am still planning to get over to the locker to pick up the cash, sweetheart?"

Damn the man, where was he that he could spot me and read my mind?

"I'm afraid I may have led you down the garden path, darlin'. I've got the cash in hand now. There is just nothing like making people second-guess themselves to get cops off my tail, though. I have a feeling two-thirds of your minders are over at the depot, checking Locker 541 one more time. Actually, this was grandstanding, pure and simple. I just wanted to let Ray and Katie know they might as well go back to chasing kiddie porn, because they are just not going to get the better of me. I'll leave your precious Babel, babe, but only because you asked so nicely. But doing so won't put so much as a dent in my livelihood, and there's not much you can do about it. Face it. Systems are my business. Once you see the whole world as one code or another, there's nothing you can't manipulate. This is the new world order."

"You don't scare me, Tremor."

"Sure I do. And you're wise to be scared. Stay scared, doll. After all, I know everything there is to know about you. It wouldn't take much, believe me."

"They'll get you," I whispered. "Wherever you are."

"You want to know where I am? Turn around, why don't you?"

Slowly I turned, my back to the bus depot. I was facing east now, toward City Hall, and about sixty yards from me and one storey up was another walkway.

There, silhouetted against the lit interior of the glass corridor, was a man in black, a sports bag slung over his shoulder. He might be an executive heading home after hitting the gym. I couldn't make out his features, but I could see one hand held up to his ear. Tremor waved with his free hand, and then reached for something hanging around his neck. My heart lurched until I remembered that people don't carry guns slung around their necks like cameras.

Cameras? Sure enough, I could see the glint of a huge lens and realized he was staring at me through a zoom that could likely spot blackheads and the filling on the front of my left bicuspid. I moved my free hand up to my neck in an automatic gesture, as if by taking my picture he was somehow going to steal a part of my soul, located near my thyroid.

"Kiss kiss bang bang, sweetheart." I didn't see a flash, but then again, I doubt he would have used one to good effect, with all the glass to glare off. I heard the click of the camera, though, very clearly, through the phone, just before I heard a dialtone.

We stood there, watching each other. As I watched him transfer the money from the gym bag to a backpack,

I dialed the number of Kate's cell phone, and very calmly told them where I was. Steve was fine. Winston/Sanders was winning at Scrabble with "quixotic" on a triple-word score. Ray was raising hell with the folks at the bus station, and Kate was dispersing the troops to the airports and highway roadblocks. Apparently, Michele Armstrong and Iain McCorquodale were close behind me in the pedway system, and I was to wait for them where I was. Fine by me. This was surreal. Tremor waved, turned, and walked briskly toward the shopping mall, from which he could get to two parkades, another LRT station, an express bus top, or a cab stand. I could hear sirens in the distance, but I was pretty sure the cops didn't stand a chance.

I had to hand it to Tremor. He'd hacked his way into my city, finding its quirks and vulnerabilities, like a master. I'd bet, in forty-eight hours, he had come to know Edmonton better than most of us residents. What was more, he knew all about me. I only had his word he wouldn't be back to use any of that knowledge. I slid to a crouch against the glass wall, suddenly too exhausted to move.

Chapter 53

They never did catch him. After a couple of more days of coffee and takeout, though not all of it consumed in my little apartment, Ray and Kate and the other assorted traveling Banzai Web crusaders packed their tents and headed home to Austin. They charged Thea as an accessory to murder, using the transcripts of the chat discussions with Alchemist and Tremor and my cell-phone discussions as evidence. Apparently there had been a few other cases that they were tying to Tremor, as well, so the Babel connection was enough to get them some warrants on other clients of the big bad wolf.

His word was good on staying out of Babel. It had been over a month since our standoff downtown, and neither Alchemist nor I had spotted him in the chat room. I found myself feeling really odd for about ten minutes in my first conversation with Alchemist after his outing as a machine. It was probably how chess master Gary Kasparov felt, shaking hands with Deep Junior on the draw. It was so tough to stay mad at him, though, since he was so tuned in to me. It was like having a totally empathetic best friend for a workmate. A best friend with a brain the size of a planet. We made up and got on with things, and pretty soon we were exchanging bot jokes—but tasteful ones, if you know what I mean. Monitoring on Babel continued to be alternately fascinating, maudlin, and church-potluck-supper enjoyable. The money was good, the hours reasonable, and it looked to be pretty steady for the future, which was a good thing, with education cutbacks in this province being what they were. I was still trying to figure out how to make some money writing about my adventure, but so far I hadn't managed to organize it into anything pertinent.

Sanders continued to hang out in Babel and was good enough not to expose me as a paid monitor to the rest of the crowd, which would have meant the end of my job. I think he was placated by the allowance to interview the Banzais and write up the group psychology of stakeouts from a phenomenological perspective. Talk about pertinence, eh? Supposedly, the article would be in next June's issue of *Psychology Today*. I heard through Steve that he and Detective Lewis meet for drinks and Scrabble on a semi-regular basis.

Speaking of semi-regular, Steve and I are back together for sure, which pleases Denise no end. We keep extra toothbrushes and sweats in each other's apartments and see each other more days than not, but, although we're rumba-ing around the idea of marriage, we're not quite there yet. Anyhow, I wouldn't tell Denise even if we were. If I know her, she'd haul me off on another shoe-buying expedition.

I ran into Dr. Flanders again at the Safeway the other day, and he gave me the URL to his home page. He has posted three of his scholarly articles and a jillion pictures of the trip he and his sister took to the newly rebuilt Globe Theatre last summer. He was asking me whether I would be interested in contributing to his local theater blog. I told him I'd think about it. I still don't like writing for free.

Of course, I will chat on a dime.

ALSO FROM
JANICE MACDONALD

Sticks and Stones

How dangerous can words be? The University of Alberta's English department is caught up in a maelstrom of poison-pen letters, graffiti and misogyny. Part-time sessional lecturer Miranda Craig seems to be both target and investigator, wreaking havoc on her new-found relationship with one of Edmonton's finest.

The men's residence at the U of A wants to party and issues invitations to the women's residence, each with specific and terrifying consequences if female students don't attend. One of Randy's star students, a divorced mother of two, has her threatening letter published in the newspaper and is found soon after, victim of a brutal murder followed to the gory letter of the published note.

Randy must delve into Gwen's life and preserve her own to solve this mystery. Is someone trying to kill Randy, and if so, who? An untenured professor? An unknown student? Gwen's killer?

0-88801-256-X /pb $14.95 Cdn./$12.95 U.S.

Where Shadows Burn
Catherine Hunter

Kelly, a young costume designer, is struggling to put her life together after the recent suicide of her husband. After a series of disturbing phone calls, as well as more unearthly dangers, she finds herself on the lam with her young nephew, looking over her shoulder and wondering if the danger she faces comes from the living . . . or the dead.
0-88801-231-4/pb $16.95 Cdn./$14.95 U.S.

Dying by Degrees:
An Emily Goodstriker Mystery
Eileen Coughlan

Psychology grad student Emily Goodstriker quickly becomes uneasy with her maniacal professor's experiments. Could a rash of student suicides somehow be connected to the psych department's extracurricular activity?
0-88801-247-0/pb $14.95 Cdn./$12.95 U.S.

The Case of the Reluctant Agent:
A Sherlock Holmes Mystery
Tracy Cooper-Posey

When Sherlock Holmes' brother, Mycroft, is shot and left for dead, Sherlock is forced to go to Constantinople to uncover the man behind the deed.
0-88801-263-2/pb $14.95 Cdn./$12.95 U.S.

Chronicles of the Lost Years:
A Sherlock Holmes Mystery
Tracy Cooper-Posey

Cooper-Posey picks up where Sir Arthur Conan Doyle left off. *Chronicles of the Lost Years* is the "real" story of Holmes' adventures in the Middle East and Asia during the three years Watson believed him dead—commonly referred to as the Great Hiatus.

0-88801-241-1/pb $16.95 Cdn./$14.95 U.S.

Hoot to Kill:
A Robyn Devara Mystery
Karen Dudley

Biologist Robyn Devara is surveying the old-growth forest for spotted owls. If she finds any, it's going to mean big changes for the logging town of Marten Valley. Caught between hostile locals and militant environmentalists, Robyn tries to remain neutral, until she discovers a body in the forest.

0-88801-291-8/pb $10.99 Cdn./U.S.

The Red Heron:
A Robyn Devara Mystery
Karen Dudley

A contaminated industrial site, a fragile wetland, sabotage and snipers complicate an already diffucult job. But fears over poisons in the ground and hints of long-buried secrets in town take a bizarre turn when a missing garden gnome shows up alongside a brutally murdered man.
0-88801-240-3/pb $16.95 Cdn./$14.95 U.S.

Macaws of Death:
A Robyn Devara Mystery
Karen Dudley

Hot on the trail of the mysterious macaw, Robyn finds herself stationed at an isolated field camp in the Costa Rican jungle. It's certainly an exciting change from routine paperwork. Exciting, that is, until communication with the outside world is cut off, deadly snakes start slithering into cabins, and members of the field team begin to die . . .
0-88801-274-8/pb $10.99 Cdn./U.S.

Available at your local bookstore.
www.ravenstonebooks.com

ABOUT THE AUTHOR

Janice MacDonald teaches undergraduate English courses, much like her heroine, Randy Craig, at Grant MacEwan College in Edmonton, where she lives with her husband and her two daughters. She has written children's books, musicals and textbooks. She has also worked as a monitor, host and cybrarian for several Internet sites. *The Monitor* is her third Randy Craig mystery.